SMOKY
THE COW HORSE

Written and illustrated by WILL JAMES

D0109895

SCHOLASTIC INC.
New York Toronto London Auckland Sydney

ISBN 0-590-43685-6

12 11   6 7/9

Printed in the U.S.A.   40

First Scholastic printing, February 1991

PREFACE

To my way of thinking there's something wrong, or missing, with any person who hasn't got a soft spot in his heart for an animal of some kind. With most folks the dog stands highest as man's friend, then comes the horse, with others the cat is liked best as a pet, or a monkey is fussed over; but whatever kind of animal it is a person likes, it's all hunkydory so long as there's a place in the heart for one or a few of them.

I've never as yet went wrong in sizing up a man by the kind of a horse he rode. A good horse always packs a good man, and I've always dodged the hombre what had no though nor liking for his horse or other animals, for I figger that kind of gazabo is best to be left unacquainted with, no good would ever come of the meeting.

With me, my weakness lays towards the horse. My life, from the time I first squinted at daylight has been with horses. I admire every step that crethure makes, I know them and been thru so much with 'em that I've come to figger a big mistake was made when the horse was classed as an animal. To me, the horse is man's greatest, most useful, faithful, and powerful friend. He never whines when he's hungry or sore footed or tired, and he'll keep on a going for the human till he drops.

The horse is not appreciated and never will be appreciated enough,—few humans, even them that works him, really know him, but then there's so much to know about him. I've wrote this book on only one horse and when I first started it I was afraid I'd run out of something to write, but I wasn't half thru when I begin to realize I had to do some squeezing to get the things in I wanted, and when I come to the last chapter was when I seen how if I spent my life writing on the horse alone and lived to be a hundred I'd only said maybe half of what I feel ought to be said.

The horse I wrote of in this book is not an exception, there's quite a few like him, he's not a fiction horse that's wrote about in a dream and made to do things that's against the nature of a horse to do. Smoky is just a horse, but all horse, and that I think is enough said.

As for Clint, the cowboy who "started" Smoky, he's no exception either. He's just a man who was able to see and bring out the good that was in the horse—and no matter how some writers describe the cowboy's handling of horses, I'm here to say that I can produce many a cowboy what can show feelings for a horse the same as Clint done.

But Smoky met other humans besides Clint, many others, and of all kinds, and that's where the story comes in. And now, my main ambition as I turn Smoky loose to making hisself acquainted is that the folks who will get to know him will see that horse as *I* seen him.

Will James

CONTENTS

ILLUSTRATIONS

ILLUSTRATIONS

ILLUSTRATIONS

CHAPTER I

A RANGE COLT

IT seemed like Mother Nature was sure agreeable
that day when the little black colt came to the
range world and tried to get a footing with his long
wobblety legs on the brown prairie sod. Short stems
of new green grass was trying to make their way up
thru the last year's faded growth and reaching for the
sun's warm rays. Taking in all that could be seen,
felt, and inhaled, there was no day, time, nor place
that could beat that spring morning on the sunny side
of the low prairie butte where Smoky the colt was
foaled.

"Smoky" wouldn't have fitted the colt as a name
just then on account he was jet black, but that name
wasn't attached onto him till he was a four-year-old,
which was when he first started being useful as a saddle horse. He didn't see the first light of day thru no
box stall window, and there was no human around to
make a fuss over him and try to steady him on his
feet for them first few steps. Smoky was just a little
range colt and all the company he had that first morning of his life was his watchful mammy.

Smoky wasn't quite an hour old when he begin to
take interest in things, the warm spring sun was doing
its work and kept a pouring warmth all over that
slick little black hide and right on thru his little body

1

till pretty soon his head come up kinda shaky and he begin nosing around them long front legs that was stretched out in front of him. His mammy was close by him and at the first move the colt made she run her nose along his short neck and nickered. Smoky's head went up another two inches at the sound and his first little answering nicker was heard, of course a person would of had to listen mighty close to hear it, but then if you'd a watched his nostrils quivering you could tell that's just what he was trying to do.

That was the starting of Smoky. Pretty soon his ears begin to work back and forth towards the sound his mammy would make as she moved. He was trying to locate just where she was. Then something moved right in front of his nose about a foot; it'd been there quite a good spell but he'd never realized it before; besides his vision was a little dim yet and he wasn't interested much till that something moved again and planted itself still closer.

Being it was right close he took a sniff at it. That sniff recorded itself into his brain and as much as told him that all was well, it was one of his mammy's legs. His ears perked up and he tried nickering again with a heap better result than the first time.

One good thing called for another and natural like he made a sudden scramble to get up, but his legs wouldn't work right and just about when he'd got his belly clear of the ground and as he was resting there for another try at the rest of the way up, one of his front legs quivered and buckled at the elbow, and the whole works went down.

He layed there flat on his side and breathing hard, his mammy nickered encouragement, and it wasn't long when his head was up again and his legs spraddled out all around him the same as before. He was going

His ears begin to work back and forth towards the sound his mammy would make as she moved. His vision was dim yet, and he was trying to locate just where she was.

to try again, but next time he was going to be more sure of his *ground*. He was studying, it seemed like, and sniffing of his legs and then the earth like he was trying to figger out how he was going to get one to stand up on the other. His mammy kept a circling around and a talking to him in horse language; she'd give him a shove with her nose then walk away and watch him.

The spring air which I think is most for the benefit of all that's young had a lot to do to keep Smoky from laying still for very long, his vision was getting clearer fast, and his strength was coming in just as fast. Not far away, but still too far for Smoky to see was little calves, little white-faced fellers a playing and bucking around and letting out wall-eyed bellers at their mammies, running out a ways and then running back, tails up, at a speed that'd make a greyhound blush for shame.

There was other little colts too all a cavorting around and tearing up good sod, but with all them calves and colts that was with the bunches of cattle or horses scattered out on the range the same experience of helplessness that Smoky was going thru had been theirs for a spell, and a few hadn't been as lucky as Smoky in their first squint at daylight. Them few had come to the range world when the ground was still covered with snow, or else cold spring rains was a pouring down to wet 'em to the bone.

Smoky's mother had sneaked out of the bunch a few days before Smoky came and hid in a lonely spot where she'd be sure that no cattle nor horses or even riders would be around. In a few days and when Smoky would be strong enough to lope out she'd go back again, but in the meantime she wanted to be alone with her colt and put all her attention on him without having to contend with chasing off big inquisitive geldings or jealous fillies.

She was of range blood which means mostly mustang with strains of Steeldust or Coach throwed in; if hard winters come and the range was covered with heavy snows she knowed of high ridges where the strong winds kept a few spots bare and where feed could be got. If droughts came to dry up the grass and water holes, she sniffed the air for moisture and drifted out acrost the plain which was her home range to the high mountains where things was more normal. There was cougars and wolves in that high country but her mustang instinct made her the "fittest." She circled around and never went under where the lion was perched a waiting for her, and the wolf never found her where she could be cornered.

Smoky had inherited that same instinct of his mammy's, but on that quiet spring morning he wasn't at all worried about enemies, his mammy was there, and besides he had a hard job ahead that was taking all of his mind to figger out, that was to stand on them long things which was fastened to his body and which kept a spraddling out in all directions.

The first thing to do was to gather 'em under him and try again, he did that easy enough, and then he waited and gathered up all the strength that was in him, he sniffed at the ground to make sure it was there and then his head went up, his front feet stretched out in front of him, and with his hind legs all under him he used all that strength he'd been storing up and pushed himself up on his front feet, his hind legs straightened up to steady him and as luck would have it there was just enough distance between each leg to keep him up there. All he had to do was to keep them legs stiff and from buckling up under him, which wasn't at all easy, cause getting up to where he was had used up a lot of his strength and them long legs of his was doing a heap of shaking.

All would of been well maybe, only his mammy nickered "that's a good boy," and that's what queered Smoky. His head went up proud as a peacock and he forgot all about keeping his props stiff and under him. Down he went the whole length of his legs, and there he layed the same as before.

But he didn't lay long this time. He either liked the sport of going up and coming down or else he was getting peeved, he was up again, mighty shaky, but he was up sure enough. His mammy came to him, she sniffed at him and he sniffed back, then nature played another hand and he nursed, the first nourishment was took in, his tummy warmed up and strength came fast. Smoky was an hour and a half old and up to stay.

The rest of that day was full of events for Smoky, he explored the whole country, went up big mountains two feet high, wide valleys six or eight feet acrost and at one time was as far as twelve feet away from his mammy all by himself. He shied at a rock once, it was a dangerous *looking* rock, and he kicked at it as he went past. All that action being put on at once come pretty near being too much for him and he come close to measuring his whole length on Mother Earth once again. But luck was with him, and taking it all he had a mighty good time; when the sun went to sinking

over the blue ridges in the West, Smoky, he missed all
the beauty of the first sunset in his life, he was stretched
out full length, of his own accord this time, and sound
asleep.

The night was a mighty good rival of what the day
had been, all the stars was out and showing off, and
the braves was a chasing the buffalo plum around the
Big Dipper, the water hole of The Happy Hunting
Grounds, but all that was lost to Smoky, he was still
asleep and recuperating from his first day's adventures,
and most likely he'd kept on sleeping for a good long
spell, only his mammy who was standing guard over
him happened to get a little too close and stepped on
his tail.

Smoky must of been in the middle of some bad dream,
his natural instinct might of pictured some enemy to
his mind, and something that looked like a wolf or a
bear must of had him cornered for sure. Anyway, when
he felt his tail pinched that way he figgered that when
a feller begins to *feel* it's sure time to act, and he did.
He shot up right under his mammy's chin, let out a
squeal, and stood there ready to fight. He took in the
country for *feet* and *feet* around and looking for the
enemy that'd nipped him and finally in his scouting
around that way he run acrost the shadow of his
mammy,—that meant but one thing, safety, and that
accounted for and put away as past left room for a
craving he'd never noticed in his excitement. He was
hungry, and proceeded right then and there to take
on a feed of his mammy's warm, rich milk.

The sky was beginning to get light in the East, the

stars was fading away and the buffalo hunters had
went to rest, a few hours had passed since Smoky had
been woke up out of his bad dream and there he was,
asleep again. He'd missed his first sunset and now he
was sleeping thru his first sunrise, but he was going to
be prepared for that new day's run, and the strength
he was accumulating through them sleeps and between
feeds would sure make him fit to cover a lot of territory.

There wasn't a move out of him till the sun was
well up and beginning to throw a good heat. He stacked
up on a lot of that heat, and pretty soon one of his
ears moved, then the other. He took a long breath and
stretched. Smoky was coming to life.—His mammy
nickered, and that done the trick, Smoky raised his
head, looked around, and proceeded to get up. After
a little time that was done and bowing his neck he
stretched again. Smoky was ready for another day.

The big day started right after Smoky had his feed,
then his mother went to grazing and moving away
straight to the direction of some trees a mile or so to
the south. A clear spring was by them trees, and water
is what Smoky's mammy wanted the most right then.
She was craving for a drink of that cold water, but
you'd never thought it by the way she traveled. She'd
nose around at the grass and wait for spells so as little
Smoky could keep up with her and still find time to
investigate everything what throwed a shadow.

A baby cottontail had jumped up once right under
his nose, stood there a second too scared to move, and
pretty soon made a high dive between the colt's long
legs and hit for his hole; Smoky never seen the rabbit

or even knowed he was there or he might of been running yet, cause that's what he'd been looking for, an
excuse to run.   But he finally made up an excuse and

His long legs tangled and untangled themselves as he run, and he was sure making
speed.

a while later as he brushed past a long dry weed and
it tickled his belly, he let out a squeal and went from
there.

His long legs tangled and untangled themselves as
he run, and he was sure making speed. Around and
around he went and finally lined out straight away
from where his mammy was headed. She nickered for

him and waited, all patience. He turned after a spell and headed for his mammy again the same as tho he'd run acrost another enemy at the other end and as he got close to his mammy he let out a buck, a squeal, a snort, and stopped,—he was sure some little wild horse.

It took a couple of hours for them two to make that mile to the spring. The mother drank a lot of that good water, a few long breaths and drank some more till the thirst was all gone. Smoky came over and nosed at the pool, but he didn't take on any of the fluid, it look just like so much thin air to him, the same with the tender green grass that was beginning to grow in bunches everywhere; it was just growing for him to run on.

The rest of that day was pretty well used up around that one spot; adventures of all kinds was numerous for Smoky, and when he wasn't stretched out and asleep there was plenty of big stumps in the cotton-wood grove that could be depended on to give him the scare he'd be looking for.

But there was other things and more threatening than stumps which Smoky hadn't as yet spotted, like for instance,—a big cayote had squatted and been watching him thru dead willow branches. He wasn't at all interested in the action Smoky was putting into his play and only wished the colt's mammy would move away a little further when he would then take a chance and try to get him down,—colt meat was his favorite dish and he sure wasn't going to let no chance slip by even if it took a whole day's waiting for one to show itself.

A couple of chances had come his way but they was queered by Smoky's mammy being too close, and he knowed better than show himself and get run down by them hoofs of hers. Finally, and when he seen his appetite wouldn't win anything by sticking around that spot any longer, he took a last sniff and came out of his hiding place. Keeping the willows between him and the horses he loped out till he was at a safe running distance and where he could see all around him and there he squatted again, in plain sight this time. He hadn't quite made up his mind as yet whether to go or stick around a while longer.—Just about then Smoky spots him.

To him, the cayote was just another stump, but more interesting than the others he'd kicked at on account that this stump moved, and that promised a lot of excitement. With a bowed neck and kinked tail Smoky trotted up towards the cayote. The cayote just set there and waited and when the colt got to within a few feet from him, he started away and just fast enough so as the colt's curiosity would make him follow. If he could only get the colt over the ridge and out of his mammy's sight.

It all was only a lot of fun to Smoky, and besides he was bound to find out what was that grey and yellow object that could move and run and didn't at all look like his mammy. His instinct was warning him steady as he went, but curiosity had the best of him, and it wasn't till he was over the hill before his instinct got above his curiosity and he seen that all wasn't well.

The cayote had turned and quicker than a flash made a jump for Smoky's throat.—The generations of mustang blood that'd fought the lobo and cougar and which was the same blood that flowed in Smoky's veins is all that saved the colt. That inherited instinct made him do the right thing at the right time, he whirled quicker than lightning and let fly with both hind feet with the result that the cayote's teeth just pinched the skin under his jaws. But even at that, he wasn't going to get rid of his enemy (it was a sure enough enemy this time) that easy, and as he kicked he felt the weight of the cayote, and then a sharp pain on his ham strings.

Smoky was scared, and he let out a squeal that sure made every living thing in that neighborhood set up and wonder, it was a plain and loud distress signal, and it was answered. His mammy shot up the hill, took in the goings-on at a glance, and ears back, teeth a shining, tore up the earth and lit into the battle like a ton of dynamite.

The battle was over in a second, and with hunks of yellow fur a flying all directions it wound up in a chase. The cayote was in the lead and he stayed in the lead till a second hill took him out of sight.

Smoky was glad to follow his mammy back to the spring and on to the other side a ways. He didn't shy at the stumps he passed on the way, and the twig that tickled his tummy didn't bring no play, he was hungry and tired, and when the first was tended to and his appetite called for no more he lost no time to picking out a place to rest his weary bones. A thin stream of

blood was drying on one of his hind legs, but there was
no pain, and when the sun set and the shadow of his
mammy spread out over him he was sound asleep, and
maybe dreaming of stumps, of stumps that moved.

When the sun came up the next morning, Smoky
was up too, and eyes half closed was standing still as
the big boulder next to him and sunned himself. A

His mammy shot up the hill, took in the goings-on at a glance, and ears back,
teeth a shining, tore up the earth and lit into the cayote like a ton of dynamite.

stiff hind leg was a reminder of what happened the
day before, but the experience was forgotten far as
dampening his spirits was concerned, even the stiffness
wouldn't hold him back from whatever the new day
would hold. He'd always remember the cayote, and
from then on never mistake him for a stump, but that
sure wasn't going to take any play out of him.

He was two days old now and strength had piled
up fast, he felt there was no trail too long for him and
when the sun was a couple of hours high that morning and his mother showed indications that she wanted
to drift he sure wasn't dragging along behind. The stiff-

ness gradually went out of his hind leg as he traveled, and by the afternoon of that day he was again shying at everything and sometimes even shying at nothing at all.

They kept a traveling and traveling, and it seemed like to Smoky that the trail was getting pretty long after all. They skirted the flat along the foot of the mountains, crossed one high ridge, and many creeks, and still his mother was drifting on. She wouldn't hardly even stop for him to nurse, and Smoky was getting cranky, and tired.

The pace kept up till the sun was well on its way down, when it slackened some and finally the mother went to grazing. A short while later Smoky was layed out full length and dead to the world.

Smoky didn't know and didn't care much just then, but his mammy was headed back to her home range, where there was lots of horses and other little colts for him to play with, and when late that night she lined out again traveling steady he wasn't in any too good a humor.

Finally it seemed like they'd got there, for his mammy after watering at a creek went to grazing at the edge of some big cottonwoods, she showed no indications of wanting to go any further. Right there Smoky was willing to take advantage of the chance and recuperate for all he was worth, the sun came up, but Smoky was in the shade of the cottonwoods what was beginning to leaf out. He slept on and a twitching ear once in long spells is all that showed he was still alive.

That day never seen much of him, once in a while

he'd get up and nurse but right away after he'd disappear again and stretch out flat on the warm earth.

He kept that up till way in the middle of the next night, and it was well towards morning before he felt like he was all horse again.

He come out of it in fine shape though, and he was stronger than ever. His vision was taking more territory too, and he was getting so he could see near half as far as his mammy could. She was the first to see the bunch of range horses trailing in to water early that morning, Smoky heard her nicker as she recognized the bunch and it drawed a heap of interest as to what she was nickering about, for he was right there alongside of her and he couldn't see nothing for her to nicker at, but pretty soon he could hear the horses as they trailed towards him, his ears straightened towards the sound and a while later he could make out the shapes of 'em. Smoky just kind of quivered at the sight of so many that looked like his mammy. He was all interested, but at the same time and even tho his instinct told him that all was well he had no hankering to leave his mammy's side till he knowed for sure just what was up.

The mother watched the bunch coming closer with ears pointed straight ahead, but soon as some of the leaders discovered little Smoky there was a commotion and they all begin crowding in to get a look at and greet the newcomer, about which time the mother layed her ears back. It was a warning that none of 'em come too close.

Little Smoky's knees was a shaking under him at

the sight of so many of his kind, he leaned against his mammy half afraid, but his head was up far as he could get it and facing 'em and showed by the shine in his eyes that he liked the whole proceeding mighty well at that. He rubbed nostrils with a strange gelding which was braver than the rest and dared come close, and when that gelding was nipped at by his mammy he had a mighty strong hankering to help her along just for fun, and nip him himself.

The preliminary introduction took a good hour, and the mother stood guard; not for fear that any of 'em would harm Smoky, but she wanted it understood from the start that he was her little colt and she had the say over him. It finally *was* understood, but it took all that day and part of the next for the bunch to get used in having the new little feller around and quit making a fuss over him.

They was all jealous of one another and fought amongst themselves to be the only one near him, and his mother, of course she'd declared herself from the start, and it was took for granted from all around that her place in Smoky's heart couldn't be considered, and all knowed better than try and chase her away from him. Fillies and old mares, young geldings and old ponies and all, had it out as to which was the most fit to tag along and play with Smoky and keep a watchful eye over him along with his mammy. All wanted the job, but a big buckskin saddle horse who all the time had been the boss of the herd took it to hand to show them that *he* would be the all around guardeen for Smoky, and second only to his mammy. He delivered a few swift kicks, pounded on some ribs, left teeth marks on shiny hides, and after taking one last look and making sure that all was persuaded grazed out towards Smoky who by his mammy had watched the whole proceeding with a heap of interest.

There was three other little colts in the bunch besides Smoky, and each time one of them little fellers came the buckskin horse had to whip the bunch so as he'd have the say over the newest one. Now Smoky was the newest one, and the buckskin horse had first rights as an outsider once again. He was an old horse full of scars showing where he'd had many a scrap, there was saddle marks on his back and at one time had been a mighty fine cowhorse. Now he was pensioned, he'd more than earned a rest and all he had to do for the rest of his life was to pick out good feed grounds for the winter, shady places and tenderest green grass for the summer, and his other interest in life was them little colts that came in spring time.

Smoky's mother was young, at least ten years younger than the buckskin horse, but the buckskin was like a colt compared to her when it come to be playful. She had the responsibility of Smoky and while she let him play with her, kick or bite at her, she never played with him and once in a while if he'd get too rough she'd let him know about it. She loved little Smoky with all her heart and would of died for him any time, and her main interest was to see that she kept in condition so that Smoky would never be stunted by lacking of rich milk. She had no time for play.

And that's where the old buckskin came in. Him and Smoky was soon acquainted, in a short while they was playing, Smoky would kick at him while the big buckskin nipped him easy and careful along the flank, then he'd run away from him, and the little colt had a lot of fun chasing that big hunk of horseflesh all over the country. The rest of the bunch would watch the two play and with no effort to hide how jealous they felt.

Smoky's mother kept her eye on the buckskin, but never interfered, she knowed, and it was only when Smoky came back to her, tired and hungry, that she put her ears back and warned him to keep away.

It took a few days before the buckskin would allow any of the other horses to get near Smoky, and then he had no say about it for he found that Smoky had his own ideas about things, and if he wanted to mingle in with the other horses that was his business, and all the buckskin could do then was to try and keep the other horses away. That was quite a job, specially if Smoky wanted to be with them. So the buckskin finally had to give it up and do the best he could which was to see that none of 'em done him any harm. But none of 'em had any intentions of doing the little colt any harm, and as it was it looked like Smoky had 'em all buffaloed. He'd tear in after some big horse like he was going to eat him up and all that big horse would do was to scatter out like the devil was after him.

Smoky was the boss and pet of the herd for a good two weeks and then one day, here comes another little feller, a little bay colt just two days old and trailing in alongside his mammy. Smoky was left in the background and witnessed the same fuss and commotion that was done over him that morning by the creek. The buckskin horse once again fought his way in that new little feller's heart, and right away he forgot Smoky.

But Smoky never seen anything wrong to that, he

Smoky had 'em all buffaloed.

went on to playing with every horse that would have him and it wasn't long till he picked up with a young fillie and afterwards went to mingling with other young colts.

From then on Smoky had more freedom, he could go out a ways without having some big overgrowed horse tagging along, but he never went far and if he did he always came back a heap faster than when he started out. But them spring days was great for Smoky, he found out a lot of things amongst which was, that grass was good to eat, and water mighty fine to drink when the day was hot, he seen cayotes again and the bigger he got the less he was afraid of 'em till he finally went to chasing every one of 'em he'd see.

Then one day he run acrost another yellow animal. That animal didn't look dangerous, and what's more it was hard for Smoky to make out just what it was, and he was bound to find out. He followed that animal plum to the edge of some willows, and the queer part of it was that animal didn't seem at all in a hurry to get away, it was mumbling along and just taking its time and Smoky was mighty tempted to plant one front foot right in the middle of it and do some pawing, but as luck would have it he didn't have the chance, it'd got in under some willows and all that was sticking out was part of the animal's tail. Smoky took a sniff at it without learning anything outside that it shook a little, there didn't seem to be no danger, so the next sniff he took was a little closer, and that done the trick. Smoky let out a squeal and a snort as he felt his nostrils punctured in half a dozen places with four-inch porcupine quills.

But Smoky was lucky, for if he'd been a couple of inches closer there'd been quills rammed into his nose plum up to his eyes, which would've caused a swelling in such size that he couldn't of been able to eat and most likely starve to death. As it was there was just a few of them quills in his nostrils, and compared to the real dose he might of got, it was just a mild warning to him. Another lesson.

It was a few days later when he met another strange animal, or strange animals, for there was many of 'em. He didn't get much interest out of them somehow, but while they was handy maybe it was just as well for him to have a close look at one. Besides he had nothing else to do, and his mammy wasn't far away.

His instinct had no warning to give as he strutted towards the smallest one of the strangers which he'd picked to investigate. He wasn't afraid of this animal and this animal didn't seem afraid of him so Smoky kept a getting closer till one was within a couple of feet of the other. Both Smoky and this stranger was young, and mighty inquisitive, and neither as yet knowed that they'd sure be seeing plenty of each other's kind as they get older, that they'll be meeting thru the round-ups at the "cutting-grounds," on "day-herd" and on "night-guard," on the long, hot, and dusty trails. A cowboy will be riding Smoky then and keeping a whole herd on the move, a whole herd of the kind that little Smoky was so busy investigating that day. They'll be full grown then, and there'll be other young ones to take the place of them that's trailed in to the shipping point.

But Smoky wasn't as yet worried or even thought on what was to come, neither was the little white-faced calf he was exchanging squints with, and when the critter called her long-eared, split-hoofed baby to her side, Smoky just kicked up his heels, put his head down, and bucked and crowhopped all the way to where his mammy and the rest of the bunch was grazing.

CHAPTER II

SMOKY MEETS THE HUMAN

THE long spring days followed by the warmer days of middle summer had took away all signs of snow excepting where the peaks was highest and the canyons deep and narrow. Up there was crusted hunks still holding out against the sun and hugging the shady sides of rocky ledges, and leaving out moisture that kept the springs and creeks running to the flats below.

The grass was greener up there, the flies wasn't so bad, and besides there was always a breeze and sometimes a wind which made things mighty cooling, specially in the shade of the twisted pines scattered over the country where Smoky, his mammy, and the bunch was ranging.

That high, rocky, and rough territory had a lot to do in the makings of Smoky. Playing down the steep ridges where shale rock made the footing slippery and mighty uncertain had took all the wobble and shake out of his legs, they fit to his body more and rounded up in size so as they looked like they really belonged to him. His hoofs had long ago lost their pink soft shell and turned to steel grey and were near as hard and tough as steel itself, and the way he'd buck and play down a rocky canyon and jump over down timber, may not of compared with a mountain goat for sureness, but he more than made up for that in speed and recklessness, and somehow he'd always hit the bottom right side up.

It was in one of them wild scrambles down a mountain side one day that Smoky near run into a cinnamon cub which had been curled up and sleeping on top of a big stump. Smoky stood in his tracks for a second, and in that second the cub fell off the stump with a snarl and lit a running on the other side.

The action of the cub is what decided Smoky whether to stand still, turn back and high-tail it, or follow and investigate, but his curiosity was still with him, and bowing his neck he paced high and mighty on the trail of the hairy puzzle.

Over dead timber he went, sailed acrost washes, and ducked under branches. He was gaining and would of kept the chase up for quite a spell, only, and just when things was getting real interesting, there was a crash, and to his right a dust and a commotion which sounded like a landslide. In half a second more, a big round brown head showed itself thru a tangle of broken limbs and underbrush, Smoky got a glimpse of two small eyes afire, long white teeth a gleaming, and when all the sudden apparition was backed by a roar that near shook the mountains, Smoky left. He tore a hole in the earth as he turned tail, and he wasn't pacing high and mighty as he made distance and raced back towards his mammy and safety.

His heart was thumping fit to bust as he cleared the timber and got out in open country, and for the life of him he couldn't figger out how that little bunch of

fur he'd been chasing could turn out into such a
scenery-tearing cyclone as what he'd got a glimpse of.
He'd never reckoned the little cub had a mammy too.

But Smoky was learning fast, and along with his
own experiences he learned from his mother just what
was what in the timber and on the flats;—like another
time on the foothills, his mammy was in the lead and
him following close behind on a hot dusty trail towards
a shady spot. Of a sudden there was a rattling sound,
and just as sudden his mammy left the trail as though
she'd been shot. Instinct made Smoky do the same
and none too soon, for on the left just a foot or so off
the trail was a wriggling thing that'd just struck, and
missed to reach his ankle by an inch.

Smoky stood off at a safe distance and snorted at it
as it coiled up ready. Somehow he had no hankering to go stick his nose nowheres near or take a sniff
at the grey and dirty yellow colored rattler, and when
his mammy nickered for him to follow there was a
warning in her nicker, he took another look at the
snake. He'd remember, and do the same as his mother
had done whenever the rattling sound would be heard
again.

Taking in all, Smoky was getting mighty wise along
with being mighty lucky in getting that wisdom,
scratches is about all he ever packed out of any scramble, and scratches didn't count with him. His hide was
getting tough and the blood that flowed in his veins
wasn't from a heart that'd peter out very easy.

The little horse was having a great time up in that
high country, and if he'd seen more of life, he'd most

likely wondered how long it all was going to last, it would of struck him as too good to last much longer, but as it was, Smoky took in all that life could give and enjoyed it to the limit. He never passed anything which had him wondering for fear of missing something. If a limb cracked anywheres within hearing distance he'd perk his ears towards the sound and seldom would go on till he found out just why that limb cracked that way, he'd follow and pester the badger till it'd hunt a hole, he'd circle around a tree and watch the bushy tailed squirrel as it'd climb up out of his reach.—Skunks had crossed his trail too, but somehow, the atmosphere around 'em would sort of dampen his curiosity and he always kept his distance.

Smoky had met and had experiences with all the range country's wild animals excepting the lion and the wolf. His mammy kept clear of the territory where them outlaws ranged, and if by scent the bunch suspicioned them two as neighbors they'd drift, or else keep on the lookout till the others had drifted. Smoky met them too and had scrambles with 'em, but that came later in his life, and it's a good thing it was later, for I most likely wouldn't be telling about Smoky now.

The first big event of Smoky's life came when he was four months old. There was nothing to tell him anything would happen, no dark skies nor ill winds to threaten or warn, and as it was, the little feller was just in the steady motion of keeping one end of himself clear of the few flies that was around, that short tail of his was working like a pendulum, he was standing up and asleep, the breeze blowed thru his mane and that same breeze made a sort of lullaby as it passed thru the branches of the big pine that shaded him and his mammy.

His mammy was asleep too, and so was the rest of the bunch, and when the cowboy that was riding up the canyon spotted 'em he knowed he could get above 'em and be where he could start 'em down before any of the bunch would see him.

It was a mighty good thing he done that, for soon as one of the bunch got wind of him and raised a head, there was a snort, they came to life and was on the run in a split second. Down the side of the canyon they went, a cloud of dust and the cowboy following.

Smoky was right with the bunch from the start, he stampeded with the leader and once in his life it never came to him to wonder what it was all about, he just run and plum forgot to investigate.

Tails was a popping as the horses slid off the mountain, jumped off ledges and sailed acrost washouts. Loosened rocks bumped against boulders, boulders crashed into dead hanging timber and pretty soon a landslide brought up the rear, but even that was too slow. The ponies and the cowboy behind 'em hit the bottom of the canyon first, and when the slide reached that spot and filled the canyon with ten feet of boulders, timber, and dirt, the whole wild bunch was half a mile away and kicking up dust on the foothills at the edge of the flat.

It was away out on the flat and where the dust wasn't so thick that Smoky took a back slant over his withers and got his first sight of the human. The way his mammy and the rest of the bunch acted, the way they run and tried to dodge or leave that human behind sure put the impression in Smoky's mind that here was a different kind of animal, the kind that no horse would stop to fight or argue with but instead run away from, if it was possible.

But it didn't seem possible, for the rider was still right on their tails, and stayed there till he drove 'em into the long wings of big log corrals which to Smoky seemed like trees growing sideways instead of up and down. But the little horse knowed that there was no going thru them trees. He stuck close as he could to his mammy's side, she and the bunch milled around for a spell around the big pen, the big gate closed on 'em and wild-eyed the bunch turned and faced a bow legged, leather-covered, sunburnt human.

Smoky shivered as he watched that strange crethure get off one of his kin, a horse just like any of the bunch him and his mammy was running with, all excepting for that funny hunk of leather on his back; pretty soon the human fumbled around a while and then that hunk of leather was pulled off, the horse was turned loose, shook himself, and walked towards Smoky and the bunch.

The colt was stary-eyed and never missed a thing, and soon as the loose horse came his way he took a sniff at his sweaty hide for some kind of a clue as to just what had been setting on him all thru that long run. The sniff left him more puzzled than ever, and forgetting the horse he put all his attention on the crethure which was standing up and on two legs.

There'd been a lot of lightning up in the mountains where Smoky had been ranging that summer, he'd seen some fires up there too. That lightning and them fires was great puzzles to the colt, and when he seen the human make a swift move with a paw, and then seen a fire in one of them paws, and later on, smoke coming out of the mouth, it all made things more than ever impossible for him to figger out. He stood petrified, and watched.

Pretty soon, them same paws that'd held the fire, reached down and picked up a coil of rope, a loop was made, and then the human walked towards him and the bunch. At that move the bunch tore around the corral and raised the dust; then Smoky heard the hiss of a rope as it sailed over past him and the loop settled on one of the ponies' heads. The pony was stopped and led out to the hunk of leather on the ground, it was cinched on him the same as it'd been on the other horse, and when the human climbed on is when Smoky first set eyes on one of his kind in a fight with the two-legged crethure.

It was a great sight to the colt. He'd seen some of his bunch play and kick often, and he'd done a lot of that himself, but he'd never seen any get in the position and tear things up the way that pony was doing. He knowed that pony was fighting, bucking for all he was worth, and doing his daggonedest to shed that sticking and ill built wonder that was on top of him. Smoky watched and shook when he heard the pony beller. He'd never heard one of his kind make that noise before, and he knowed without wondering just

what the beller meant. He remembered doing near
the same that time when the cayote had nipped him
in the ham strings.

Smoky's eyes was blazing as he watched on thru the
fight and the pony's hard jumps dwindled down to
crowhops and then a stop. He watched the man as he
got off the horse, opened the gate, led the horse out
and after closing it, watched him ride on and out of
sight. It wasn't till then that he came back to himself
and it come to his mind to investigate the kind of
place it was that cooped him in. He rubbed noses
with his mammy and went to scouting around the
big corral. Long strands of mane which had caught
in slivers of the logs told him there'd been lots of
horses here before, sniffs at the ground and more sniffs
at pieces of calves' ears that'd been cut while earmark-
ing reminded him of the critter he'd seen while he was
only a couple of weeks old. Many calves had been
branded in the big corral, and with all them signs
which was plain enough reading to Smoky it only
made him all the more suspicious and spooky.

He was trying to get up enough nerve to go near
and take a sniff at a pair of chaps hanging on the corral gate, when he noticed a dust, and under it a band
of horses being hazed towards the corral he was in.
With that band was a half dozen riders or more, and the
sight of them made Smoky hightail to his mammy's
side in a hurry. Once there, he took in all that could be
seen and watched the riders drive the horses thru the
gate and turn' em in with his bunch. There was a lot
of dust, milling around, and confusion, for there was

now near two hundred head of horses in the one big
corral, but to Smoky all that company was mighty
welcome, they meant more protection, he could hide
better in that big bunch and be able to always keep
some of the horses between him and them two-legged
crethures.

He kept hid as well as he could while the bunch
milled around the corral, and in a short while, as he
watched thru the horses' legs, he seen where on the
outside and close to the pen a fire was started, long
bars of iron was passed thru between the logs and one
end of 'em sticking in the hot blaze. Then, pretty soon
a commotion was stirred, and the bunch went to racing around the corral and snorting. Many was cut out
into another corral, till there was only about fifty left,
mostly young colts about Smoky's age, and a few quiet
old mares.

Smoky had no chance to hide, and as he seen the
bow-legged humans uncoil long ropes and heard the
loops whiz past him at the speed of a bullet, terror
struck in his heart and he was ready to leave the earth.
He heard some of the colts squeal as they was snared,
throwed, and tied down, and that sure didn't help to
ease the fear that'd took hold of him.

He was doing his best and keeping as far out of reach
as he could but it seemed like them crethures was
everywhere, and no place where them long ropes
couldn't reach. It was during one of his wild scrambles
for a get away that Smoky heard the close hiss of a
rope, and like a snake coiled itself around both his
front legs, he let out a squeal, and in another second
he was flat to the ground and four feet tied up.

Smoky figgered the end of the world had come as he
felt the human touch him, and if it'd been in his blood
to faint away, he'd a done it easy, but as it was he
never missed a thing. He seen one of the crethures run
towards him with a hot iron, smelled burning hair and
hide—it was his own that burned, but it felt cool and
there was no pain, for he was at the stage where the
searing iron was no worse than a touch from the human hand. But there's an end to all, whether it's good
or bad, and pretty soon, Smoky felt the ropes come
off his legs, a boost to let him know that all was over,
and when he stood up and run back to the bunch,
there was a mark on his slick hide that was there for
life,—as the brand read, the little horse belonged to
the ℞ (Rocking R) outfit.

It was all a mighty great relief to Smoky and
the other colts when the branding come to an end, the
bunch all put back together, and when the colts found
their mammies all was turned out and free again, free
to go back to the high mountain range, or run on the
flats.

Smoky's mammy took the lead, and after the rest
of the bunch was thru parleying with the strange horses
they joined in with her and the colt and all strung out
for the foothills. The next day they all was up in high
country again and everything of the day before was
forgotten, forgotten, all excepting with Smoky and
the other little colts. They still remembered some, on
account that it had all been mighty new to 'em, and
besides, the sting of the fresh brand was there on their
left thigh to remind.

But as the days went by, and new things happened

right along to draw Smoky's interest in life, the happenings at the corral was gradually left behind like a bad dream; the burn healed quick and left a neat brand all of which growed right with him.

Fall came, skies clouded and the rains was getting cold, and each time it cleared up again it was a little colder, the sun wasn't making as high a circle and was steady losing some of its heat, and when after a few mornings' frost the skies clouded again and the wind blowed a light snow over the high pinnacles, the bunch gradually ranged lower and lower, till, when they reached the foothills and finally the flats, the first of the winter had set in and it was time for 'em to drift to their winter range.

Their winter range was low ridges and benches that raised up in the middle of the prairie. There was steep ravines where willows and cottonwoods growed in big patches, the shelter of them was mighty fine when the cold north winds blowed and the howling blizzard made every living thing hunt a hole. Tall grass was there too and could always be reached by pawing for it. In quiet winter days, when the sun came out and the wind went down the bunch could always leave their shelter and find places on the ridges where the winds had swept the snow away, and where the grass was in plain sight.

Drifting acrost that flat open country and investigating that new winter territory had kept Smoky's eyes, ears, and nostrils mighty busy. There'd been a lot to keep him looking, listening, and sniffing. Every buffalo wallow, coulee, and rise had kept his senses on hair-trigger edge, and when the first snow had come, he'd enjoyed that too. It made him want to buck and play as it fell on his withers and rump, and along with the cold weather that'd turned the range brown and then white he was finding more ambition to keep on the jump. He wasn't looking for shade no more.

If Smoky minded the cold he sure didn't show it, and if you could of felt his warm hide and seen how thick the hair had growed on it, and how long, you'd never wondered why it was that the cold raw winds never fazed him. Mother Nature had seen to that and brought on the winter gradual, till, when the time come for it to set in, Smoky was well prepared, he was packing a natural fur coat on a good thick hide, and with an inch of tallow for a lining, and along with the rich, thick blood which he kept in good circulation he was mighty able to compete with the snows and freezing weather, and was never found to hunt shelter till the blizzard blowed over the ridges from the north.

He pawed snow for his feed that winter, for it had been quite a few months before when he found that his mammy's milk wasn't quite enough, and later turned out to be just a taste, and finally, she give him to understand that he was weaned. There was no arguing with her, and Smoky knowed better than try, so he pawed and hunted for grass like a big horse. He et snow and could stay away from water as long as any of the bunch, and even tho he lost some of his roundness thru the worst of the winter, you couldn't of noticed it on account of his hair being so long.

Being that Smoky was still quite a privileged character it helped him considerable thru them long winter months, if he'd see some big horse dig down into a special good grassy spot, he'd take advantage of his standing and chase the big horse away. He looked mighty wicked as he put his ears down, showed his teeth, and delivered a side kick, and the big horse would *act* scared to death, and get away from the dangerous Smoky in a hurry. There was only one in the bunch that wouldn't scare worth a bit, and that was his mammy, he could paw in the same hole with her and maybe steal a bunch of grass right from under her nose, but there was no chasing *her* away, most likely there was no such intentions in Smoky's mind anyhow, for the little horse did think an awful lot of that mammy of his, and even tho she never played with him, and even nipped him for some things he'd do, he knowed if a showdown ever come she'd fight to a finish for him.

So, as the snows piled high and the ravines filled with drifts, Smoky went on and passed the hard of the winter in near the same carefree reckless way he'd passed the summer before. Of course, pawing for his feed the way he had to was taking some of his energy, but he'd manage to reserve some for play, and many is the time when you'd see the bunch a pawing all intent to reaching the grass, you'd see Smoky tearing up clouds of light snow and a playing for all he was worth. Other colts would join him, and pretty soon the young ones would have the white scenery all tracked the same as if a thousand head of horses had stampeded thru.

The winter wore on that way, no events came to shake the quiet and peace of that part of the range, only, one day a rider had showed up against the skyline. Smoky had been the only one to see him on account he was a little ways from the bunch and where he could see around a point. With the sight of that rider Smoky remembered ropes, a corral and human hands, and he sashayed back to the bunch fast as his legs could carry him.

Finally, the first sign of spring came, Smoky couldn't appreciate it very much on account that the warm winds which was starting the snow to melting only left him weak and lazy. His blood hadn't started to thin down as yet, and for the first short spell in his life, he had no hankering to crowhop around and play.

Then a few weeks later the bare earth begin to show in big spots and on the sunny side of the buttes green grass begin to shoot up. That new green grass tasted mighty good to Smoky, it tasted so good that the dry feed he'd wintered on and which could now be got without pawing for, was only stepped on in hunting for them first blades of green. Nothing but that would do, and as it was still scarce and hard to find that early in the year he covered a lot of territory and got very little feed.

But the rest of the bunch was afflicted the same way, the long dry grass wasn't good enough no more, and consequences is the bunch lost some weight. But Mother Nature was on hand there again, she knowed that's what the bunch needed to condition 'em for the change of season, and sure enough, pretty soon the warm weather didn't leave 'em so drowsy no more, and as the grass kept a growing, and finally got to be everywhere, on the ridges as on the flats, the bunch perked up again; the long winter hair was loosening and big hunks of it was left wherever they rolled.

Smoky's winter coat had faded to a brown at the first sign of spring, and now that the warmer weather had come and green grass was a plenty there was another color showed where he'd shed off the long hair. It was what we call "mouse color" only maybe darker, no more of the slick black hair that decorated his hide the summer before could be seen, the change of color had showed itself around his ears and flanks but it wasn't till winter came that the real change had took place and turned him to a grayish mouse color.

His head and legs was a little darker than his body and showed brown, and with that little blaze face of his a looming up, he made a mighty pretty picture, a picture of the kind once you see you never forget; for Smoky was perfect any way you looked at him and it seemed like as you sized him up that the other of his kind hadn't been played square with and some of their good points stole away so as Smoky would be the perfect little horse.

Smoky had never thought of his good looks and strong body, his good looks was only a sign of his good health, he felt it all and used it to the limit for his own benefit and for whatever fun his strength and energy could afford him. That never lacked, and if he layed

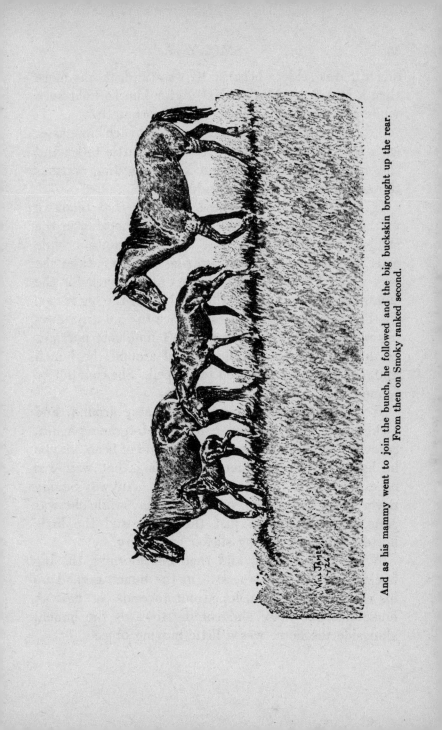

And as his mammy went to join the bunch, he followed and the big buckskin brought up the rear. From then on Smoky ranked second.

down it was seldom because he was tired, it was more
thru a hint from Mother Nature for him to hold on a
while and store up on life and more strength.

The spring rains came and went, and each time after
each spell of moisture the grass was a little taller and
the country greener, the sun kept a getting warmer
too and some days was already hot.

It was during one of these hot days that Smoky's
mother disappeared. Smoky had been snoozing in the
shade of a creek bank and it wasn't till quite a while
after he got up and started grazing that he noticed she
was gone. The bunch had been drifting back for the
summer range and was at the foothills of the big range,
the big flat below was an easy place to spot any moving object on, but Smoky couldn't find hide nor hair
of that mammy of his, he trotted around the bunch
and, nickering, investigated for a spell. She couldn't be
found.

He took another look at the country around, and
nickering in kind of wonder, he went to grazing again.
Somehow he wasn't fidgety as he should of been, maybe
he had a hunch that her disappearing that way was
necessary and that all was hunkydory. Anyway Smoky
never missed any sleep, or feed, or play while she was
gone, things went on just the same, and the little
horse's hide was getting slicker every day.

A few days passed, and then one morning the big
buckskin horse that was still in the bunch perked up
his ears, nickered, and loped out towards the flat. A
horse was out there and coming towards the bunch,
alongside the horse was a little moving object.

Smoky and the bunch stood in their tracks and watched. Pretty soon Smoky noticed something familiar in that lone horse coming towards him, but that little object a tagging along puzzled him, and head up, he trotted out a ways to investigate. Then it all came to him, for the lone horse was none other than his mammy.

He lit out on a run a nickering as he went till he got to within a few feet of her, and then he got a slant at the object a tagging alongside, a brand new little wobblety legged colt it was, shining black, and awful timid at the sight of so many strangers. It was Smoky's new little brother.

Smoky couldn't keep his nose off the baby, and his mammy had to cock one ear back at him the same as to say "careful, Son," but Smoky was careful, and as his mammy went on to join the bunch, he followed and the big buckskin brought up the rear. From then on Smoky ranked second.

CHAPTER III

WHERE THE TRAILS FORK

MIDDLE summer had come, the day was hot and still; even up amongst the high peaks and where the snow was making a last stand the heat was strong, for the sun was shooting straight down and the crags could give no more shade. Up on a rocky trail of that country a small bunch of range horses was drifting one behind the other and following the leader,—the leader was Smoky's mammy, the new little black colt right at her heels and next the blaze faced, mouse colored, yearling, Smoky. A little further back was a big buckskin horse and there followed eight or ten others which made up the rest of the bunch.

They all trailed along seemed like headed for nowheres in particular. They passed under wind-twisted trees and right on thru the shade they'd give. Cool streams wasn't even sniffed at, and the long stems of grass that was everywhere wasn't at all noticed, they was all just drifting and maybe only hitting out for another special good part of the high range.—A feller watching 'em would of figgered that something or other had started 'em on the move, maybe a rider had been spotted that morning which had kettled 'em into a run, or else cougars might of been too numerous for comfort.

The little bunch kept a trailing along till they came

to where the trail branched and the leader took the lower one, the little black colt and all the rest followed, all excepting the mouse colored yearling. The upper trail had drawed that one's interest, and nothing would do but what he had to investigate it for a ways. He kept his nose on the ground as he went and sniffed for clues of anything that might be of interest to him, he could see the bunch below and he figgered on cutting across to 'em soon as his curiosity was satisfied.

Ahead of him a ways and above the trail was a big granite boulder a good ten feet high. A scrub mahogany had found root in a crack of the big rock and was spreading its branches well over it and making a good shade. In that shade and mighty hard to notice, was an object, a long, flat, dark buckskin object, which looked a lot like part of the rock. It was stretched out full length and seemed like without life only maybe for the tip of its long, round tail which was jerking up and down. The round head raised an inch at the sound of hoofs on the rocky trail, the ears flattened and the yellow eyes turned jet black at the sight of Smoky, the mouse colored yearling.

Smoky was coming right on the trail and would pass to within a couple of feet of the big rock that was the mountain lion's game hunting perch, many a deer he'd pounced onto and killed from that perch; and not far away from that spot was bones scattered around which showed where he'd drug his victims and et his fill. Wolves, cayotes, and other varmints had cleaned up what the big lion would leave and the result was white bones a shining to the sun.

The lion had a big territory which he claimed as his, but in all that rough country there was no better place than the one he was now getting ready to spring from, he'd got meat from that spot when he failed at others, and the trail he overlooked was tracked with many hoofs, hoofs of all the kind that ranged up there,—it was a main trail to a main pass.

Why Smoky's mother didn't take that trail can't be explained much; may be it was instinct that warned her, and then again she might of got a glimpse of the tall rock and past experience made her turn to the left, but anyway she and her young colt and the rest of the bunch was safe and had left Smoky till he was thru investigating and ready to catch up with 'em.

Smoky kept on a coming and edging closer to the rock, he nosed every twig and stone along the trail till he got to within a few feet of the spot where the lion would spring. The lion wasn't a stretched out shadow no more. He still looked like part of the rock and fitted pretty well with the stump of the scrub mahogany, but he was in a position that sure tallied up with all what was about to happen. He was ready, and still as the rock he was on, and the quiver of his long tail was a plenty to show that his wiry frame and brain was sure together and intent on one thing.

Another foot ahead and Smoky would be seeing his last of daylight, the colt had one leg raised to make that last step when there's a rattling buzz comes from the foot of the rock, a four foot rattlesnake stretched out and reaches for Smoky's nose and that one leg

The lion had figgered on his victim a jumping to one side at his leap, and he'd allowed for that.

which was raised to go forward went back instead. It was all that saved him.

The lion had figgered on his victim a jumping to one side at his leap, and he'd allowed for that, but the way it happened this time was that the snake caused Smoky to jump away just as he'd started which was a little too soon according to the lion's figgering, and what's more Smoky went to the wrong direction about a foot with the result that he just got his claws full of Smoky's mane and no more. He scrambled in mid air and done his best to get a hold in Smoky's neck but even with all the action he put in his trying he struck mostly air, and then hard ground.

Smoky never waited to see if that flying shadow of sharp claws was after him or not, he'd started at the sound of the rattler and had kept a moving mighty fast ever since. A few feet of drop in the scenery only helped him make more speed and the short cut from the trail he'd left to the trail his mammy and the bunch was on was covered in no time.

He lit in the bunch a running, and the bunch getting a hint from his wild eyed actions that all wasn't well started a running too and for a ways they all went as tho the devil was after 'em.

But the devil (if that ain't too mild a name for the lion) wasn't after 'em. He knowed the colt had too much speed for him and never even thought of following him, and as it was he was just a lashing himself with his long tail and mad clear thru at the thought of missing such a nice fat yearling colt as Smoky was.

From that day on Smoky dodged high rocks unless

he could see the top of 'em, pine trees with stout lower limbs had him a circling too, or any other place where a lion could perch on and spring from. The little horse was gradually getting so he was satisfied to be more with the bunch and not do so much investigating, besides he'd got first hand acquaintance with most all

He got strong headed and full of mischief, and then's when the older horses figgered him to be a regular pest.

that prowled the range, and everything in general was getting to be less of a puzzle to him.

It all kept a getting to be less of a puzzle to him till finally there come a time when Smoky got so he thought he knowed it all. He figgered he had the world by the tail and with a downhill push. Like all the other colts of his age he was just where conceit had the best of him, he got strong headed and full of mischief, and then's when the older horses figgered him to be a regular pest and begin knocking on him.

He was getting to be of a size that could stand
knocks too. They all took turns at him and pounded
on his ribs every chance they had thru the rest of that
summer and tried to set him where he belonged; but
it was slow work and Smoky was still getting away
with some of the bluffs when the first snows came.
He was ornery all that winter, and even tho none of
the horses would let him steal the grass they pawed
up he aggravated 'em a lot by making 'em think he
would; and when they'd kick at him, and miss, there
was some more about his actions that sure let 'em know
he was getting away with something.

Then one day a strange horse showed up on the skyline and joined the bunch. A strange horse is always
sort of timid when first joining a new bunch that way,
and Smoky took advantage of that to show there was
at least one he had buffaloed,—he run the stranger
around and around and kept a nipping him on the rump
till the old pony was on the point of leaving to hunt
new territory. That sport lasted off and on for a few
days, and then one day the older horse turned and lit
into Smoky. There was no battle, for Smoky was just
running a bluff, and at the first turn of the events he
evaporated and kept on evaporating till the stranger
got cooled down a bit. After that Smoky kept his distance and acted willing to let the stranger stay with
the bunch.

The winter wore on that way, and as Smoky was
met hard at every ornery thing he'd do, it all got to
finally leave an impression on him and he gradually lost
some of his conceit and hard headedness. But spring

came, other seasons and all kinds of weather followed and it wasn't till Smoky was a three year old that he really come anywheres living up to good range horse etiquette. There was so much life wrapped up in that pony's hide that it was mighty hard for him to settle down and behave, and even as a three year old he sometimes had to bust out and do things that wasn't at all proper and which made the old horses set their ears back and show their teeth.

The start of Smoky's third year was all to his favor,— the spring rains was warmer than on average, the green grass shot up half an inch to the day and more than met up with the hard to satisfy appetite which was his, consequences is, when he shed off his long winter coat he was slicker and rounder than ever and looked like he was wrapped up in fine mouse colored silk. His blazed face loomed up snow white and to match his trim ankles. He was a picture to make any cowboy miss a few heart beats as he sometimes raced acrost the prairie sod and with head and tail up showed off the qualities that stuck out at his every move.

But to the bunch, all them qualities and good points of Smoky's was lost and not at all noticed, his mammy or any of the others would of thought just as much of him if he was just an ordinary horse or even an ill built scrub. They'd all liked him better if he wasn't so ornery and didn't need so much convincing, for Smoky was getting to be of a size and temper along with it where it was mighty hard for some to try to eddicate him and *show* that they could.

His eddication kept on tho for there was still a few that packed a convincing hoof, but them few was dwindling down fast and Smoky was steady getting where he could hold his own with most any of 'em, till finally, and after many showdowns there came a time when there was only two left in the bunch that he wouldn't stop and argue with, them two was his mammy and the big buckskin.

Smoky felt some superior and mighty proud then for a while, and it's a good thing he was a little wiser and quieter and not so full of mischief no more or he'd sure dealt them ponies misery; as it was he was now willing to leave them alone if they'd do the same by him.

Things went on that way for some time and as the days went by, the bunch was getting to be more willing to accept Smoky as a full size range horse with brains according. None tried to eddicate him no more, and if once in a while he showed young blood and some foolishness they was all careful to overlook it, of course Smoky was wise enough to keep away from his mammy and the buckskin at them times.

Peace was with the little bunch, all had some understanding and every horse knowed his ground. It was all so peaceful that Smoky felt it and it all begin to wear on him to the point where he felt like tackling the big buckskin, just to start something—then relief came one day and scattered that peaceful monotony from hell to breakfast.

It all happened as the little bunch strung out, was heading for water, Smoky's mammy was in the lead as usual, and she was the first to turn the point of a ridge and find herself to within a few yards of a big black stud. Smoky was close second on the sight, and somehow as he snorted at the long-maned thick-jawed black a hunch came to him that peace had come to a sudden end.

He stood in his tracks kinda doubtful as to what to do and watched the black cloud of horseflesh, he'd let the stallion make the first false move— Proud as a peacock came the black, mane and tail a waving and stepping high, his little bunch of mares and colts had stayed back at the first sight of the strange ones and was now watching the proceedings of the meeting.

That meeting impressed the young horses a whole lot, the white of their eyes showed their interest as the stud came up to within a few paces of the new bunch, stopped, and with a powerful neck bowed to a half circle, ears pointed ahead, and eyes a shining, stood and sized up the strangers.

He'd had plenty of experience in meeting strange bunches that way before which all left him kinda cautious, for many a time he'd left quicker than he'd come and lost some hide to an older stud what was more up to the game of fighting, and he soon learned that it wasn't a wise idea to ram into a strange bunch and go to appropriating mares without first investigating what kind of a leader that bunch had.

He'd got wised up in many ways thru them meetings, and he learned to be some careful. He'd also learned to handle his hoofs and teeth till there hadn't been any stud on that range that'd been able to whip him the last three years—he'd evened up scores.

Smoky hadn't moved, and as the stud still kept a standing in one spot with no indication of wanting to start anything, he got restless. Pretty soon it came to his mind that the stallion was leary of starting anything, it was a big mistake, but Smoky'd had no way of knowing better. The big buckskin did know better and if Smoky had noticed, he'd seen him out there on the far side of the bunch, and willing to keep neutral.

A move from the black stud decided Smoky. He'd stepped close to his mammy and nostril to nostril was exchanging sniffs with her when she let out a squeal and struck at him, all of which the stallion didn't pay any attention to. But right about then Smoky landed on him, or, *at him*, for his striking front feet and bared sharp teeth missed him, missed him just enough to be a clean miss.

Smoky had never reckoned with the fighting qualities of a stallion, and he couldn't figger out how it was he'd struck just thin air when he was so sure his enemy had been right there in front of him and within easy reaching distance, and what's more that puzzled him was that the stallion never offered to show fight when he landed at him so furious, instead he'd just got out of the way of his rush, kept his ears ahead, and went on sizing up the bunch the same as if nothing had happened. Smoky felt like he hadn't even been noticed, and the actions of the stud had said plainer than words "fool kid."

A swift kick in the ribs couldn't of done any better

towards putting Smoky down a peg or two, and that simple quick move of the stud's went a long ways to show what could of happened if he'd been in mind to fight. All that left Smoky kinda uncertain as to how to proceed, he didn't know whether to go back and try it again or let things rest for a spell till another chance showed up.

In the meantime the black stud had found out that there was none in that bunch he'd need to watch, and head down to the ground, ears back, he started cutting out the geldings, keeping the mares and fillies to put in with the bunch he already had. That was a harder job than it might sound here, for none of the geldings wanted to be cut out of the bunch they'd been with so long, and even tho they went out easy enough they'd turn back as the stud would be cutting out another and would have to be headed off and cut out again and again.

Then the big buckskin which had been neutral all this time finally got riled up at being separated from the mares that way and when the stud headed for him he stood his ground. A few seconds more and there was buckskin and black hair a sailing in the air, then hoofs a pounding away which would of kept up with machine-gun fire for speed, only the pounding wasn't sounding so sharp it was hitting something solid, and there wasn't many misses.

Finally out of the dust that was stirred there came a streak of buckskin and right close to it was a streak of black, away from the herd they went, and pretty soon the black stud came back shaking his head the same as to let every horse know that he wasn't going to stand for no foolishness.

There was one more to be put out of the bunch, he was that mouse colored gelding, Smoky. He'd got in while the stud was chasing away the buckskin, he'd stood alongside his mammy and watched the fight, and there was a light in his eyes that showed he was ready to start another battle if it was necessary, but he sure wasn't going to be put out without he was convinced it could be done,—he wasn't built that way.

The stallion spots him there and never went thru no preliminaries nor tried to scare him out with just a look, he dived right into him and Smoky met him halfways. That battle was short and wicked and Smoky managed to land some good hard kicks, kicks that'd knocked the wind out of any ordinary horse and sent 'em a sprawling; but the stallion wasn't no ordinary horse and them kicks only shook him a little and made him all the madder. He'd fought too many hard battles to let any gelding faze him and besides he was in the habit of winning.

His chance came when Smoky turned to land a couple more hard ones. The stud was broadside to the gelding, and as the hard ones came, he just reared up out of the reach of 'em, made a big lunge to one side and coming down he made a quick grab and fastened his teeth in Smoky's withers. When Smoky pulled away and the stud's teeth snapped together there was some of his silky hide between 'em.

Smoky squealed and kicked some more, then he whirled and faced the stud figgering on doing some

damage with teeth and front hoofs. Just about then the
stud whirled too and planted his two hind hoofs smack
bang into Smoky's ribs. There was an echo which
sounded like a steam engine ramming into a stone wall,
that echo was followed with a mighty grunt as Smoky
was lifted off his feet and throwed out a ways to a
staggering standstill.

Smoky was in a daze, his vision was dim, and maybe
it was all instinct that warned him of the dark cloud
that's turned and was now a tearing down on him,
anyway something made him move in a hurry, all the
strength that was left in him was used to make distance away from the black devil which now looked to
Smoky like a big centipede, it had so many legs.

His life depended on the speed he could make, and
Smoky was running, running like he'd never run before,
it seemed like there was no shaking the mad stud, and
just when he was on the point of giving in and make a
last stand for his life that destroying hunk of horseflesh left him— When Smoky stopped, looked back
and seen the stud hightail it back to the mares he had
no hankering to follow, he was convinced.

The next few days that followed was mighty aimless
to Smoky, him and the big buckskin had formed a
pardnership in that time and the two wandered around
like they was lost and didn't care where they went.
They covered a lot of territory, passed up a lot of good
grassy hollows and shady places but they kept a drifting on. They grazed as they drifted and natural like
followed up the canyons and crossed over the high

passes that'd been the summer range of Smoky's mammy and the bunch.

They came acrost other little bunches, but it seemed like in each of 'em there was a wild-eyed thick-jawed stud come out ready to kick the daylight out of 'em if any symptoms of them wanting to trail in with the bunch was showed.

In their roaming around they passed other geldings which like themselves had been kicked out of the stud bunches; the meeting with them was just plain "how-dedo's" and each and all passed on and headed their own wandering way.—All would be hunkydory again for the buckskin if he could find another bunch to run with where there was mares and little colts. He had a mighty strong failing for the little fellers and most any bunch would do if there was only a few of them in, but with Smoky, it was his mammy he missed most, his brother, and the other colts he'd growed up with.

No other bunch would do as well, and the nicker he'd send echoing acrost canyons and over ridges every once in a while was just for them certain few.

Smoky's mammy had no choice when that black stallion came and scattered them out to his liking that way. She was made to join that little bunch of his and she knowed better than try to do different; she knowed she'd only lose some hide in any attempt to get away and that in the long run she'd have to do as he pointed out.

She was wise to the range and the ways of her kind, and even tho she was as strong for Smoky as Smoky was for her she didn't miss him so much as he did her.

She felt in a way that he was now big and mighty able to take care of himself, and then there was other youngsters which called for all her attention. But it was different with Smoky, she was his mammy and there was none other that could take her place. He'd growed up at her side and even tho other little colts had come she was and always would be the mother he knowed when he was wobblety legged and needed her.

Then one day and as time had wore on in lonesomeness that way, there came a short break in the monotony which helped Smoky forget some. Him and the buckskin had run acrost a little bunch of mares,—there was some little colts in the bunch, and a stud, a young stud.

The big buckskin sized up the stud the same as he'd sized all the others he'd met, and as this young feller came up full of pride and confidence to meet the two strangers, the big buckskin found a flaw in him,—the flaw was nothing more or less than just *youth*, he showed it in every move he made and every action.— From past experience the buckskin had figgered youth and ignorance to go together, and that's what made it interesting.

Interesting by the fact that thru youth and ignorance the young stallion wouldn't maybe be able to compete against the fighting ability of the buckskin, the younger horse hadn't as yet fought many battles, that the buckskin could feel at a glance of him. He didn't turn away like he'd done before,—as the stallion came on he just stood in his tracks and watched him. Smoky was doing the same.

There's bowed necks as the three touch nostrils, there's some squealing and striking and then a kick is planted,—the young stud had started things.

Smoky had caught the kick, which left him out a ways. In the meantime the buckskin followed up the lead and went at it from there. It was all a mighty fair exchange from the start, kicks and bites was averaging pretty well on both parties, and for a young horse that chestnut stud was sure doing well. All might of come to a draw and both fighters might of quit about the same time, if it hadn't been for Smoky.

Smoky which had got to be pretty thick with the buckskin and had been a good pardner of his thru their lonesome roamings found it mighty natural-like wanting to help when trouble came that way; besides he was holding a grudge against the stud for kicking him the way he did, and all them things together kinda had him worked up to mix in.

His chance came as the chestnut whirled to plant a hard one on the buckskin's ribs, there was only a few feet between Smoky and the stud right then and double action started from there. The stud felt hard-hitting hoofs and teeth a getting him from both sides and the punishment he received all at once wouldn't of been worse if he'd a lit in a stack of wild cats.

It was then that it come to his mind, and sudden, that he should let up on the fighting and start to do some running if he wanted to keep hisself all in one piece. Smoky and the buckskin kept a pounding on him and a helping along on the good hunch till finally it was all made mighty plain. The chestnut picked

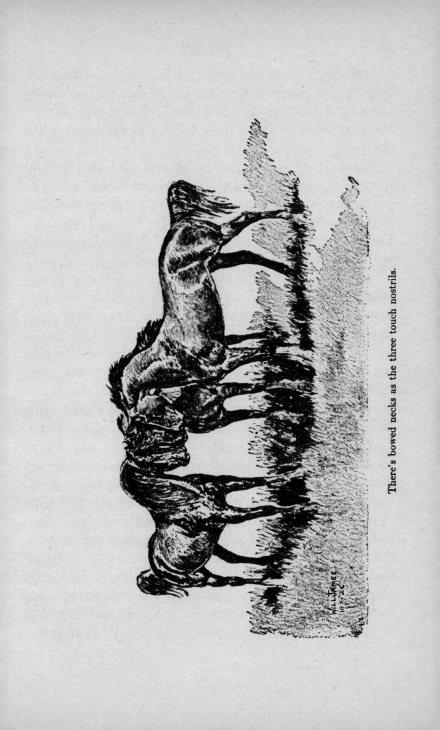

There's bowed necks as the three touch nostrils.

himself up as best and quick as he could and made a leap out of reach of the too many wicked hoofs and teeth, and tore up the earth for a change of scenery, the two pardners done their best to escort him on his way.

But as that day came to an end and as the sun passed over and beyond the blue ridges Smoky and his pardner could see a lone horse outlined against the sky, the chestnut was following. He followed 'em and the bunch they'd chased him out of for three days, and once he started a fight to win back what he'd lost, he just lost more hide and won nothing but another boost out of that territory.— Smoky and the big buckskin had handed him the same medicine another stud had handed them.

The days that followed was mighty peaceful to the big buckskin, and Smoky seemed some contented too, he was gradually getting used to being away from his mother and new young fillies and colts he was running with made it all a heap easier to forget. Then again, the knocks he'd got ever since that day when things had been so peaceful with his mammy, when he just figgered he'd have to start something to bust up the monotony of that peace, all took the mischief out of him. The fight with the black stallion, the lonesome ramblings with the buckskin, and the other fights with the chestnut stud all helped eddicate him and shape him into a full sized, serious thinking gelding. It didn't take so much to keep him contented no more, and somehow or another he was seeing a heap more in life.

That's the way things stood with Smoky that sum-

mer, him and the buckskin ranged high up in the
mountains with the little bunch of mares and colts,
they all snoozed and grazed thru the days and done
the same thru the nights. A little play was brought on
once in a while by some of the young colts and Smoky
and the buckskin was always the steady victims of
them. Them two older horses was colts themselves at
them times and the way they'd all nip one another and
then sashay around hell bent for election, a human
would wonder at the care Smoky and the buckskin
was taking so that the colts would feel winners in all
they'd start.

Summer passed, the grass had gradually turned to
a yellow brown and the leaves of the aspens begin
banking up on the edges of the streams, fall had come,
and one day the bunch started a grazing steady lower
and lower till a few days later the foothills was reached.
It was there that Smoky took the lead and headed for
the winter range where his mammy had put him thru
that first year, the big buckskin followed till, glancing
back over his withers he noticed that the mares and
colts had left off and branched out another direction.
The buckskin stood in his tracks, watched Smoky line
out straight ahead and then looked back at the mares
again. For the time being he wasn't sure whether to
go on with his pardner or turn back to the bunch. It
was hard for him to decide, he wanted to go with Smoky
and still them little colts sure had a mighty holt on
his heart strings, it was just about as he was doing the
hardest figgering when one of them little fellers came
out of the bunch a ways and nickered for him. That

little nicker decided things for the buckskin, he answered it and loped back to join with the other little fellers and the mares.

Smoky went on straight ahead. Maybe he was thinking strong, thinking that he'd see his mammy again on that winter range. Anyway, it never come to him to look back and see if the bunch was following him, and finally when it did come to him that he was drifting on alone, he stopped and looked around in a sort of vacant stare, his instinct had been controlling him and was taking him back to his home range, but when he found himself alone that way it all left him surprised at first and then doubtful as to what to do. He was mighty attached to that buckskin, the little colts, and the bunch in general.

He looked at the far away hills of his range and he seemed like to think on the subject for quite a spell, then of a sudden his head went up, a loud nicker went out and away in the distance he could hear an answer,—the answer had come from his pardner, the buckskin.

Smoky nickered again and loped back to the bunch. He'd come to feel that it didn't matter so much which range he wintered on, he was a big horse now, and a few ridges to the north or south of that range he was raised in didn't make much difference.—An old mare had took the lead and from then on Smoky just followed side by side with the buckskin. A little colt nipped him in the flanks, and all was well.

CHAPTER IV

THE END OF A ROPE

SNOW layed heavy on the range that winter, grass was hard to get at, and the little bunch of ponies that tracked the low hills which raised up on the prairies was finding themselves doing a lot of rustling and pawing, and getting very little feed. Bunches of cattle followed 'em wherever they went and rooted with their nose for the few blades of dry grass them horses had pawed the snow off of and left.

Hay couldn't be bought that winter and the stockmen found themselves where they had to take a chance and pull their cattle thru with whatever little hay the dry summer before could let 'em have. Cattle had been in fine shape that fall, but as the snow kept a piling and a drifting and covering up the feed the tallow kept a dwindling away from under the critters' hides and lean ribs begin to show more and more thru the long winter hair.

Then came a time as the blizzards blowed and regardless of what all the stockmen done (which was to the limit of what any human can do) when mounds of white begin to show here and there in that part of the range. Underneath them white mounds was the dead carcass of a critter. Some was dug up by the varmints, cayotes was licking their chops, and to make things worse, there appeared three big grey wolves on the skyline one day.

Smoky and the big buckskin horse was the first to see the wolves. Their ears was towards 'em as the three outlaws of the range trotted along and then stopped to look at the horses.

Smoky had never seen a wolf before, but the big old buckskin had seen too many of 'em and had scars to show for his meetings with the kind. He let a loud snort at the sight of the three grey shapes and from that Smoky got a hunch that these was more to be reckoned with than the cayotes he'd chased when he was a yearling. He had a hankering to go and give them a chase too, but the nervous way the buckskin was acting kinda warned him that it'd be best for him to stick with the bunch.

The weak and dying cattle is what had really drawed the wolves, of course they would just as soon tackle a strong animal as a weak one but the scent that scattered over the range from the dead stock and which would reach no less sensitive a nose than theirs was a lot to their liking, and they'd just drifted in to investigate.

It was below them to touch any of the carcasses they'd passed, for these was old wolves well up to the game of killing, and nothing but fresh meat would do. A good fat yearling or two year old colt is what came highest and most to their tastes, and when they skirted that ridge and spotted that little bunch of ponies in the draw below, it was the sight of them that reminded their appetites how long ago it was since they'd et last, and they'd traveled a long ways.

But it was still daylight, and according to their natural way of doing things they'd wait till night come before making the kill. They skirted on and out of sight of the horses, nosed the snow and the air to make sure that the coast was clear and after another look at the country so they'd know it when they returned the wolves trotted on. They showed what old timers they was as they circled well away from a carcass for fear of a trap, they'd had their toes pinched in the steel jaws, scars showed where bullets had grazed 'em and one was still packing a piece of lead which a cowboy had fired at him from a long shot with a 30–30.

The big buckskin back there in the draw knowed their way, and it showed in his action, he'd quit pawing for grass and instead put all his attention to the tops of the ridges that was all around him and the bunch. The way them three wolves had sized up the bunch and then disappeared had made him restless and mighty spooky and finally that draw got to be too much of a hole for him, too good a place for an enemy to come into without being seen till that enemy was too close.

The older mares showed a lot of spookiness too which all got Smoky riled up so that he begin acting the same, and when the buckskin took the lead out of the draw to where a good look of the country around could be got the whole bunch was mighty anxious to follow, even the little colts seemed to have the hunch that something was up, the white of their eyes showed and they stuck mighty close to their mammies' side.

A big moon came up and the light of it reflected a path that shined on the crusted snow, the air was mighty still, still with the cold that'd gripped the range and made everything that lived and carried hoofs come to a stand so that no air would be stirred; a breeze at that temperature would froze stiff every standing animal in that territory.

Smoky, the buckskin, and the bunch stood on a knoll where they could see well around 'em, they looked like petrified or froze there so still they all stood, there was no sign of life from 'em excepting for an ear that moved once in a while and which was on the job to catch any sound that might come from near or far.

The "yip, yip," and howl of a cayote was heard, another answered, and pretty soon them two filled the air with their serenading—. The echo of that hadn't quite died down when the long, drawed out, and mournful howl of a wolf made that of the cayotes seem like a joke. The little bunch of horses on the knoll hadn't blinked an eye while the cayotes was serenading, but at the sound of what followed, every head in the bunch went up, every ear pointed towards the sound, and the buckskin with a few others snorted.

Restlessness had got in the bunch, Smoky started out a ways and came back, then pretty soon and keeping as close together as they could they all begin moving. They moved on like shadows, and like more shadows three grey shapes had took up their trail.

The big buckskin had stayed in the rear of the bunch and he was first to notice the wolves, a loud whistling snort was heard from him as he landed in the middle of the bunch and kettled 'em into a stampede and the run for their lives. The cold air was split forty ways and crusted hunks of snow was sent a flying as the ponies all wild eyed broke their way thru the drifts at the edge of a ridge and run on towards the big flat.

Smoky had stampeded with the rest and kept pretty well up in the lead thru the run, but now that his blood was warming up in plowing thru the deep snow, and being that that blood was circulating more free up his neck and into his brain, it all put somewhat of a different light on the subject. That brain of his was all het up, on hair trigger with the waking up the run was giving it, and pretty soon something hatched up in there that made Smoky slow down till the bunch went past and ahead of him.— He was wanting to see what was all fired dangerous about them wolves so as to make the bunch run that way.

The big buckskin was the last to pass Smoky, he was busy keeping two little colts just a few months old from lagging behind too far, bucking the deep snow at the speed the bunch was making was beginning to show on 'em and it was taking a lot of persuading from the big horse to keep them little fellers on the move.

The wolves was steady catching up with the bunch and the attack would of took place some sooner if it hadn't been for Smoky. His lagging behind had fooled the wolves into thinking that the mouse colored gelding had quit and was ready to make his last stand. It had been Smoky's intention to wait for the killers and paw the daylight out of 'em, but as the three rushed in on him he figgered it a good idea to postpone the pawing for a while and do a little running till he was some acquainted with their ways and tricks.

Head and tail up and fire in his eyes he lined out and *led the wolves away from the bunch,* they'd figgered on making him their victim on account he was the handiest but as the chase kept up they found the gelding had a powerful lot of speed left in him. In the meantime Smoky had somehow lost all hankering of stopping and fight it out with 'em, there was something about the three hungry looking crethures that kept him a moving and his instinct was warning him strong that he should keep some safe distance between him and them.

He was doing that the best he could and as the running kept up and the wolves couldn't get any closer they finally figgered they was wasting their time. May be he got to looking too old and tough for 'em and calculated they'd rather have younger and more tender meat, besides he was leading 'em straight away from the bunch which might make 'em lose their chances of getting anything at all.

Smoky's play of leading the wolves off that way had been a great relief to the bunch and mostly the young colts, they'd had a chance to slow down some and get their second wind, and when the killers showed up on their trail once again they was all more able to sashay on and keep from reach of their tearing fangs.

When Smoky found that the wolves had left him and turned back towards the bunch, it was his natural instinct to turn too and follow up in their tracks, he had a hunch somehow that he'd be needed there and he hadn't altogether lost the hope of a chance of taking apart at least one of the outlaws.

It was a long and mighty hard run back till he caught up with the bunch again, but Smoky wasn't the horse he was for nothing, he made it in near as good a time as the wolves themselves, and he got there just as the wolves circled around past the buckskin and headed for one of the colts he'd been hazing.

The buckskin hadn't hardly been noticed, the wolves had passed him up as too old specially when there was such as the young colts which could be got easy. The old horse had watched 'em catch up with the bunch and go past him for a younger victim, he had no way to know that they didn't want him, and he could of kept well in the lead of the bunch if he'd wanted to but he'd made hisself guardian over the little colts and he couldn't for the life of him have left 'em behind, of course the little fellers' mammies would of fought for 'em too but they was at the stage where they felt every horse was for himself, they'd scared into a stampede and was all a running for their own lives.

The old buckskin knowed wolves, he knowed they had their eye on him and it was best to keep neutral till they'd got over being watched of every move he'd make, and as the three greys passed him and was gaining on the scared little colts he kept to one side and watched. It was just as the leader made a leap for one of the little fellers' ham strings that the big buckskin came to life, made a leap too and went to fighting at the risk of his own life.

The wolves hadn't looked for no such move from him, they'd got over watching and figgered he was far

behind and had put all their attention on dragging
down the victim they'd picked. It was a mighty big
surprise for them when from behind the big buckskin
landed on the second wolf and buried him in the snow
while on his way to the first. A good sized hoof came
down just as that first wolf turned his head to meet
the fighting buckskin. That hoof connected with his
lower jaw as he made the turn and left that jaw hanging limp and plum useless.—When the old pony looked
back for the other wolves there was long grey hairs
sticking between his teeth.

It was about then when Smoky arrived on the scene,
he'd come up right behind the buckskin and when the
second wolf picked himself up out of the snow and
made a grab which would of been the death of the old
horse Smoky done a side swipe that was quicker than
chained lightning. A hind hoof came up and caught
that wolf right under a front leg close to the body and
took that leg off of him like it'd been a tooth pick;—
another horse that'd come up from behind and hadn't
been reckoned with.

It was during this commotion of biting and kicking
mixture of buckskin and mouse colored horseflesh and
flying grey wolves that the third and only able wolf
disappeared into thin air. Them two fighting ponies
had took away all his appetite for colt meat and left
a hankering only to be gone from the reach of their
destroying hoofs. Three of his kind could of competed
with the mad ponies if their attention had been on
them from the start, but that's where the slip had been
made, and as it was that lone wolf didn't feel at all

Smoky done a side swipe that was quicker than chained lightning.

equal of resuming what the leader of the pack had
started.—He left.

The moon faded away into the sky, break of day
had come. Out on the flat the little bunch of ponies
was knee deep in the snow and a pawing away for the
grass that was underneath, there wasn't a scratch on
nary a hide to show that any had ever seen a wolf,
but if Smoky and his pardner the buckskin hadn't
been in that little bunch there would of been another
story to tell. The little colt which was so busy digging
up feed for himself and plum ignorant of the close call
he'd had would of been amongst the missing and just
easing the appetites of three gray wolves, and who
knows but what a couple more colts might of been
killed along with him, for once a wolf gets a taste of
warm blood there's no telling how far he'll go.

The "yip, yip" and howl of a cayote sounded off
from the hills, and gradual as the sun came up big
clouds showed over the skyline from the northwest and
seemed like headed to meet and kill that sun's warm rays.
By noon that day a blizzard had come and the little
bunch of ponies faced it on the way back to the shelter
of the hills from where they'd left in their run for life.

The howl of a lone wolf was heard that night, and
away off to the south there came an answer, an answer
that was more drawed out and mournful than any
that'd ever been heard. Smoky snorted, but with the
buckskin, only his head went up, his ears pointed towards the sound. He knowed wolves and he knowed
they wouldn't be back, not that night.

The blizzard hung on for a day and filled the ravines with deep drifts, then the wind died and it settled down to a slow falling snow. There was more white mounds where that snow had covered the carcasses of dead critters, but amongst them mounds there was one that wasn't made by any of the bellering grass eating kind.—A big gray wolf layed there, a broke jaw had been the cause of his death.

(Some months later a cowboy run down and roped a three legged wolf and remarked as he looked close to where a front leg was missing, how "it must of been an awful wicked bullet to've took that leg off so neat.")

The already long winter dragged and hung on like it never was going to quit, snow was deep, and even tho the sun climbed higher and stayed longer there seemed to be no more heat from it than there'd been two months before and when it was at its lowest. The ponies was having a hard time and as the feed kept a getting to be harder to reach right along they was steady losing on weight and strength. The roundness that'd been theirs a few months before was all gone and instead they showed lean and slab sided.

Finally, and after it seemed there'd be no end to the rough weather there came a break, it turned warmer, and some time later the snow begin to sag and then melt on the sunny side of the hills, gradually, and after what seemed weeks instead of days the grass showed in plain sight more and more till the time come when the ponies didn't have to paw for their feed no more.

Then after a while there was green stems showing thru the dry grass.—The dangers of the winter was over.

The range had turned from white to brown and then green and the little bunch of ponies begin to perk up considerable, the winter hair was a slipping, their eyes showed more bright, and pretty soon ribs begin to disappear under layers of fat and glossy hides. Then to make this new green world as great and wonderful as the winter before had been hard and cruel there begin to appear brand new little colts in the bunch, all slick little fellers and full of play. And as the bunch drifted to the open prairie they came acrost little calves their little white faces a shining in the sun.

Smoky had more than kept with all the changes to the good, he showed it in every move he made, and as him and the old buckskin (which had got young again) played around and showed jealous over the new colts it made a sight that was complete in all that life could give.

There was months of peace that way, the little bunch roamed the prairies not at all seeming to care where sunup found 'em. Tall green feed was a plenty and everywheres, clear swift mountain streams slowed down on the flats and furnished moisture for the big cottonwoods that reached out in the sky and made cool shade, and as it was, time was just let slip by and enjoyed only as a free range horse with little colts for company can enjoy it.

It was more thru habit than heat that the little bunch drifted on up the foothills one day and then higher in the mountain. Maybe they liked the breeze up there better, or the change of feed, or maybe it was that too many riders had been showing up off and on and which kinda disturbed 'em.

But them riders couldn't be dodged that easy, and one day for a whole half hour there was one to within a half a mile of 'em a setting on his horse, field glasses in his hands and looking at the little bunch as they fanned themselves on a high ridge plum ignorant of the eyes that was on 'em.

That rider had spotted the mouse-colored blaze-faced gelding, and at the sight of him let out a whistle of surprise of seeing such a horse. He'd rode a little closer then and watched that horse some more, he'd of come still closer only he didn't want to kettle the bunch and make 'em suspicious, besides he'd just wanted to locate where that horse was running so he'd know where to find him when he wanted to.—He was one of the Rocking R men.

Smoky had stood the whole watchful spell without a hunch of it, and as him and the little bunch started a grazing on up the mountain there was nothing further away from his mind than the thought of a human on his trail. Of course there wasn't any human on his trail that day, but there would be soon, for the way that rider talked that night and described Smoky to the bronco buster of the outfit all indicated that it wouldn't be long when the little horse would be finding himself in a high pole corral.

Smoky was now a four year old going on five, the age when most all range geldings are run in and broke to either saddle or harness, for use on the range or to

fit 'em for market. The little horse'd had a good long
time of freedom and if he was kept with the outfit
he'd get more, but his time for usefulness had come.
The free roaming of the hills and flats was past for a
while till the work he'd be cut out for was done, and
Smoky's experiences from his colt days on till now
would go on with more learning and experiences with
the human.

Smoky's waking up to realizing them things came
sudden and all mighty unexpected. A long legged rider
on a long legged horse had showed up on a ridge above
him and the bunch; there'd been a lot of territory covered in mighty fast time as all lit into a run and they
was hazed down onto the flats and then into long pole
wings towards the corral, then first thing Smoky
knowed he was penned in, he couldn't go no further.
A big gate was closed and all around him was big
cottonwood bars.

In another pen joining the one Smoky was in there
was other horses, all geldings and along about Smoky's
size and age. The gate between was opened and Smoky
was cut out of his bunch by that same long legged
rider that'd run him in, and put thru that gate to join
them other geldings, the gate was closed again after
him.

Smoky peeked thru the bars and watched the rider
open the outside gate and leave out the bunch he'd
run with. He watched one of the mares take the lead
and in a long lope, head back to the high territory from
where they'd come, he watched the little colts running
to keep up and then he seen the big buckskin tagging

along. His pardner and all was leaving him amongst strange horses, in a high corral, and not far away was a human which to Smoky was ten times worse than any wolf.

He nickered, and there was a sound to it that made the buckskin stop, look back, and nicker an answer. The old horse stood there a while kinda like he was waiting but pretty soon he started again and caught up with the bunch. The old buckskin knowed humans, he'd packed many a one of 'em on many a long ride, his freedom had been handed back to him for the good work he'd done, he'd experienced what Smoky was going thru now and knowing what he did it was all plain to him just what was up. There was no use of him waiting.

Smoky watched him and the bunch disappear in a cloud of dust and out of sight. If only there was no bars holding him it wouldn't take him long and he could still catch up with 'em, but— He was brought back to hard facts by the squeak of the heavy gate as it was pulled open and the cowboy walked in with a long coil of rope on his arm.

Smoky let out a snort at the sight of the human and tore up the earth for the far side of the corral. Natural fear of the crethure had a hold on him and once against the solid bars he turned and quivering faced what he felt was his worst enemy.

If Smoky could only knowed, there'd been a lot of suffering which he wouldn't had to've went thru on account of that fear, if he'd only knowed that right then that human was just admiring him for all he was worth and that doing the little horse any harm was the furthest thing away from his mind. But the wild gelding had no way of knowing and every word that human was saying sounded to him like the growl of a flesh tearing animal, and every move was a step closer to the victim;—he was the victim.

The cowboy well understood his kind. He'd been raised on the backs of such as him and he was making his living by gentling that kind and making good saddle horses out of 'em, and as he stood there, his eyes taking in every move the mouse colored gelding was making, there was a smile showed under the stetson. That smile was just for the glad way he felt as he sized him up and seen where he was all saddle horse, not the kind that'd fit in harness and to be shipped to farming countries. He was glad to know that he'd be the first to touch that pony's hide, and as he kept his eye on the gelding, at the same time shaking out a loop, he felt there'd be no end of patience for such a horse as that one looked to be.

His loop ready he walked towards the gelding. Smoky watched him come and that pony's actions showed where he just wanted to shrink away to nothing and disappear, but he stayed full size, and seen where his next best move was to just move, and away to most any old place. The other geldings scattered as the human came on and Smoky piled in amongst 'em full speed to the other side of the corral; about that time he heard the hiss of a rope and that thing which he likened to a snake coiled up and right around both his front feet.

Them front feet was jerked away from under him as he sailed in the air and tried to get away, and then he made a circle in the atmosphere and came down to earth flat on his side. He no more than hit the ground when he tried to get up. He tried it again and again, and as the cowboy talked to him and advised him to ease up on the fighting Smoky turned a wild eyed look his way and snorted.

"Now lay down and be good" says that cowboy. "I sure don't want to skin up that pretty hide of yours."

Smoky did lay down, he had to, for in another few seconds his four feet was tied together. He breathed hard as he layed there plum helpless, his mind wasn't working no more, his heart was a thumping fit to bust and the racing of the blood thru his body only stampeded his brain. He was past trying to figger out how he was throwed so easy and then held down where he could move only his head. No cougar or bear could of made him so helpless, he could of fought with them, but with this human it all seemed like he had no chance and the mystery of that human's power is what put the fear in him, a fear the likes of which was a heap worse than he'd felt if he'd been cornered by a thousand bears, cougars, and wolves.

In a dazed way he seen the cowboy bend over him; a knee touched his neck and the muscles along there quivered the same as if a snake's fangs had been feeling for a holt. A hand touched his ear and another his forehead; there was no pain but if there had been the little horse would of never felt it.

Pretty soon a hackamore was slipped on his head, he

felt the rawhide "bosal" around his nose and then the "feador" rope around his neck, all the while the creuture was making a low, and *somehow* not aggravating noise. It was a talking to him.

The cowboy gave his forehead a couple of rubs, then stood up and walked around to the pony's feet, Smoky felt the tight ropes loosening up from around his ankles and pulled away; his feet was free but his mind was confused a lot and he still layed there; then he felt a pull on the hackamore rope.

"Come on up and stand on your legs" says that cowboy,—and Smoky came to life.

He came to life a pawing and rearing and a snorting. His feet was free and he could handle 'em again, he did handle 'em and put in all the strength and action he had a trying to pull away from the cowboy which was holding him with a long rope.—There's some talk of the skill that's showed between the angler and the trout, but the skill that was brought out from that hundred and fifty pound cowboy a holding that eleven hundred pounds of kinky, wild horseflesh was past talking about and beyond the figgering out of any human that's not up to the trade of bronco busting.

The cowboy played his rope and held his horse, he'd held many like him before and most all had fought the same as Smoky was now fighting. That pony's eyes was afire as he seen there was no chance for any get away even when he was on his feet, he couldn't at all shake that two legged hunk of terror, and as he snorted and fought the rope that still held fast around his head and neck he begin to tire some, and came a

time when as the cowboy stood still a few yards away
he stood still too, and legs wide apart, sweat a dripping
from his slick hide, he took in a breathing spell.

He stood there as he watched the cowboy back away
and let the rope slide thru his hands; he watched him
open the gate and get the saddle horse that'd been
left to stand on the other side, seen him get on that
horse and then pick up the slack of the rope that was
holding him. There was thirty feet of it between him
and the mounted human, and when that rope was
tossed a little as the rider circled around him, Smoky
made a leap and shaking his head like trying to slip
what held him he headed straight on for the open gate.

But once past it Smoky was jerked to a fighting
standstill, he hadn't as yet reckoned that a rope *could*
hold him—. The gate was closed after him and the
rider had went thru and then Smoky felt some slack.
He took advantage of that and started out full speed
again; he was out of the corral and in the open, the
rope that was still on him was only felt and wasn't
holding him from lining out.

A shallow creek bottom full of tall green feed was by
that corral and Smoky headed down it; any place
would do so long as he could run and keep a distance
between him and that rider, but that run wasn't to
last long, once again he felt the rope tighten till he was
brought to a stop, and facing the rider once more
watched him get off his horse and fasten the end of the
long rope to a log.

"Well, little horse" says the cowboy as he stood
there and watched him for a spell, "don't play too

rough with this rope, the better you treat it the better it'll treat you," and with that he got on his horse and rode off towards the corrals where more broncs waited for the same eddication that Smoky had just got.

That long soft and thick cotton rope, and that log which held Smoky was the means of his first learnings as to ways for usefulness to the human. The more he'd fight that rope and try to get away from it the more he'd learn that his fighting and tearing was of *no use*. That rope was on the job steady and to learn him to turn as he run and hit the end of it, it would take the stiffness out of his neck and there'd come a time when he'd give to a pull from either side without fighting and wanting to be convinced that it could be done. The log which the rope was tied to was part of the teaching apparatus, heavy enough to hold the pony, and even tho it could be dragged around some Smoky couldn't get very far with it.

The little horse realized somehow as he sized up the contraption that the end had come to all he'd enjoyed with the freedom he'd had, cool shades,—clear streams, and grassy ranges to all roam on as he pleased had been took away from him; he didn't know what was to come next, but he did know that he was on that creek bottom, close to corrals, and there to stay for a spell.

CHAPTER V

THE BRONC TWISTER STEPS UP

A CLOUD of dust was hanging on over the big corrals where Clint, the bronc twister of the Rocking R outfit, was busy starting raw broncs under the saddle and "twisted" 'em in shape for good saddle stock. It was long, hot, and hard days for that cowboy as he wrestled with the slick, fat, and snorty ponies and convinced 'em that they all could be led, rode, and handled according to the way he seen fit; but Clint was used to that, he'd been at it for years with nary a rest or relief from the work that was beginning to tell on him.

He'd take ten broncs at a time and soon as he'd took the rough off them ten he'd turn 'em over as broke and run in ten more raw, wild ponies. Each green colt was rode every day if even only for half an hour, and gradually learned to behave under the saddle. There was a few that wouldn't learn to behave, but the Rocking R outfit had good men and all them ponies was put in to their work whether they was good or bad.

Clint had been with the layout for near two years, and in that time had broke to ride somewheres around eighty head of horses. He'd broke many more for other outfits and never made an outlaw, if one did turn out-

law once in a while it was because of that pony's
natural instinct to be that way, but Clint handled and
rode 'em all just the same,—if a perticular horse
couldn't be learned it sure wasn't his fault and none
had better try to learn that same horse *anything*.

As has been said before, bronc fighting was beginning
to tell on Clint,—none of them ponies he'd broke had
spared him, and instead they'd called on for all that
was in him. Many had tried to tear him apart and
scatter him in the dust of the big corrals; hoofs had
come like greased lightning and took hunks off his bat-
wing chaps, teeth had took a few shirts off his back,
and as he'd climbed on one after another of these
wild, kinky ponies they most all tried to see if they
could move the heart of him from one side of his body
to the other.

There was many times when he was layed up with
dislocated shoulders, ribs broke and legs the same.
From the root of his hair to the toes in his made to
order boots there was signs, if not seen they was felt,
where some horse had twisted, broke, or shook something loose. Each happening had come more or less
separate, and healed some in time, but as some kept a
repeating off and on there was some parts of him which
never got strong again, and as time went on and as
Clint said, "he was beginning to feel loose like an old
clock and figgered that some day some bucking hunk
of horseflesh would take the *tick* out of him and scatter him out so that none of the parts would never be
found again."

Clint had started riding rough ones long before he

quit growing and that's the condition he was in at
thirty, an old man, far as riding was concerned. The
horses of the same big outfit he'd rode for was worked
on the average of only four months in the year, and in
them four months the broke horses was rode only four
or five hours once every three days. That might show
some of the difference in the work the cowboy and the
cowhorse does with a real cow outfit.—The men go to
pieces young and early and the ponies stay fat,—but
there was no grudge for there's nobody in the world
likes to see and ride a fat strong horse more than does
the cowboy.

They'll keep the ponies fat and feeling good, and
some of them horses find it hard to behave and will try
to jar loose the eye teeth of their riders. The cowboy
wants 'em that way tho ,—it's a pride of his to have a
kinky horse under him that's feeling good rather than
some gentle old plug that's leg weary. That all gets
him in time, but there's a grin on his face when that
time comes, a grin from the pride of knowing that he
never was seen on no horse that was against the prin-
ciple of a cowboy to ride.

Like with Clint, horses was the life of him. He loved
'em for all he was worth and the greatest pleasure in
the world for him was in just being with a corral full
of 'em, handling 'em and feeling of their hides. The
satisfaction he'd get out of seeing some four year old
colt learn the things he'd teach meant a heap more to
him than the wages he drawed for that work, and there
was times as he'd be breaking some right brainy gelding and watch the horse pick up fast on the eddication

he'd give him, when he'd feel real attached to the pony. He'd hate to give him up when the time came for all half broke horses to be turned over to the round up wagons and where more teaching in the handling of the critter begin.

"I feel sort of married to them kind of ponies" he'd say, "and I sure don't hanker to part with 'em just when we're beginning to get along good together, but" he'd go on "I guess as long as I'll be breaking horses this way I can't get too sensitive."

But Clint kept a being sensitive that way, and he never was happy when he'd see riders coming in on him and then ride away hazing a bunch of the broncs he'd "started." "Some day," he was heard to say once "I'm going to meet a horse I'll really get married to, and then there'll be things a popping."

Clint would have such a liking for some of them ponies that he'd forget and didn't want to think that they belonged to the company and not to him. He was just hired to break 'em. He'd reason that out often but that reasoning never fazed the hankering he felt and that's how come when he run in the mouse colored gelding he begin to do some tall figgering.

He had a hunch when he first set eyes on that pony that he'd met the horse which would start "things a popping" when any rider showed up to claim all that's half broke. Clint had dreamed of such a horse as the mouse colored gelding but he'd never expected to see one really living, that pony had got holt of his heart strings from the start, and as he watched thru the bars of the corral out to where the horse was picketed he felt him to be the kind he'd steal if he couldn't buy, and if he could neither steal nor buy he'd work for.

It'd been two days since he'd run him in and put him on the picket rope outside the corral a ways, and in them two days Clint had been mighty fearful lest somebody rode up on him, seen the horse and took possession of him as private saddle stock for the superintendent or some other what owned shares in the outfit and liked pretty horses that way. Clint wanted that horse mighty bad and he was just leary something would happen so he'd be took away from him, but as he'd reason some he was less worried and he'd wind up by saying as he'd take another peek towards the gelding. "They'd have to let me break him first, and before anybody else gets him I'll sure make an outlaw out of that horse."

That was no way for Clint to feel maybe, but that's sure enough the way he figgered on doing rather than lose the horse to anybody else;—that feeling was past skin deep with him and that I think excuses him some.

In the two days that Clint'd had the horse up, there was no chance passed where he could show his feelings and win that pony's confidence,—if the picket rope tangled him up too much Clint was right there to untangle him and each time the gelding fought less when he came. That pony was gradually losing his fear of being et up or tore apart by the human and pretty soon he felt as Clint came and went that each visit from that crethure brought some comfort in a way.

It was on the second evening and when the day's work was all done that Clint made his way from the bunk house to where the gelding was picketed. He went up to within a rope's length of the horse, rolled a smoke, and stood there watching him.

"Smoky," he says, "you're some horse"—Clint hadn't hardly realized he'd spoke a name, he was too busy watching and admiring that pony's every move, so as it was that name came unconscious like to the cowboy and it was used and repeated from then on as natural as tho that name had been thought and decided on.

He'd named many horses and had always let the name come to him either by the color, size, or shape of each horse, and sometimes by the way they acted. He'd called one tall rangy horse "Shorty" and another low built small horse "Skyhigh." Often the name didn't at all fit the horse in that way but there was some reason there, the same as there was a mighty good reason to call the mouse colored gelding "Smoky."

He did look like a rounded shiny cloud of grey smoke, and as he held his ground and watched the cowboy, he acted as tho he might live up to his name and really go up in smoke,—his acquaintance with the human hadn't been very long and he wasn't as yet any too confident.

Clint could tell as he watched just what was going on in that pony's think tank, he could still see fear in his eyes, but mixed in with that fear was a lot of nerve that showed fight. He knowed that pony would fight and make himself hard to handle, and he'd of been mighty disappointed not to've seen them signs in the horse. It was only natural that any of his kind should

act this way and he figgered the wilder the spirit the
bigger and more worth while would the winning be.—
He would take his time, do a good job and turn Smoky
from a wild raw bronc into a well broke and eddicated
cowhorse.

He took a few steps closer and Smoky backed away
to the end of the rope,—he snorted when he found he
couldn't back no further and pawed at the rope as the
cowboy kept a coming still closer and closer. Clint
took his time but came on steady and a talking the
while till he finally got within a couple of feet of the
horse and where he could touch him. Hanging on to
the rope with the right hand he reached out with the
left and touched him easy between the eyes. Smoky
flinched and snorted but he stood it,—he stood it for
quite a spell and felt the hand rubbing on his forehead
and working up and up towards his ears.

Clint had just about got to one of them ears when
Smoky rubbed his nose along the cowboy's sleeve, took
a sniff, and then of a sudden nipped him on the arm.
That had happened to him before many a time and
he'd been ready for it with the result that the pony
got only a piece of shirt and no flesh.

"Now, don't be so daggoned ornery," says that
cowboy as he kept a rubbing the same as tho nothing
had happened, "I only want to reach between them
ears and touch that knowledge bump of yours."

Finally he did reach the bump and rubbed around
there a spell. Smoky struck once, Clint dodged the
front hoof and kept a rubbing. He rubbed past the
left ear and down his neck till the withers was reached,

the mane was worked on and all the knots in it un-tangled. The little horse quivered and flinched every once in a while but the rubbing process went on till Smoky begin showing symptoms that he could stand it all easy enough.

In the meantime Clint talked to him like he'd never took time to talk to another horse before, and if Smoky could of understood he'd knowed by that talk just what was ahead for him; but Smoky wasn't thinking on what was ahead,—the present had him worried enough as it was, and he was kept busy watching every move that human was making.

Smoky had lost considerable wildness during the two days on the picket rope. He'd learned there was no use in fighting the rope that held him, that it was best to turn when he came to the end of it, and gradually he was getting used to have that rope touch him here and there and he'd quit kicking at it. He was more familiar with that than with the human who put him there, but the rope done the trick of getting him used to having anything touch him,—it kinda broke him to stand the touch of the hand.

He was learning to stand that well enough too, but the movements of that hand had to be just right, not too quick and no jabbing done or there'd be a scatter-ing of something mighty quick.

"I'm sure making a lot of fuss over you" says Clint as he rubs on past the withers and along his back a ways. "If you was just an ordinary bronc you'd be missing most of this attention and you'd be finding yourself in the corral with me on top of you by tomorrow, and turned in the 'Remuda' by another month, but I got a scheme up on account of me liking you the way I do: I'm going to take my time and make you my private top horse and when that's done I'll have every cowboy in the country jealous of me for having such a horse as you're going to turn out to be."

With Clint's scheming that way there was a good chance of him winning out, and gradually, steady, the eddication of Smoky started in. That cowboy called on for all he knowed in the profession of horse breaking and used it all with a lot of time to shape out Smoky the way he wanted him. No company time was used on the horse on account Clint felt it wouldn't been doing the square thing "cause" as he says "it'll be bad enough if I have to steal him."—Of course Clint wouldn't steal that horse or no other one, but he felt like he'd sure do something out of the ordinary rather than let Smoky go to any other rider.

Every evening after that last meal of the day was over, Clint would be down in the creek bottom with Smoky. What went on there showed some of what Clint really thought of the mouse colored gelding, and there was no disappointed look on his face when dark made him return to the bunk house.

Smoky had been on the picket rope about a week. In that time Clint had kept his eye on him thru the day while working in the corral and spent a couple of hours with him every evening. The little horse had got used to the rope and wouldn't pay no attention to it no more, but as for the cowboy he was just neutral, it was hard for him to shed off the fear of the

human and which he'd inherited,—that human was still
a mighty big mystery to him even after a week's acquaintance. It'd done him no harm but his wild instinct kept a warning him to expect most anything.
The power that two legged crethure had over him kept
him leary and watching for the next move, whatever
that would be—and that's why Smoky was still neutral, his confidence for the human hadn't come to the
top as yet and not a move did that cowboy make which
he didn't see.

"You sure got your eye on me, ain't you, little horse?"
Clint would say, "but that's the way I want you to
be," he'd go on, "for the more you watch the more
you'll see and the quicker you'll learn."

Smoky did watch and see and learn, and then one
evening Clint untied the long picket rope from the
log and started leading him towards the corral; the
little horse was broke to lead by then and he followed
easy enough. His heart was a thumping in wonder of
what was due to happen as the cowboy led him thru
the big pole gate, he stepped high and careful and his
eyes took in everything that looked suspicious,—a
slicker hanging over one side of the corral made him
snort and try to pull away. Clint talked to him, and
kept on a leading him thru another gate into another
smaller and round corral. A big snubbing post stuck
up in the center of it and by that post was a big brown
and shiny hunk of leather, it was Clint's saddle.

"Well now, little horse, the performance is about to
begin, you're going to get your first smell of saddle

leather." Clint had turned as he spoke and begin rubbing on Smoky's forehead. For once since Smoky had been caught his attention wasn't on the cowboy, that hunk of leather was drawing all his interest and ears pointed straight at it, eyes a shining, he snorted his suspicions and dislike for the looks of the contraption that was laying there, waiting it seemed like to jump at him and eat him alive.

"Look, snort, and paw at it all you want," says the cowboy. "You'll get well acquainted with it before you get thru, and I won't rush the acquaintance either."

Clint didn't. He kept Smoky to within a few feet of the saddle and grinning some at the pony's actions kept a rubbing him back of the ears while the investigation was going on. Smoky was for getting away from there but Clint was persuading him to stick around close, and there was nothing for him to do but just that.

A move from the direction of that saddle right then would of queered things and made Smoky scatter, and Clint couldn't of held him either for a ways, but the hunk of leather layed still, mighty still, and pretty soon it kinda lost its dangerous look to the little horse,— he begin looking around for other things in that corral which wouldn't be to his liking and not seeing anything that was worth getting spooky at, Smoky begin watching the cowboy again.

It was about then that Clint reached over and picked up the saddle slow and easy and drug it closer to Smoky. At the first move of the riggin' the little horse snorted and backed away but Clint and the saddle kept a coming straight towards him, slow but steady. One side of the high corral finally was reached. Smoky had backed against it and couldn't go no further. The cowboy, still hanging onto the rope that held his head, came on, saddle and all with him, and quivering with fear the little horse layed low. Feet straight out in front and head near to the ground he stayed there, and got another and different eddication with the saddle, this time it was dragging.

When Clint thought that had gone far enough and seen where Smoky had got over the worst of his fear he layed the saddle down again, and picking up an old saddle blanket he begin fanning the air with it, closer and closer to Smoky came the blanket as the fanning motion kept on, and stary eyed the little horse watched. He struck at it and snorted a couple of times and he even tried to turn and kick, but the blanket came on till finally one corner of it grazed his side. He flinched and kicked and tried to jerk away but there was no dodging that spooky looking thing.

Not a word was heard from the cowboy as the "sacking" went on, this was a part of the eddication that was necessary and which should be put thru mighty quiet. It was all a spooky enough performance to a raw bronc without adding on any talking, and even tho the goings on scared the pony near out of his hide, that blanket done the trick of showing him that no matter how bad it looked it wasn't going to hurt him, it was one mighty good thing to teach him general confidence in the cowboy and his riggin'.

Smoky fought like a cornered wolf and tried to get

The cowboy still hanging onto the rope that held his head, came on, saddle and all with him, and quivering with fear the little horse layed low, feet straight out in front and head near to the ground he stayed there.

away, but he had no chance,—Clint had "sacked" many a bronc that'd fought as much and the cigarette between his lips noticed no change of spells between puffs. Smoky showed hate and fear of the human once again the same as when he was first caught, his instinct had warned him to expect most anything from that crethure, and he wasn't surprised at the way things had turned;—but that didn't help any, he just wanted to sail clear over the corral and disappear.

Thru all that fighting and goings on the sacking kept up in steady motion. Wherever the long blanket touched Smoky he flinched, and kicked at it and squealed. He was too scared to realize that there was no sting or any kind of a hurt felt. It was just the looks of the thing which had him going and his fighting instinct just had to answer every swish of that thing that circled around a leg one time and his neck the next.

Finally, and whether it was from being tired or fighting or that he was dazed past caring of what was going on Smoky begin to let up; his kicks begin to get less wicked and his eyes lost some of the fiery look till came a time when he stood near still and he'd only flinch as the blanket kept a touching, going away, and touching him here and there and all over.

Clint noticing the little horse calming down remarked, "You'll get so you'll like it pretty soon." But Smoky wasn't showing no such symptom as yet, he was just standing it best as he could and that was all.

Both sides and all around Smoky went Clint with his blanket till the little horse finally even quit flinching. The cowboy then dropped the rope that was holding the horse and worked his blanket wilder than ever, that blanket was layed everywhere on that pony's hide and around his legs, he layed it on the ground and drug it under him and all Smoky would do was to cock one ear and watch it, but he never moved. A half an hour before such a play would of sent him straight up.

Clint worked on for a while longer till he was sure there wasn't a spot on that pony that'd flinch at the feel of the blanket, then he begin to notice that Smoky was finally getting so he kinda liked the performance, no flies could touch him while that was going on, and that blanket being pulled all over him that way seemed to kind of soothe some.

It was about when Clint figgered he could do no more good in the way of sacking that he picked up his saddle again and came straight towards Smoky with it. The squeak of the riggin' brought some interest from the horse, but Clint was careful to bring the old blanket with him and keep a fanning the same as to let him know that one was no worse than the other.

In the first saddling of most broncs Clint generally tied up one of their hind legs so as to hinder 'em from kicking the saddle out of his hands and at the same time learn 'em to stand still while that went on;—a few of 'em he'd just hobble in front. And being that Smoky'd had more teaching than the average colt generally gets before first saddling, Clint figgered that just hobbling his front feet would do.

The sacking had helped a lot and Clint had no trouble fastening the rawhide hobbles around Smoky's ankles, the pony snorted at him a little but stood still, for Clint

was waving that blanket around as he worked. Once
the hobbles was on he picked up his saddle and *eased*
it up and on that pony's back, Smoky had a hunch
that something new was going on, something different
than the sacking performance which he'd just went
thru; but as nothing happened outside of the flapping·
of stirrup leathers and cinches he stood in one spot,
only a quiver in the muscles along his shoulder showed
how much alive he was, and how quick he could leave
the earth if anything "goosed" him.

Plenty of practice had made Clint past master at
putting a saddle on a green colt, nothing happened to
make Smoky want to move out of his tracks, and even
when the cinch was reached for and drawed up under
his belly he never batted an eye. The sacking had all
been a mighty fine preliminary for all this that followed
and cured the horse from scaring at everything that
flapped on or around him.

As it was Smoky hardly realized that he was saddled till Clint took the hobbles off his front feet and
pulled him to one side, at that pull he felt something
fastened to him and hanging on, that was a new kind
of feeling to Smoky and it kettled him, down went his
head and he lit in to bucking.

Clint had expected that, for no bronc likes the feel
of the cinch no matter how loose it might be, and when
Smoky bogged his head that way he was ready,—he
let the hackamore rope slide thru his hands for a ways
and till he could get a good footing, then he give that
rope a little flip and set down on it. That done the
trick and it come daggone near upsetting the little

He didn't forget how he was stopped, and so sudden, that first time he'd tried to break with an empty saddle.

horse, but Clint let out just enough slack and that saved him. He didn't want to throw the horse but then he didn't want to have that horse buck with an empty saddle either.

"Now Smoky," says that cowboy as the horse jerked to his senses, turned and faced him, "I don't want you to waste any of your energy that way, if you want to do any bucking you just wait till I get in the middle of you."

Smoky waited, but it wasn't thru the talk the cowboy had handed him that he did wait; it was that he remembered how that rope had upset him that first day he was picketed to the log outside the corral, and he wasn't hankering to be "busted" that way again.

There's folks that's read some on how horses are broke on the range, and from that reading they get the idea that the cowboy breaks the horses' spirit, that it's the only way a wild horse can be tamed. What I've got to say on the subject if that's what's believed, is that either them folks read something that's mighty wrong, or else they got the wrong impression and misunderstood what they read, and breaking a horse the way he's broke on the range is about the same on the animal as schooling is to the human youngster. The spirit of the wild horse is the same after years of riding as it was before he ever felt a rope, and there's no human in the world wants to preserve that spirit in the horse like the cowboy does;—he's the one what knows better than anybody else that a horse with a broken spirit is no horse at all.

To them that *only* sees a wild horse roped and rode and don't know the insides of the game, horse breaking might seem a little rough; but I'm here to say that it's not near as rough as it is necessary, and in the long run it's the rider that gets treated the roughest. You let a wild horse get away with something once and he'll try it again till there will come a time when even if there's no meaness in him he'll develop some. That's what makes outlaws.

Outlaws are made mostly when a horse proves too much for the man that handles him. A wild horse will turn outlaw often if handled by any other than them that knows his kind, and there'll be no way of breaking him only thru starvation and abuse. His spirit would be broken then too, and that proves that the cowboy, knowing his business, will see that the pony's heart is kept intact.

There's a variety in horse minds as big as there is amongst human minds. Some need more persuading than others, and a few of 'em, no matter how firm they're handled will have to be showed again and again that they can't get away with this or with that,—they'll keep on a trying and if ever once they do put a bluff thru there's most generally enough meaness in their system to make 'em plum worthless.

And like I was saying with Smoky, "he remembered how that rope had upset him that first day he was picketed to that log outside the corral, and he wasn't hankering to be 'busted' that way again."—That little horse had brains. If he was convinced a few times he had the sense to realize it, but at the same time, *he had* to be showed, and more because it was part of his necessary eddication than because of any meanness of his.

He was willing to learn but the teaching had to come from one who *could* teach him. There was no meanness in Smoky, not an ounce of it, he was honest clear thru, but meanness would develop if a slip was made. He fought and bit and kicked but Smoky was a wild horse and he was going only according to his instinct and more to protect himself from the strange human.

That's the caliber of most range horses. Clint had handled many of 'em and always won out with their confidence and turned 'em over as broke with their spirit intact. He'd savvied Smoky the minute he dabbed his rope on him that first time: that pony was wild, wild as a horse or any animal can get, and he had the strength to go with it; but Clint seen where that little horse also had a mighty fine set of brains between them little pointed ears of his.

He treated him like a grown up would treat a kid, a kid of the kind that'd learn a lot if the chance showed up, and he missed no chance to show that pony all he should know and how good he wanted to be to him.

"Daggone it Smoky" he'd say, "it's too bad you can't know without I have to use a lot of ropes, as it is sometimes. I bet you don't think I'm a friend of yours, none at all."

Clint was right. At first Smoky had took him as an enemy and fought him according; then had come a time when he was willing to trust him some, specially when Clint had come and untangled him out of that long picket rope, talked to him, and rubbed his ears. His heart had got over thumping so much when he'd see the cowboy coming of evenings, and even tho the little horse didn't realize it as yet, he'd got to expecting him.

Then, and just about when his liking for the cowboy was coming to the top fast, something happened that'd make him wonder for a spell if that cowboy was a friend or still an enemy. The "sacking" he'd went thru in the corral had sort of jarred the confidence that'd begin to sprout for the bowlegged crethure, and then the way his head was jerked up out of his bucking spell with the empty saddle, all had left him puzzled as whether to start in and do some fighting or else be good and take his medicine.

Smoky had no way of knowing as yet what was expected of him, and it was a ticklish time for him. It was right then that he'd have to be handled just right and when the turning point for the good or the bad would be decided on. But Clint knowed how the turn to the good layed and it was right there that he proceeded to bring it out.

There was only one way to it and that was for Clint to *show* Smoky he had to be good. The cowboy knowed Smoky had brains a plenty to realize once he was showed, that he had to do just what he wanted him to do, that of course would take a little time, the pony would fight some more and *want* to be showed, and to keep him from getting frustrated that horse would have to have his own way, some.

CHAPTER VI

"THE SQUEAK OF LEATHER"

TWENTY feet of rope is laying between the cowboy's hand and the pony's head. The cowboy is standing there just watching and smiling some at the surprised look that's in the pony's face, that pony had just been stopped sudden in his bucking with an empty saddle;—it was the first time a saddle had been on his slick back and it was no wonder he tried to get out from under that thing, nothing had ever clung there before.

"Now, you just take it easy for a spell, and keep your head up" says that cowboy as he started walking towards the pony.—Legs wide apart, a wild look in his eyes, and a snorting his surprise Smoky watched him come; he didn't know whether to stand his ground and start fighting or back away as the cowboy came. —On he came, and as Smoky was seeing no sign of harm, he stood in his tracks, watched, and waited. A hand touched him on the forehead and moved on down his neck, the cowboy was a talking to him the while, and pretty soon Smoky's heart wasn't thumping so hard no more.—

He was then led a little ways, and as he heard the squeak of leather and felt the weight of the saddle with each step he took, an awful hankering came to

him to put his head down and try to buck it off, but
the cowboy was right there in front of him and he
didn't want to be stopped again and so sudden as he'd
been stopped that first time.

A hand touched him on the forehead.

The other side of the corral was reached and there
Clint turned and rubbed Smoky on the ear. "Well,
old boy, lets see how you're going to behave when I
get up in the middle of you."

Smoky watched the man reach for the latigo and
felt the cinch tighten up; a hump came in his back and
which made the saddle set near on end,—it was the
hump that carried the punch in the buck, and most
likely Clint could of led the pony around some till the

hump wore down and his back straightened up again, but that rider wasn't for taking the buck out of a bronc too quick. He believed a good sensible horse should buck at the first few "settings" and he wasn't the kind of rider that'd smother that natural feeling and have it come out later, when the horse is supposed to be broke gentle.

He let the hump be and never moved the pony out of his tracks;—he knowed that just one move would be enough to start that pony to exploding, and Smoky was set and just a waiting for that signal to start. He watched the cowboy raise his chaps so the belt wouldn't hinder his leg action, watched him pull his hat brim down solid, and then he couldn't watch no more. Something had come between him and his vision, it was the cowboy's thumb which had layed over his left eyelid and pulled it down over his eye— In the next second he felt a weight added on to that of the saddle, and all of a sudden he could see again.

But what he did see left him stary eyed and paralyzed. For half a minute he just stood like petrified, that cowboy had disappeared from the side of him, and instead, there he was right in the middle of his back and on that hunk of leather he'd been hankering to shed off ever since it was put on there.

Instinct pointed out only one way for him to act,—it was telling him that neither the human nor the leather belonged up there in the middle of him that way, and that if he tried he could most likely get rid of 'em. There was nothing else to do that he could see, and right then he felt that he sure must do *something*.

His head went down, and a beller came out of him that said much as "I want you"— Up went Smoky's withers followed by the hump that made the saddle twist like on a pivot, and last came steel muscles like shot out of the earth and which carried the whole mixed up and crooked conglameration of man and horse up in mid air and seemed like to shake there for a spell before coming down. All seemed heads and tails and made a picture of the kind that was mighty hard to see, and still harder to figger out.

Saddle strings was a popping like on a whip lash, leather was a squeaking, corrals shook as the hard hitting hoofs of the pony hit the earth, and a dust was stirred that looked like a young cloud. Smoky was scared, mad, and desperate. All the action, strength, and endurance that was in him was brought out to do its best. Not a hair on his hide was laying idle thru the performance,—every muscle tightened and loosened in a way to shake the weight on his back and make it pop.

Clint felt the muscles work even thru the saddle, and every part of that pony which his legs touched seemed as hard as steel and full of fast working bumps which came and went, twisted his saddle under him, and made him wonder if it was going to stay. It seemed like sometimes that Smoky was headed one way and his saddle another,—he wasn't always sure of the where-abouts of that pony's head; and in all his riding that's what he wanted to keep track of most, cause losing track of a horse's head at them times is something like riding blindfolded—a rider would prepare for one kind of a jolt and meet another, which would cause things to scatter considerable.

Clint was still straight up and on top when Smoky's hard jumps finally dwindled down to crowhops and then a stop. That pony was needing wind mighty bad, and as his nostrils opened wide, was taking in the necessary air, he felt a hand a rubbing along his neck, and wild eyed, ears cocked back at the cowboy that was still there, he stood and heard him talk.

"You done a mighty fine job little horse," says Clint, "and I'd of been disappointed a lot not to've found that kind of spirit in a horse like you."

If Smoky had been raised amongst humans like a dog and been with 'em steady that way, he'd of had a hunch or felt what Clint said and meant. But Smoky was a wild horse of the flats and mountains, and even tho the sound of Clint's tone and the feel of his hand soothed him some, he would buck again and again. It was his instinct to fight the human, and he would fight till that human showed he could handle him and proved a friend.

That had to be done gradual, and Smoky had no way to know as yet that man could be a friend of his, not while the breaking was going on anyway, for thru that spell a horse is *made* to do things he sometimes don't want to do and which all keeps down the confidence that would come faster if that didn't have to be done.

Smoky was doing some tall figgering as he stood there trembling and wondering if there wasn't anything that he could get by with. He'd been made to do things just as that cowboy pleased and he'd found no say in the goings on, none at all. If he could only've bucked him off that would of pleased him a lot, but the little horse didn't know that he wouldn't of won anything by that;—he didn't know he was on this earth for the purpose of the human and that if he did throw one man another would climb him till finally he'd have to give in and go thru a lot of grief the while.

Smoky felt a light slap on his neck. "Come on, young feller," says the cowboy. "Let's see you trot around the corral a while."

But Smoky bucked more than he trotted, the cowboy let him, and when his head would come up he'd keep him on the go till finally there seemed to be no buck in the horse at all.

"I reckon that'll be enough for you today" says Clint, as he headed Smoky for the side of the corral and made him face the bars to a stop. He then reached for the pony's left ear and twisted it some, just enough to keep that pony's attention on the twist of that ear most while he got off.—

Clint touched the ground with his right foot, and keeping his left in the stirrup, at the same time keeping close to the horse's shoulder and out of the reach of his hind feet, he held that position for a few seconds. Smoky was watching him, shaking like a leaf and ready to paw the daylight out of the cowboy at the first wrong move or sudden jab of a knee.

Clint *wanted* him to watch. This was part of the eddication, and all that cowboy wanted to teach right then was for Smoky to stand and not to go to acting up.

Slow and easy, at the same time having complete control of himself and his horse, Clint raised himself up in the saddle again. It was done in a way that only bronc busters know. Smoky never even felt the pull on the saddle as the cowboy climbed on, and if that saddle hadn't even been cinched it wouldn't of budged then, so neat it was done.

Clint climbed on and off a few times that way, Smoky stood and shivered, scared, but willing it seemed like to take his medicine. Maybe it'd come to his mind that there was no use fighting that cowboy, or else he was getting tired—anyway that was the last of it, Smoky felt the cinch loosen and then slow and easy the saddle was pulled off. About that time he whirled and faced the rider who was holding the saddle, he took a sniff at the hunk of leather and snorted like to say, "Gee! I thought that thing was on me for good."

The saddle was set to one side and the cowboy begin rubbing Smoky's back with a gunny sack, and according to the way that pony acted that felt mighty good, his upper lip stuck out and twitched with every motion of the rubbing, and when Clint finally quit, the little horse's action showed plain that he should do it some more, Clint rubbed again.

"I'm afraid," he says as he grinned and rubbed, "that I'm naturally going to spoil you. Here we just got thru with the first saddling and you're beginning to look for favors already."

Smoky's picket grounds was moved to a fresh one for that night and where the grass was tall, a plenty and green,—but somehow his appetite wasn't at its best, and when the break of day come there was very little sign (as Clint noticed) that the pony had et at all. He'd just stood in one spot, looked like, and seemed to've done tall wondering and figgering instead of feeding. He was ganted up the same as if he'd been rode all that night, and still there was no show of any appetite for the feed that was under and all around him.

As Clint worked in the corral busy with other broncs he'd look thru the bars for any show of interest in the little horse, he'd look often but most every time that pony's position was about the same, and if he did catch him with his head down he noticed how Smoky was just nibbling at the feed, and not eating much.

Smoky was taking the change, from the life he'd led to what he was now going thru kinda hard, harder than the average wild horse ever does, and Clint layed it that the little horse had more brains than the average, more sensitive maybe, and more able to realize.

"I guess I'd better lay off of him to-day," decides the cowboy, as he noticed very little change in him even late that afternoon, "he's having a hard time trying to figger things out as it is."

It was bright and early the next morning when Clint looked out of the bunk house door and noticed Smoky out on the creek bottom. It appeared that the little horse, after figgering and figgering, had come to some sort of decision, and that done and settled had went to eating again, for that's what he was doing when Clint looked out,—Smoky was eating like he was trying to make up for the time he'd lost, and he seemed all at peace with everything in general.

The cowboy grinned, "I know what that son of a gun has decided on," he remarked. "He's going to fight, and I see where I'm sure due for a tossing from that pony to-day."

Clint done his day's work, and after riding and lining out nine head of rough and kinky broncs, went to where Smoky was picketed and led him into the corral where he'd been initiated a couple of days before. He was some kind of a different horse than what he'd been that day, his head was higher and more with just one purpose. He didn't shy and snort at every little thing like he did that first time, and Clint noticed that he never seemed to see the saddle as it was eased on his back and cinched.

"I don't like the sound of them 'rollers' that's making that noise in them nostrils of yours," he remarked; "they sound to me like you meant business."

Smoky did mean business, and even tho Clint was doing considerable kidding, he meant business too, he wasn't going to let the little horse get away with anything, for he realized that if he did it'd be harder than ever to persuade him to be good, he'd have to be treated rough, and Clint didn't want to treat him rough.

The cowboy seen the light in Smoky's eyes and understood it, he understood his every action, and they all meant fight.

"I'm glad to see so much spirit in you old boy," he says as he pulled his hat down, "but if you want to

fight I'll have to fight too, and here's hoping the best
one of us wins;—let's go."

Smoky only shook his head a little as Clint put his
hand on his left eye and mounted, he didn't want to
notice a little thing like that, which was just as much
a warning from him for that cowboy to get set, set
well and solid, for in this next performance things was
a going to pop worse than ever.

There's a big difference between the bucking that
comes with the first setting of a bronc and the bucking
that comes with the settings that follows afterwards
on that same bronc. The first time Smoky was rode he
was just a plain scared pony, of course his intentions
was all to the good towards throwing that cowboy,
saddle and all, off, but he was too scared and desperate to try and figger out how that should be done.
He'd learned from that first setting that plain bucking
wouldn't faze that rider, he'd have to use some science,
and with a cool head, study out the weak points the
rider might have, and work on them weak points till
a shadow on the ground tells him the cowboy is *leaving*.

Smoky had learned that it wouldn't get him anything to stampede hot headed into bucking like he did
that first time, maybe that's what he'd been studying
on the last day or so. Anyway, he was some cool horse,
and when he "bowed his head" this time it was all
done deliberate and easy. He lined out with a few easy
jumps just to sort of feel out how that cowboy was a
setting as a preliminary, and with an eye back on all
the movements of the rider as he went, he layed his
plans on just how to proceed and get his man.

It was just when Clint seemed to be riding his easiest when without warning Smoky "broke in two" and brought out some mighty wicked saddle-twisting, and cowboy-loosening jumps; crooked, high, and hard hitting was them jumps. It looked to the horse like his man was loosened at the sudden turning of events and had been shifted to one side a little,—and that's just what Smoky was looking for to carry on the program he'd mapped out.

It was the first encouragement that pony'd got since he first felt a rope on him, maybe he could get it over that cowboy yet. He bucked all the harder from the new energy the signs of winning brought him. No chance did he give so that the cowboy would ever get back in the saddle and straight up, and every jump from then on was used as a kind of leverage against the rider,—he bucked in a circle and every time he'd hit the ground he was his whole length back from where he'd started up.

The cowboy was well up on the fork of the saddle and still to one side. Smoky bucked on, and cool as a cucumber in a mountain stream, kept a watching and took care that he didn't buck back under him. He was holding his own, and looked for signs of the rider loosening some more, but no sign of that showed. The cowboy was still to one side and well up in the saddle, but he sure hung there, and with his left hand on the "Mecate" (hackamore rope) he kept his right up in the air and fanned on the same as ever.

As the fight kept on and no show of the cowboy ever loosening up any more was seen, Smoky begin to won-

And when a glance back showed Smoky the rider was still there, he got desperate again and begin to see red.

der. He'd tried different tactics and with all his figgering and variety of sidewinding he couldn't tear away from that hanging hunk of humanity. He was getting tired, his lungs begin to call for air and pretty soon he wasn't so cool no more.

All that was in him, science and everything, was brought out on a few more earth shaking jumps, and when a glance back showed Smoky the rider was still setting there, he got desperate again and begin to see red. He bellered and at the same time forgot all he'd studied on in the ways of getting his man.

The fight didn't last long after that, it was too furious and unscientific. Smoky fought the air, the earth, and everything in general,—nothing in perticular was his aim, and pretty soon he lined out in long easy crow-hops and then a standstill.

Clint climbed off as Smoky stood spraddle-legged and took in the air, the little horse never seemed to no-tice him and in a hazy way felt the rider's hand rub-bing around his ears and straightening out his mane.

"I knowed you'd give me a tossing to-day," says Clint.

And there was one thing Smoky didn't know: it was that no time during the fight did the cowboy feel he was losing his saddle; a setting to one side the way he had been was just a long-staying holt of his, something like a half nelson with the wrastler.

Poor Smoky had lost again, but in a way he'd won,— he'd won the heart of a cowboy, cause, thru that fight that cowboy's feelings was for the little horse. He'd seen, understood, and admired the show of thinking qualities and the spirit which was Smoky's.

The idea might be got, on account of Smoky being

the steady loser, that his spirit would get jarred and
finally break, but if anybody thinking so could of seen
that horse the next day that idea would of been scattered considerable. His time on the picket rope had
been spent on *more* thinking and figgering, and the
way he went after the tall grass showed he meant to
be in shape to carry thru whatever the new scheme
was.

And some would of thought it queer to've seen how
Smoky, the steady loser in the contest, seemed to hold
no grudge or hate against the winning cowboy. As it
was, that pony seemed to welcome that human a lot
as he walked towards him the next morning, and the
way he rubbed his head against the shoulder of that
smiling rider showed that the fights in the corral had
got to be some friendly. Both was mighty serious, and
both meant to win in them fights, but soon as they
was over and the dust cleared there was a feeling the
likes of when two friends have an argument, when the
argument comes to an end both the loser and winner
are ready to grin, shake hands, and be friends again.

Smoky had lost out twice in trying to dodge out
from under his man, but he was nowheres near convinced as yet that it couldn't be done. The third time
Clint climbed him that pony bucked harder than ever
and that cowboy just sat up there and let him. Clint
had whipped *some* horses for bucking that way, but
he'd whipped them because it was natural orneriness
that made 'em buck. With Smoky it was different,
there was no meaness in him so far,—that pony was
confident that nothing could set him once he got onto

the hang of knowing how to buck real well, and all
he wanted was to be *showed* for sure that Clint could
really set there and ride him thru his worst that way.
After that was done he'd most likely quit.

The first couple of times Smoky was rode and after
he'd quit his bucking, there hadn't been much more to
it excepting that Clint would just run him around a
bit and turn him a few times till the hump was well
down on that pony's back. Smoky had got to thinking
that was all would ever come of being corralled and
saddled, and so, he was some surprised, when after
the bucking spell was over at that third setting, to see
the corral gate opened wide, the cowboy on him again,
and heading him for open country.

Smoky took to the high ridges like a duck takes to
water, he trotted out like a good horse, and then was
put into a long lope. Covering territory felt mighty
good to the little horse for a change and he wasn't
caring much where the cowboy lined him out to. For
a spell he'd forgot the weight on his back, his ears was
straight ahead, and the hand he felt on his neck only
reminded some that somebody was *with* him.

He was needing that change after being bested again
like he'd been that third time. Clint had won once
more and Smoky was a lot in favor of something, most
anything, to drive off the feeling he'd got in losing.
He was taking advantage of the run in that way and
sashayed at a good clip, all went fine, till, of a sudden
a jack rabbit scared out of his hiding place jumped
up and right under Smoky's nose,—he shied straight

up and to one side, and at the same time he was scared more by the wing of Clint's chap which had curled up and slapped along his shoulder. Away he went to bucking once again.

The first few jumps was mighty wicked but they didn't last; he'd already had his buck out not long before and pretty soon he straightened into a lope once again. Clint let him lope a ways then turned him and headed him back to the corrals, stopped him there, turned him a few times and started him out a ways only to turn him and bring him back again. That went on for a few minutes, and then Smoky was unsaddled and put on the picket rope once more.

The run had tired Smoky a little and give him an appetite. He didn't do so much figgering on how to get his man that night, and instead he grazed more, rested some, and even slept a little. When he was led to the corral the next day and the saddle put on he even neglected to watch the cowboy and begin to show interest in the broncs that was in another corral. His ambitions hadn't allowed him to do that before, but somehow, things had changed.—Figgering ways and means of throwing off that rider had got to be tiresome, specially when nothing but disappointment was ever got by it; and besides that saddle and man was getting so they wasn't so bad to stand up under no more.

But as neutral as Smoky showed and felt, that little son of a gun bucked again. Of course there was nothing in his bucking that was so wicked as it had been in them first three saddlings; it was more that he felt he should buck *some*, it made him feel better, and besides he was wanting exercise; but he raised the dust and pounded the earth in good shape even at that, and that play of his would of throwed many a man.

Another run like the one of the day before, a few turnings and teachings on the feel of the rein, and Smoky was thru for another day. He was getting used to the lay of the program Clint had set, and the new game that was brought on right along as he was rode begin to draw the pony's interest.

Then one day, the cowboy begin dragging a rope on him; he let it drag quite a ways, and even tho Smoky watched it mighty close so it wouldn't circle around his legs and throw him like most ropes always did, it didn't worry him much. Pretty soon Clint coiled the rope up and made a loop which he started whirling in the air,—the whirling was slow and easy at first and done with a small loop. Smoky looked back all interest and snorted a little; he wondered what that rope was doing up there and what Clint was up to.

But nothing happened only that the whirling kept up, the loop was gradually made bigger and then it was throwed on the ground a ways in front of him. Smoky shied and snorted and the coils shot out, straightened, and all of it pulled up again by the cowboy, but he didn't try to run away from it, he hadn't forgot the eddication he'd received from the long soft picket rope. He'd learned from it that it didn't pay to stampede when a rope was around, on account that them ropes had a way of stopping him that couldn't at all be argued with.

Loops was made, throwed out, and drug in again

Smoky wondered what a rope was doing up there.

one right after another. They went one side one time, and another side the next, then in front and back, till Smoky begin to lose fear no matter which way the rope went or how it coiled up. It was at the point when he was beginning to lose interest in the game that Clint roped a small bush. The rope tightened on it and Smoky pulled,—he pulled more in wonder what was holding him than with the idea of what he should do, but anyway the bush came out and headed straight for Smoky as it did, he struck at it and would of left from there, but Clint held him and made him face it.

Smoky shook like a leaf as slow but sure the cowboy kept a pulling the bush towards him, he struck again and snorted as it touched his front feet, and he bucked a couple of jumps when he felt it up along his shoulder, but there was no getting away from it; the way that bush moved, it looked like something vicious to Smoky, and when Clint took the rope off of it, and held it out under the pony's nose for him to see what it was the little horse near showed signs of shame for getting scared.

Loose stumps, branches, pieces of old wagons, and everything that could be drug or moved was roped,— anything that was light enough was pulled up for Smoky to investigate, and each time he was showed that he'd been shying and fighting for no reason, till finally, nothing could be found that brought any more than a snort from him. An old coal oil can was then roped and brought up a rattling under Smoky's nose, but he even stood his ground at that.

He was learned to pull on the rope and made to drag

things as heavy as a yearling critter. Then gradually
Clint made him keep the rope tight and hold it that

The bush came out and headed straight for Smoky.

way till a couple of light jerks on it made him give
slack. All that took time, and the cowboy learned him
only one thing each day, sometimes very little of that

one thing,—but as the days went by it all accumulated to a lot.

It done Clint's heart good to watch the way Smoky was taking to things, his little ears worked back and forth, and with his eyes he never missed a move that went on, his nostrils quivered at all that was new, and the cowboy was noticing with a glad feeling that the pony was putting a lot of trust in him, a word from that cowboy, or a touch from his hand was getting to mean a lot when that pony was dubious or at the point of scaring at some new happening.

Clint hunted up a bunch of cattle one day and acquainted Smoky with some pointers in the handling of the critters. He'd haze the horse in the bunch, cut out some fat kinky yearling, and make him put his interest on that yearling only. All was a puzzle to Smoky at first, and he had no idea of what he should do, but Clint give him his time, and coaching him along it wasn't but a few days when the little horse understood some of what was wanted of him. In the meantime the teachings with the rope wasn't left behind, that went along with working cattle, and once in a while Clint would snare some big calf and make Smoky keep his nose along that rope while the calf circled, bucked, and bellered.

Smoky showed signs of liking all that went on. He took interest in it the same as a kid would to some new game,—he liked to chase the wild eyed cow, turn her when she didn't want to be turned, and put her where she didn't want to be put, he liked to hold the rope tight on one of the critters and feel that *he* was

He liked to chase the wild-eyed cow, turn her when she didn't want to be turned, and put her where she didn't want to be put.

the one that was keeping 'er down. It all struck him as a kind of a game where every animal before him had to do as *he* and the cowboy wished.

He was all for catching on and not a nerve in him was idle as Clint would take him of evenings and ride him out for a spell, and chase, cut out, or rope at the critter. Them goings on had his mind occupied and the fact that he'd figger and think on the subject between times was proved by the way he'd go at things in a decided and knowing how way, when the day before the same thing had left him puzzled and wondering.

That little work he was getting and the all heart interest he was finding in it, had settled him to the big change from the free life he'd led with the old buckskin horse and the bunch of mares and colts,—his mammy was even forgotten, and instead there'd sprouted in him something that made him take a liking for the long lanky cowboy that came to see and *play* with him every day. He'd got to finding a lot of pleasure in doing just what that cowboy wanted him to do, and when that was done there was a hankering in him to do just a little bit more.

That's the way Clint wanted to keep him; just a hankering to do more would get results, and he was careful to see that the little horse didn't tire on the work. He wanted to make it play for him and keep it that way as long as he could, for he knowed that was the way to keep Smoky's heart and spirit all in one hunk and intact.

CHAPTER VII

SMOKY SHOWS HIS FEELINGS

JEFF NICKS, cow foreman of the Rocking R outfit, was riding along and headed for the horse camp where Clint was breaking horses. Spring works was over and Jeff thinking it was a good time for him to do a little lone riding and kinda visit the camps of the outfit, had left his straw boss in charge of the wagon, caught his best horse and strung out to cover some of the Rocking R territory.

It was a hot day, not a breath stirred the air, and as the old cowman rode he lifted his hat often to kinda let a fresh supply of atmosphere come in underneath. His big brown horse was covering ground in a running walk, and Jeff keeping him down to that gate wasn't passing a coulee nor a draw without a glance in it and then to the skyline above. It was his habit as a cowman to keep his eyes on the job while riding, and for the good of the company or his own, nary a thing had ever escaped his vision unless it was just too far for that vision to reach.

It was as he was riding along natural that way, that he noticed a thin streak of dust to the right of him quite a ways; that dust wasn't made by anything traveling fast, and even tho it reached up in the air good and high Jeff could see at a glance that the dust was stirred by something dragging.

He stopped his horse so as to get a steadier view, and pretty soon he could make out the shape of a horse underneath that dust; something that looked like a turned pack was fastened or hanging on to him and dragging alongside.

Jeff had seen many happenings on the range between man and horse and from that figgered to always investigate anything that suspicioned of something gone wrong, and to investigate quick.—He put his horse in a high lope. Down draws, over rolling hills, and acrost dog towns he went all at the same speed, and pretty soon he comes to where there's only a small ridge between him and what he wanted to investigate.

It was then that he figgered it best to take it slow till he'd seen just what was up; if some rider had got caught in his riggin' some way as a horse fell, and that horse was wild and unbroke, riding in on a high lope would only make things worse and cause the horse to stampede.—Nobody knowed that better than Jeff did.

He got off his horse, walked a ways, and peeking thru the tall grass seen the whole goings on at a glance. Fifty yards below him was a mouse colored horse,—looked like a half broke bronc to him on account of the way the hackamore was rigged,—but that horse didn't act like half broke. He was going thru a performance that most gentle broke range horses wouldn't put up with, and that was to half carry and half drag a man, *and on the wrong side.*

Jeff recognized that man as his "bronc peeler" Clint, and he was all for rushing down to see what had happened and help, but he held back,—he wasn't sure but what the mouse colored horse would scare and run away at the sight of him, and he couldn't tell but what Clint's hands was fastened to the saddle horn the way he was hanging on.

He could see there was still life in the rider, but if the man was conscious he wasn't showing very good sense by hanging on the wrong side of a half broke horse that way. Still, as he watched, Jeff begin to wonder. He noticed for one thing that the horse was headed straight for camp, Clint's camp, and then there was another thing he noticed and which made him wonder and watch more than ever— The mouse colored gelding wasn't dragging his man, he was more kinda helping him along seemed like, each step that horse took was with care and in favor of the man alongside; the pony watched every move that man made, and if the steps sorta lagged or hesitated he stopped or slowed down till the man braced up some and went again.

Jeff's mouth was wide open with wonder as he watched the goings on, and when a little while later the gelding happened along a big rock, and seen him stop while the man tried to use the rock to get from it up in the saddle, Jeff wondered some more.

"By japers, I've seen and handled thousands of horses," says Jeff, "but I never thought any horse ever had that much sense."

The old cowman watched for near a half an hour while Clint tried to get on his horse. He seen the horse stand there, all patience and a helping the best he could, and finally, with the help of the rock, the favor-

ing of the horse, and the little strength the man had,
and all put together, Clint was setting in the saddle
at last. The hackamore reins was hanging loose; nothing was holding that pony from bucking, stampeding,
or do anything he pleased, but he stepped slow and
easy, and ears cocked ahead, packed his man to camp
with the same care any human would take.

Jeff got on his horse and keeping well behind followed, what he'd just seen had got him to the point
where he begin a talking to himself, his horse, and the
country around.

"Yessir, by japers, and he let Clint get on him from
the wrong side too, why this daggone old gentle horse
I'm riding now wouldn't let me do that— But then,
maybe I better not be too sure about that, I'm beginning to believe from what I've just seen that there's
things going on in horses' think tanks that's mighty
surprising and which don't come out till the right time
shows up."

A couple of hours and the camp was reached, Jeff
looked around the big corrals as he rode closer for signs
of Clint and the mouse colored bronc, and sure enough,
there the both of 'em are,—Clint is still in the saddle
and to all appearance unconscious; the gelding is
standing by the corral gate, still, and waiting.

The cowman rode on towards 'em, but he soon had
to stop, for he noticed as the gelding sees him how by
that pony's action, he wasn't for standing in one spot
no longer at the sight of a strange rider coming on him
that way. Jeff had to maneuver around considerable
to keep that horse from hightailing it. The only way

he could do it was to go back the way he came till out of sight, once there he circled around till he came up on the camp from the opposite side, the corrals and a long shed was between him and the half broke horse with his unconscious rider.

Jeff left his horse out of sight, and hugging close to the shed made his way to where the mouse colored gelding had been; a peek thru a hole in the wall showed him the horse was still there, and Clint still in the saddle. How to proceed from then on was a sort of ticklish proposition. Jeff didn't want the pony to get scared, run away and throw the hurt rider, and still, he couldn't let the rider stay where he was.

He had to take a chance and do the best he could. Around the corner of the shed he came, and slow and easy, showed himself to the wild eyed gelding; he talked to him, and that seemed to help some, for the little horse stood his ground. *Stood his ground* is correct, but Jeff had hesitated somehow from coming any closer,—he noticed a light in that pony's eyes which warned him plain to keep his distance, and even tho Jeff was half peeved and half leary at the stand the pony had took he couldn't help but admire the show of liking that half broke gelding had for the rider that was still unconscious in the saddle, and laying with his head on the pony's bowed neck.

The horse's actions had all been a puzzle to Jeff at first, and as he finally understood, it all left him mighty surprised and in a trance with wonder. He'd expected that horse to start running away at the sight of him, but instead, he was showing fight, the pony wasn't wanting to go no further with the hurt rider, he wasn't going to trust no strange human with that helpless pardner of his.

Two months or more had passed since Clint and Smoky had met in the dust of the bare corral. In that time the man and horse'd had fights, some had been mighty wicked, and the wild horse would of killed the man too if the chance had come, but all thru them fights the man had won,—slow and easy, but he'd won. Then gradually Smoky begin to get confidence in the human, and then a liking; he'd got to looking for his company and would nicker with a glad feeling as he'd see that human come towards him of evenings, and he'd go the length of his picket rope to meet him.

Steady good treatment from the rider, no matter what the horse done, had won that pony's heart, till the little horse could near be seen smiling with the happy feeling that was his every time Clint came, saddled him, and rode him out for a little play with the rope and critter.

That's the way Smoky's feelings had come to be for the bow legged rider, and taking all as was, it's no wonder the horse showed fight when a strange human appeared. In his life Smoky had seen no other but Clint; he knowed *him*, but he didn't know the others, and he had no more love for them than he had when he was first run in from his free range. Them others was still enemies to him, and right then when that pony felt his pardner was depending on him most, he was sure ready to paw the daylight out of that stranger if he came any closer. He was his enemy, and according to his way of thinking, he was or should be Clint's enemy too.

Jeff stood there figgering for quite a spell a trying to digest and believe what that pony showed, it couldn't come to him to hurt or kill such a horse so as to get the man, and he'd just decided to get his rope, throw a loop over his head and snub him close to the corral, when the rider begin to show signs of life.

"Come to, Clint," hollered the cowman as he noticed the rider move, "and get off that horse."

Clint raised his head some at the sound of the voice, and as Jeff kept a speaking to him he made a big effort to understand and try to do as he was told. Pain showed in his face as he tried to straighten himself in the saddle, and as Jeff feared that the rider would lose consciousness again he hollered at him not to try to straighten up, but just slide off and hang on.

With a lot of pain and time and coaching from Jeff, Clint finally managed to raise one leg over the cantle of the saddle and let himself slide to the ground. Smoky stood still as a statue and as solid, his eyes was on Jeff with a steady warning for him to keep his distance—and Jeff did.

"Hang on to the saddle," coached Jeff, "try and get the horse thru the gate in the corral, and I'll close the gate on him."

That was done in time, and as the gate was closed Clint's hands went limp and he fell to the ground. Lucky it was that Jeff could reach him thru the corral bars, but he had to do considerable maneuvering even then to get the cowboy thru and under so as not to stir Smoky. And it was a mighty good thing for Jeff as he picked Clint up and started towards the house that there was bars high and strong between him and that pony, for as high and strong as that corral was Jeff worried some and, looking back over his shoulder as he went, wondered if it would hold him.

The sun had sunk away, and dark had come before Clint came to well enough so things was plain to him and he could talk. Jeff had made him as comfortable as was possible, boiled some "jerky" and made a strong broth which he was holding under Clint's nose for him to sniff at.

That cowboy sniffed, looked around, and then said, "where's Smoky?"

"If you mean that mouse colored fighting son of a gun of a horse you was on," says Jeff, "why he's in the corral, and a fretting his head that I'm going to eat you up."

Clint couldn't quite get the meaning of that just then, and he asked, "I wonder if you wouldn't go take the saddle off of him and put him on the picket rope where he'd get something to eat. He's gentle, and you can handle him easy."

Jeff snorted and laughed, "gentle, ——? I wouldn't try to handle him if you'd give me this whole outfit, I'm not enough of a bronc fighter no more, and that ain't all, that pony is just a hankering for me to stick my beezer thru that corral."

Smoky circled around the corral not at all minding

Smoky's eyes was on Jeff with a steady warning in 'em for him to keep his distance — and Jeff did.

the saddle that was on him, he wasn't caring for any grass either, he was too peeved and restless. If Clint had been right side up and able, things would of been different and Smoky would of hardly even noticed the stranger.—There seems to be a heap of difference in the feelings of any thinking animal when a pardner is sick or dying,—the little horse knowed as well as any human that something had went wrong with his pardner, and the appearance of the stranger at such a time was worrying him.

The next day was well along and the sun getting high, when Jeff helped Clint on his feet and half carried him towards the corral where Smoky had put in the night. Clint staggered on alone from the gate and the little horse nickering came to meet him,—his ears was all ahead and with his eyes a shining, he looked all interest and like he wanted to ask questions. He then spotted Jeff, and at the sight of him, his expression changed, his eyes showed fire, and his ears layed back on his neck.

"Well, I'll be daggoned" says Clint as he noticed the horse's actions. He looked back at the old cowman and grinned, wondering,—but the old cowman wasn't grinning any. Jeff figgered it best for him to vanish for a spell, Smoky was unsaddled, and put on good feed and water, which all seemed to take Clint a powerful lot of time; but he finally showed up and Jeff helped him back to the house.

It was on the way over that Clint begin to speak, and on a subject that'd been on his mind for a long time. "You know, Jeff," he says, "I think the time has come for me to quit riding broncs, I feel like I better quit, specially after this last that's happened to me."

"What *did* happen anyway?" asks Jeff.

"It was all on account of a fool cow," starts Clint, "she'd showed signs of wanting to leave the country soon as she seen me riding up on her, and being she was good and fast, I figgered it'd be a good time to line Smoky out after her and let him turn 'er over a few times. I throwed my rope but the loop didn't land good, it just sorta sailed in front of her, and she stepped in it. About that time I jerked up my slack and I jerked it too hard. Down went the critter all in a heap and sudden, so sudden that with the speed Smoky was going he couldn't stop in time, and first thing we knowed we both was straddle the critter.

"But she didn't stay down long, she got up just at the wrong time and just right to yank Smoky's front feet from under him, raise him up in the air with me on top, and just turned us a couple of somersets before we landed on the other side.

"I didn't know much more after that, till now, I just sorta felt a weight on my back, and that was all. Maybe I got under Smoky somehow as we fell, but I think it's that fool cow that stepped on me and separated me from my thoughts.

"I'll most likely be all right in a few days, but I recognize this ailing. I got hurt a few years ago from an ornery black horse I was breaking for the Three C's, and being that I don't want this ailing to come back with me to stay, I figger I better quit riding rough ones. There's other parts of me that's hankering for me to quit too, and if you'll let me join the boys at the wagon, I'm mighty willing that somebody else gets my job here."

Clint was quiet for a spell, and then pretty soon he goes on, "But there's one favor I want to ask, Jeff, if you'll let me stay with the outfit, I want to ask that you let me keep Smoky in my string and as long as I'm with the company."

What the cowboy had just said come from what he'd figgered, thought out, and worried on, ever since he'd first set eyes on Smoky. Clint liked all horses, maybe a little too much, but even at that he liked Smoky still more. The fear that somebody else would lay claim to the horse'd had him doing some tall thinking. He knowed that as long as he was breaking horses his work would come with raw broncs only and all half broke horses would be took away from him as fast as he'd turn 'em out. Smoky would had to go too.

And that's where the hitch came. He figgered he'd have to quit breaking horses and go to riding the range, and take the big chance that the horse might be took away from him even then. He'd noticed how Jeff had stood, watched, and admired Smoky, and if signs of a human wanting anything right bad ever showed, there was never no signs more visible than Clint had seen on Jeff's features when the horse was in sight.

There'd been only one way out for the cowboy, and he'd took it.—There was a worried look on his face as he glanced at the foreman and waited for him to answer, but Jeff didn't seem to want to answer right then, and instead he asked:

"How long have you had that horse up, Clint?"

"Two months and maybe a little over," says Clint, wondering some at the question.

"Wasn't there a couple of boys here about a month ago to get *all* the broncs you'd started?"

"Yes."

"Well then, why didn't you let 'em have that horse Smoky, he was as well broke then as any of the broncs the boys came after, wasn't he?"

Clint begin to take interest in looking at the wall of the bunk house about that time. He grinned a little, and finally he answered:

"Well, Jeff, I guess you know why."

Jeff did know why, and knowed it a plenty. What he'd seen going on between Smoky and the cowboy the day before and that morning had already answered why Clint had hid the horse when the boys came to haze away the broncs he'd "started." The foreman grinned back at the layed up rider and placed a hand on his shoulder, the same as to say that he understood.

"As long as I'm with this outfit," he says, "and which from all indications will be a long time, you're mighty welcome to join the wagon as one of my riders. You'll be getting 'top-hand' wages too, Clint, the best string of ponies I can put together, and as for Smoky, why —I sure would like that horse."

Clint's heart fluttered up his throat and came near choking him— "Yep! I'd sure like to have him" went on the foreman "but, after thinking it all over, I figger that horse really belongs to you more than he does to the company or me. He's a one man horse and you're the one man, Clint, and even if the horse took a liking to me, which I know won't happen, I'll sure never want to take him away from you—not after what I've seen."

Clint had underfiggered considerable when he'd said how he thought he'd be all right again in a few days. A week passed and very little strength had gathered from his hips up, his back felt as broke, and he had no power to straighten up again once he'd stoop, he couldn't even pick up a spur.

A new rider came one day and took up Clint's work where he'd left it. From that time on Clint hung around the corrals a talking and watching the new "hand" ride, and when he wasn't by the corrals, he could be seen in the shade of the big willows in the creek bottom where Smoky was picketed.

Clint had looked at Smoky in a new way since Jeff had come and left. The visit of the old cowboy had brought out things in that little horse which Clint hadn't dreamed of ever being in any horse. He'd been mighty surprised, and then sort of proud that he could raise such a feeling in the gelding— The horse was good as his too,—that put the cap on his worries of losing him, and all was well.

A month went by, the round up wagons was stringing out for the fall works, and the cow with the big "weaner" calf was hunting a hole. There was twenty-two riders with Jeff Nick's wagon, and amongst 'em a grinning from ear to ear at some joke a cowboy had sprung was Clint, and riding Smoky.

Long days of rest had put that cowboy in shape to ride, but not to ride broncs, and when he at last felt that he could make a hand at riding "circle," "herd," and "night guard" Smoky had been saddled and rode to the home ranch, where the wagon was to start from.

Smoky'd had a long month's rest before Clint saddled and rode him out that morning, and even tho the rider looked O. K. again to the little horse, there was a feel from the hackamore rein that as much as asked him not to buck. He'd bucked that day when Clint had met too much cow, and far as that goes, he'd bucked some at every saddling, but as the cowboy started him out for open country and the home ranch that morning he was made to feel that he should keep his head up for once and line out without a kink.

The home ranch had been reached a couple of days later, and there's where Smoky'd got his first look at a busy cow outfit's main camp. Cowboys was everywhere, and more of 'em than he could keep track of; big corrals full of horses, and more horses under the big sheds. Wagons and tents, and when the round up cook rushed out of a log house to one side and pranced up to try and shake hands with Clint, Smoky let out a snort and shied out of reach.

"Daggone it, Clint," says that hombre, "I was told you'd quit riding broncs—what in samhill do you call that spooky thing you're setting on now?"

"Some horse," answers Clint, grinning.

Smoky felt some easier when he was finally unsaddled and turned in amongst the other saddle horses. He took a good roll, shook himself, and proceeded to get acquainted. It didn't worry him none that very few of the ponies seemed to want his company and he was mighty busy going from one of the big corrals into another and giving 'em all the once over. He finally run acrost a bay gelding which seemed some familiar, and Smoky must of seemed the same to that gelding too for both of 'em started to show interest at once and came to meet one another.

Necks bowed, they touched nostrils, some explaining and understanding must of went on cause it wasn't but a few minutes later when each was scratching the other's neck like two brothers—and that's what they was, *brothers*. The bay horse was none other than the little colt, growed up, and which his mammy had brought in the bunch one day over three years before.

Signs showed where the saddle had been on his back too. A cowboy had run him in a couple of weeks before and passed the remark as he piled his rope on him that, "This little bay horse sure showed the makings of a cowhorse."

Jeff had agreed, and that's how come Smoky found him in amongst the saddle horses that day. He'd showed some of how he'd took a *natural* liking for the bay, and if one didn't recognize a brother in the other, the way they went at scratching each other's withers couldn't of meant much.

It was thru an intermission at wither scratching that Smoky seen Clint open the outside gate of the corral and walk in. Alongside of him was Jeff Nicks who'd come along to point out Clint's string of ponies. Smoky watched them two for quite a spell, he watched Jeff the most, but pretty soon went to scratching his brother's withers again. Clint was all right now and well able to take care of himself, he must of thought— Anyway there wasn't the feeling in him that Clint needed any protection.

Clint had come to see him that evening, and he'd noticed as his pardner came that some of the cowboys was watching him from the next corral. He looked over Clint's shoulder at 'em and sent out a long whistling snort.

"I'm glad Clint didn't break all the broncs like he did that one" remarked one of the boys as he seen the fight in that pony's eyes.

"Yep!" says another, "he sure made a *one man* horse out of him."

Smoky was turned out in the big pasture that night with the other horses. Him and his brother paired off soon as they was out of the corrals and fed together till daybreak brought a rider on the sky line who corraled 'em all for the new day's work.

That day's work started early. Sun up found all the boys on their horses, the chuck wagon, bed wagon and wood wagon teams was all hooked on and ready to start at a wave of the hand from Jeff. Jeff waved, and away all went thru the big gates leading out of the home ranch, three wagons strung out, a "remuda" (saddle bunch) of two hundred saddle horses followed, and on the "swing" (sides) of the whole outfit twenty-two riders, riding good and bad horses, loped along— The fall round up had started.

CHAPTER VIII

SMOKY STARTS OUT

THE first day of the fall round up was to Smoky a whole lot like the first day of school to the kid of the settlement, only, Smoky was full grown and his brain full developed. His eyes stayed wide open and worked with his ears so that nothing of interest would be missed.

There was so much that was strange and which kept his senses on the jump. The big wagons with the four and six horse teams done a lot of spooky rattling as they followed the pilot, sometimes on a high lope, across the rolling prairie, over benches and down draws. Then trailing along close behind the thumping of hoofs of many ponies, the remuda, made a sound which hinted everything to Smoky, everything from a stampede on up, and if it hadn't been for the hand that once in a while was felt on his neck, and the voice which he heard and knowed so well the little horse would of sure left a streak of dust and away from all that confusion of wagons and men.

There was too many riders around him. They all kept too close, and once in a while as the outfit sashayed on towards the first camp grounds and some bronc would bust out a bucking and a trying to shed off a cowboy, Smoky felt a lot like doing the same. But always, and whenever he felt like "kettling" the most,

Clint's hand and voice was there to quiet him down. That hand and voice worked the same as to prove to Smoky, that as long as Clint was around close there was nothing for him to fear.

As the outfit rambled on, Clint gradually reined Smoky to one side till he was well away and where he would feel more at ease to watch without fear all what the layout had to show that was strange. Smoky's ears then perked up in a different angle, and as Clint talked to him that spooky looking outfit lining out acrost the range got to look less spooky and more interesting.

Smoky followed the outfit and watched it till the sun was well up in the middle of the sky, then the pilot raised his hand, made a circle and the wagons followed him to a standstill. A dry camp was made and the cook had the pots to working a few minutes after the outfit had come to a stop. The rope corrals was strung out in the wink of an eye and the remuda run in.

Smoky had watched the whole proceedings with a lot of interest, the many horses, men, and all had him to using his eyes and ears to the limit, and the low snorts he'd let out every once in a while as he turned to watch all that went on, was as plain as talk, that for excitement this sure had everything he'd ever seen before beat to a frazzle.

'Come and get it, you Rannies!" It was the cook's holler for the riders to come and eat. About then Smoky seen Clint headed towards him and where he'd been left picketed. A little rub back of the ear and

Smoky was led to the rope corral, unsaddled, and turned in with the remuda.

"Have a good roll, Smoky horse," says Clint as he turned him loose, "and don't let no ornery pony get the best of you."

Smoky looked back at Clint for a spell the same as to ask him where *he* was going, and as the cowboy stood there watching the little horse moseyed on and disappeared amongst the saddle bunch.

The "round-up pan" was filling up with the tin cups and plates as the cowboys, thru eating, was making their way towards their saddles by the rope corrals. A hard twist catch rope was unbuckled from them saddles, loops was shook out, and pretty soon them same loops begin a sailing and a reaching out like a mighty long arm for the horse each cowboy picked out for that afternoon's ride.

Smoky seen and heard the hiss of them loops as they sailed on over past him to settle around some other pony's neck, and even tho all was done quiet so none of the horses would start running too much, Smoky had a mighty restless feeling whenever them snaky ropes appeared. Clint hadn't roped him only once and that was when he was a raw bronc, but he hadn't forgot the feeling that'd been his when that same rope had caught him, stretched him out, and left him plumb helpless.

His brain was near stampeding with him at the sound of so many ropes, and once in a while when he'd spot some strange rider carrying one of them hated coils the sight made him hit for the middle of the herd,—

but even there he wasn't safe, for there was no telling how far them ropes could reach.

It was in winding around and thru the thick of the herd, that Smoky found himself on the edge and crowded against the big rope cable which was the corral. The sight that met his eye there had him wanting to hide back in the middle of the herd once again, but he had no chance, the herd had him wedged where he couldn't move and as it was he had to stare wild eyed at all that was there for him to see.

A few feet away was half a dozen riders saddling up, and that's what kettled Smoky,—the few feet that was between him and them strangers was too close for comfort. He was just about to try another grand rush to get back into the middle of the herd when the sound of something familiar made him hesitate. It was the ring of a spur rowel, a ring he'd heard often, and pretty soon Smoky spots Clint only a few feet away from him and leading a strange horse to his saddle.

Smoky stuck his head and neck out far as he could and nickered at the sight of the cowboy, and that cowboy having his attention some other direction at the time was made to turn mighty quick as the well known nicker was heard.—There was all in Smoky's looks and nicker that seemed to say "Pardner, I need help."

Clint laughed, but the laugh wasn't of the kind that comes from a joke.

"What's the matter, little horse?"

But Clint knowed what was the matter, he could

hear the thump thump of Smoky's heart as he came nearer, and feel the throb of it as he layed a hand on his neck. He rubbed on the slick hide a spell, and that cowboy experienced a mighty great feeling when he noticed as he stayed, that gradually the pony's heart beats begin to slow down and soon was behaving normal again.

Smoky watched the cowboy leave him to go to where his saddle was laying on the ground out a ways. He watched him put the saddle on the strange horse, and when Clint came back leading the horse and finished saddling by Smoky, that pony nipped at the cowboy's chap' leg the same as to say "Stick around a spell."

Clint did stick around for a spell. He wasted a lot of good company time fooling with the latigos and seeing that his rope was coiled up neat, and even tho he knowed that as a good cowboy he should been helping tearing down camp, he stuck by the corral and Smoky till the last rider had caught, saddled, and rode his horse away. The remuda was let out then, the wrangler circled the bunch and started grazing 'em till the wagons started again for that night's grounds.

Smoky was hazed along and lost in the big horse herd, Clint watched him and when he couldn't see him no more started coiling up the big cable, which was the rope corral used on open range, and with the help of another rider put it in one of the wagons where it'd be easy reached again.

It'd been less than an hour since the cook had stopped his team and jumped off the wagon to cook

Smoky stuck his head and neck out far as he could and nickered at the sight of the cowboy.

the cowboys' noon bait, and now he was up on the
wagon again and waiting there for the boys to finish
hooking up his team and hand him the "ribbons"—
Soon enough that was done, the pilot started and the
cook warwhooped his broncs into a running start, the
bed wagon, loaded down with twenty some odd "Mon-
tana Rolls," took up the swing, and the wood wagon
tagged along behind. Then came the remuda of over
two hundred saddle horses and hazing 'em was the
"Wrangatang" (day wrangler).

The first "circle" of the fall round up was on
that afternoon— The circle starts from wherever the
round-up wagon might be. The round-up wagon of
most countries is composed of three wagons, one for
"chuck" and pots and the cook, another for the
riders' bedding which is rolled in big canvas tarpaulins.
It takes quite some bedding for twenty or more men,
specially in countries where it's apt to snow in the
middle of June. The third wagon is for wood and water
and which is used in prairie countries where there's
neither wood or water to be found for a ways.

The cook drives his chuckwagon, the "flunky"
(cook's helper) drives the bed wagon, and the "nighthawk" (rider who herds the remuda at night) drives
the wood wagon. Them three wagons which is called
"The Wagon" is the cowboys' home while on the
range. It carries his grub, his "war bag" (bag of
clothes), his bedding, and strips of rawhide which he
salts down and sometimes cuts into strings and braids
things like "bosals" (nose bands) or such.

"The Wagon" moves camp most every day, and

sometimes twice and three times a day, all depends on how quick the country is "worked." The "circle" starts from "The Wagon." The twenty or more riders and the cow foreman ride straight to some point for ten or fifteen miles. On top of some butte the bunch stops, then the cow foreman "scatters the riders." He'll send 'em in pairs to the right, left, and straight ahead and spread 'em fan shape to a certain point where they turn, or where there's no more cattle to be seen, and they'll head back towards the wagon again, bringing with 'em all the cattle that's seen in the ride.

That's what's called a "circle." It averages twenty-five miles and ends at the wagon where all the riders meet again each bringing with 'em whatever cattle was found. The wagon might of moved and a new camp set up while the boys was out on "circle," but wherever the wagon is that's where the "circle" ends. To one side of the camp a mile or so the "cutting grounds" where the herd is "worked" is the spot where all the cattle is brought to from that one "circle" and held there for branding, and cutting out whatever is not wanted. Two "circles" are made a day.

Soon as Jeff, the cow foreman, seen the wagons lining out in good shape for that night's camp he put his horse in a high lope and looking back at the boys that was doing their best in putting up a ride on the sun-fishing ponies, he grinned as he seen that all stuck on and fanned, and felt mighty proud of being the cow boss of such a bunch of riders.

Clint was riding a big "apelusa" called Chapo, and one of the best circle horses the outfit had, but he wasn't appreciating him much just then, and as he rode along leaving the wagons and remuda to his left his eyes was a whole lot on the dust that remuda made, and a trying to get a glimpse of a mouse colored piece of horseflesh which he'd called Smoky.

But Smoky was getting along fine as he trotted and loped along on the trail of the wagons. He'd no more than left Clint by the rope corral when he run acrost that brother of his again and after the two nickered "Howdedoos" at one another they trailed along side by side, plum contented with everything in general. The sound of the dozen or so bells that was strapped to the necks of the oldest and wisest ponies was new and mighty pleasant to Smoky's ears and it was good to be roaming again and with so much company.

It was middle afternoon when the pilot came to a big creek bottom and circled by a grove of willows and cottonwoods. The second camp of that day was made, the wrangler let the remuda come to a walk and pretty soon left 'em to graze on towards the creek a half a mile below camp, and as he seen that all seemed contented to graze, drink, and roll, he left 'em to go and put up the rope corral, snake in wood for the cook, and whatever other things that's all the responsibilities of the wrangatang.

He kept one eye on the ponies as he worked and if any restless bronc showed indications of wanting to start drifting that boy jumped on his horse, turned him, and watched for a spell till that bronc seemed satisfied to stay. Many a wrangler had used the excuse of "hard-to-hold ponies" just so he could get away from too much work, and most always it was a mighty good excuse too.

But Smoky and Pecos, which was his brother, had give no such a excuse to the wrangler. They both seemed mighty satisfied, and after they'd had a good drink in the cool stream, and a good roll afterwards put their time in getting away with all the blue joint grass they could. Every once in a while Smoky would raise his head, and chewing on a mouthful of the tall feed, would look up at the ridges around him, then towards the camp and wonder at the noise the cook was making with his pots and pans. All had him interested, it was all new, and with the nicker he'd often hear from one side of the scattered remuda and then the other, the steady ring of the horse bells and all, the little horse wasn't hankering for anything only just what he was in the thick of.

He'd been grazing for a good long time, and the sun was hitting towards the ridges to the west, when to the south a ways he noticed a big dust a soaring up the sky and a mile high. There was a steady rumbling noise as the dust came closer and pretty soon he could make out the bellering of the critter. A big herd it was, the "combings" of the first "circle," and a thousand head or more of white-faced, brockle-faced, speckled, red, black, and all colors and sizes of range cattle topped a ridge and on a high lope was swung towards the "cutting grounds."

About that time the horse wrangler fogged in on the remuda, and in a short while Smoky and all the ponies found themselves in the rope corral once again; the cowboys was needing fresh horses and catch ropes begin a sailing once more as the twenty and more of 'em snared their "cut" horses, a few snaked out broncs and pretty soon all hands was mounted again, and working the herd they'd brought in.

Smoky was spooked up once more as he heard the ropes sing over his ears. He heard a familiar voice say "How's she going, Smoky?" but the little horse was busy hunting a hole about that time and he was too excited to nicker an answer. Then, after what seemed an awful long time to Smoky, the ponies was left out of the corral once more and when the wrangler checked 'em all to graze, him and Pecos was in the lead.

The ponies was grazing on a low bench and on the opposite side of the creek from where the cattle herd was being worked. Many was cut out and started back on the same range from where they come, and pretty soon Smoky's sensitive nostrils smelled the smoke from the fire that kept the branding irons hot; then the smell of burnt hair followed, he heard the beller of the critters, and snorting sorta low and in wonder the mouse colored pony watched.

He watched the riders at work, seen long ropes a swinging, and how them long ropes would stop the bunch-quitting steer; he was familiar with some of that and somehow there came in him a hunch that he'd like to be closer; there was something about the workings of that herd across the creek that had his blood racing above natural, and he felt a kind of a call for the whole of the goings on, a call of the kind he couldn't as yet understand, but it was there sure enough.

Finally, the smell of singed hair wasn't on the breeze no more, branding was over for that day, and the last rope was coiled up and fastened by the saddle horn. Smoky watched as all but a few riders left the herd and headed for camp, he went to grazing then, and neck and neck with Pecos he listened to the rattle of tin plates and the laugh of the cowboys as he nosed around for the tenderest stems of the blue joint.

Four riders on "cocktail" (hours between the last meal of the day and the first night guard) got on their horses and rode to "relieve" the riders holding the herd, and it wasn't long after that when the quiet of the evening settled on the range. Even the critter seemed to want to stop bellering for a spell at that time, most of the bells of the remuda was quiet and the ponies was dozing.

Smoky had been dozing too, but pretty soon his ears perked up at a sound the likes of which he'd never heard before, the sound came from the camp, and strange as it was there was something about it that wasn't at all aggravating.

Around a good size fire was gathered the cowboys,— the cook, the flunky, the wrangler, Jeff the foreman and all was in the circle, all but the four riders on "cocktail" and the "nighthawk" who'd took the wrangler's place for the night's herding of the saddle horses. Most of the boys was setting on or leaning against a big roll of tarpaulin covered bedding, and one closest to the fire was a working away trying to get a tune on his mouth organ.

That was the sound which'd come to Smoky's ears,

the older cowhorses all knowed that sound well, and if any of 'em could of packed a tune there'd been many in the remuda a humming.

The song that was being worked at just then had been heard at all the cow camps and round up wagons of the cow country for many years, and handed down from the injun fighting cowboy to the son that took up the trail where he left it and when the horns on the critter wasn't so long no more. There was a lot of memories stirred up whenever them songs was heard and many a cowboy got sentimental at the sound of 'em, for most all cowboys can remember some quiet night when the time of such a song was spread around the herd;—then of a sudden and for no reason a stampede is in full swing, a dead cowboy is found under his horse at the bottom of a fifty foot jump off, and leaves only the memory of the song he'd been singing that night.

"Oh, I'm a Texas cowbo-o-oy, and far away from home,
And if I ever get back again no more will I ever roam,
Wyoming's too cold for me-e-e, the winters are too long,
And when round up comes again, my money's all go-o-o-ne."

Clint had got harmonious, and with the other cowboy a trying to keep up on the mouth organ was singing the song, he mixed in about ten verses and took in other songs as he went, the tunes changed some, but the "Texas whang" he carried with the tunes made 'em more or less alike and all appreciated the same.

The last verse had died down, some of the boys looked up expecting more, and others, hat brim pulled down, was stargazing at the fire and letting the memories the songs had brought lead 'em back to times and happenings that'd been stirred the most.

All was quiet, excepting for the crackling of the fire, and one of the boys was just about to speak the name of some other old song when off from the direction where the remuda was held, a nicker was heard.

Clint looked towards where the familiar nicker had come and smiled,—the cowboy's voice had carried to where Smoky had been grazing, and the little horse had stopped grinding on his feed soon as the first verse had hit his ears, he'd listened on thru to the end, nickered, and watched the fire on the creek bottom from where the voice had come.

He watched it long into the night till all was quiet and the fire had dwindled down to coals; time for first night guard to be relieved was near and Smoky was still watching. Pecos was dozing off a ways, and pretty soon Smoky begin to feel a little groggy too and he dozed with him.

A new day was no more than hinted by the paling sky to the east when the "nighthawk" begin bunching the ponies and hazing 'em towards camp. It was still faint daylight when the catch ropes was a hissing over the ponies' heads once again and loops settled around slick necks. Broncs was drug out, and a fighting against the saddle while the sun was still back of the ridges, but the day's work had started at the round up camp.

In a short while the remuda was let out again, and the day wrangler started grazing 'em while the outfit broke camp for other grounds. When all was loaded in the big wagons the pilot took the lead, and when the sun showed up to begin its circle up above, the cook had already moved his kitchen some ten miles and the pots was beginning to feel the heat of the fire underneath.

Smoky was in another new country that day, and as he grazed with the remuda he noticed the same workings of the day before, another big herd was brought in from that morning's "circle," then one more that afternoon, more cattle was cut out and then singed hair floated on the breeze once more.

Twice again he was corralled with the remuda for fresh horses the riders was needing, and the little horse was slow beginning to get used to the sound of the ropes and the sight of the strange cowboys. Clint was to see him at the last coralling of the day and when the nighthawk took the ponies out for the night Smoky nipped Pecos in the flanks. He felt playful.

Outside of the time he spent in the rope corral the little horse was enjoying the following of the round up mighty well,—there was always so many horses around, and all with the bellering of the big herds and the dust that was kept up sure tallied up with the beat of his heart. He hadn't figgered on what to expect being one of the remuda that way, and being that he couldn't make out all that went on he didn't know just what could be expected, and that's why maybe he wasn't worried much.

"Going to make a very big circle this morning, Jeff?"

It was the morning of the third day that Clint asked the foreman that question, and when Jeff answered he understood what was on Clint's mind, he grinned at the cowboy as he spoke.

"You go ahead and ride your Smoky horse, Clint, I'll put you on the inside circle so as it won't be too hard on him."

And that's how come when it was Smoky's turn to be rode that the easiest was handed him. The horse spotted Clint coming towards him, a rope was in his hands but no loop was dragging and he met the cowboy halfways.

Of the many ponies that makes up a "remuda" there's seldom any that can be walked up to, even the gentlest has to be roped. They're broke that way and it all saves time, for a cowboy can stand off thirty feet, rope his horse and start leading him out from there. It saves him many steps and when there's so many riders and horses, them steps and the time it'd take to make 'em sure would accumulate. Then again there's so many wild ponies that would *have* to be roped anyway. So making the whole thing simple, every horse is caught with a loop. No good roper ever whirls a loop in catching horses, and the only sound that's heard is when the rope splits from the ground to the pony's head.

Once in a while, and even with real cow outfits that's well run, there's exceptions in roping every horse that way. Smoky was the one exception on the Rocking R, and every cowboy was good natured jealous at the way that mouse colored son of a gun of a horse would stick his head out every time Clint came around and then left his hiding place from amongst the other horses to meet him.

Smoky knowed that something was up soon as Clint came near him, but whatever it was he was anxious to be at it;—him and that cowboy would get along.

The little horse humped up as he felt the cinch, and Clint grinned as he remarked:

"Going to make this old broke-down cowboy ride this morning, huh?"

And Smoky did. He bogged his head soon as Clint was well set, and bucked and bellered all over the flat like he was a man-eating outlaw. It was the right thing for a live horse to do them cold fall mornings, and Clint was enjoying fanning the dust off Smoky's round rump the same as that pony enjoyed the idea that he sure was giving somebody a tossing.

"Better save some of that," says Clint as he finally pulled Smoky's head up, "cause you might need all the energy you got before you get back."

About twelve miles or so from camp a knoll was reached; from there Jeff "scattered" his riders to circle and comb the country on the way back, Clint and another rider was the last to be let go, and on the "inside" brought with 'em all the cattle they found. Half ways back to camp, Smoky begin to notice big dusts on both sides of him, them dusts kept a getting closer and closer till pretty soon he begin to see that it was more cattle making them dusts. Herds kept a being drove in with the bunch Clint and the other rider had rounded up, and by the time camp was reached, all the dusts had throwed in and made one. Twenty or more riders and over a thousand head of cattle was turned to the cutting grounds and held there a milling.

Smoky was tired, he'd been breathing dust and turning bleary-eyed critters till it seemed like there'd be no end. Besides it felt awful hot on his back where the saddle was, and even tho Clint often got off, uncinched the saddle and raised it so the cool air could circulate thru, it wasn't long when his back, not used to long saddling, would feel as hot as ever again.

It was a great relief to the little horse when the saddle was pulled off as they reached camp and the rope corral. Clint then led him to the creek and washed the dry sweat off his back with the cool water, and as that was done Smoky right away forgot the work of that first circle. He felt a lot at ease with everything in general as Clint turned him loose in the corral, and a while later when fresh horses was caught and ropes begin sailing again, Smoky wasn't for hunting a hole like the times before, he felt that he'd done his.—Pecos was snared while standing a few feet from him, and then the ponies was turned loose. But there Smoky lagged behind a little; he'd spotted Clint who was saddling another horse, and he stood in his tracks, watching, and maybe wondering. Then the wrangler came, and Smoky followed the remuda up the draw.

Plenty of grass, under, and all around him, and chance to stand still was for the first time appreciated by the mouse colored gelding. He'd had a taste of real work, the first taste, and with it had come the feeling

that he wasn't no half broke bronc no more. He was
even beginning to look at the critter with a knowing
eye and something was sprouting up in him which left
no doubt but what *he* was the boy that could handle 'er.

He never figgered on how much there was to learn
in the ways of handling that split-hoofed range animal,—he'd had no way to know as yet, and as it was
he grazed feeling sure that he knowed a lot about 'em.
He felt equal to the old saddle marked cowhorses that
was in the same remuda and he wouldn't have nothing to do with the raw broncs that was mixed in. But
there that high opinion of himself was stopped, for the
old cowhorses wouldn't let him associate with 'em and
as they'd chase him away, he failed to notice that they
felt the same about him as he did about the uneddi-
cated raw broncs.

But then, credit had to be handed to the little horse
on account that even tho he still had a powerful lot
to learn, he sure was all for learning, and the pride
he'd naturally took in the game along with the coaching of such a cowboy as Clint all promised that he'd
sure get there.

Smoky watched every herd that came in, followed
the wagon on its everyday move, and was even getting used to them ropes that sung over his head three
or four times a day. Of course Clint was always on
hand at each corralling to kind of help him get used to
all the commotion, and came a time when the little horse
knowed exactly where and which side of the corral that
cowboy would be. His saddle was always on the ground
a few feet on the outside, and every horse he caught

to ride would always be led or "snaked" to that same spot, and Smoky got so that whenever he was corralled he'd make a rush for that one spot where he could easy reach Clint's shirt whenever the attention of that cowboy was needed.

Each rider on the outfit was furnished on the average of ten horses; there was anyway three changes of horses every day which made it that every horse was rode from four to six hours every third day, and that's how Smoky's turn came. Clint rode him out on "circle" three times, and till the little horse got pretty well onto the hazing of the critter, and then that pony was of a sudden promoted to the "day-herd" class. Of course Smoky was somewhat of a privileged character or he wouldn't made that so soon, but the way he took holt of the bit and went to work he sure didn't disappoint Clint any.

The promotion started when that cowboy thought of trying him out one day as a big herd was brought in to work. He'd changed his tired "circle" horse to Smoky, and after that pony had his buck out he lined him out to a standstill close to the milling critters. It was Clint's and Smoky's job to see that none broke away outside of what was cut out to be held for the "main herd." A dozen other riders was on the same job and most all riding well reined cowhorses, and as Smoky noticed the kind of company he was keeping, a ticklish feeling came between his ears and a spark showed in his eyes.

He was about at the height of his glory and hardly able to stay on earth, when, quick as the eye could

see, a big raw-boned steer broke out, and wild-eyed
dodged past the riders and hightailed it out for open
country. In the trance Smoky was in he hardly seen
anything of the critter but a flash, but as the earth had
no strings on him either just then it only took a feel
of the rein for him to be up and a flying. That flash
that went past him a second before was recognized
as an earthly critter soon as Smoky set eyes on 'er,
and soon as he got the hunch that that critter needed
turning the distance between was et up the same as
tho that horse had been starving for such.

There was a mighty satisfied smile on Clint's face
as the steer was shot back in the herd the same way
he'd come out, and as for Smoky, there sure was nothing about him that suggested "the end of the trail."
He was brought to a mighty proud standstill by the herd
again, and no critter broke out that he wasn't right
on the tail of from the start, unless it was in some
other rider's territory.

Working the herds that was drove to the cutting
grounds, and holding the day herd, was from then on
Smoky's work. He liked working the herds best on
account there was more to do, but then day herding
wasn't so bad either, Clint always seen that his rope
was kept well stretched, and soon as he knowed the
foreman was gone on circle with the other riders he
could easy find some critter he had a grudge against
and pile his rope onto, and Smoky sure enjoyed turning 'em over.

All the boys, excepting the "reps" from other outfits, had one half a day of day herding every three days.

Smoky's time to be rode came on the dot of that time, but Clint didn't always take him out on that, and often he'd switch so that the little horse would get plenty of work cutting out or bringing big calves and "slicks" to the branding fire, and that pony was sure beginning to shine there.

Once in a while tho Clint would get sort of selfish and want Smoky's company on that long half a day's herding, and it was during them spells that the two got to be more understanding, if that's possible, to one another. Neither was so rushed for work then, and there was times when the big herd of beef steers and cows and weaners would want to graze and not try to drift away or scatter. At them times Clint would rein Smoky up a knoll, and where both could see the whole of the herd, he'd get out of his saddle and stretch out in the shade Smoky made and take it easy, and there, with one eye on the cowboy the other on the herd, and swishing flies, Smoky would stand.

CHAPTER IX

FIGHTS FOR RIGHTS

THE fine, cool, and sunshiny days of fall was making a last stand,—rains begin to come, and as time was a crawling towards early winter, them rains got colder and then turned to a wet snow. Mud was where dust had been, the hard-twist throw ropes had turned stiff as steel cables, saddles and saddle blankets was wet, heavy, and cold, and the shivering ponies met the feel of them with a hump and a buck.

The cowboys, all a packing long, yellow slickers, was beginning to tally up on how much wages would be due 'em. As the end of the fall round up drawed near, and as they waded thru slush and mud from the chuck wagon to the rope corral, not many was caring. Wet socks, damp beds, two hours of shivering on night guard, saddling ornery ponies in daytime and when a feller can't even get a footing, and then riding 'em a wondering if them ponies will stand up as they beller and buck on the slick and muddy ground, all left a hankering only for a warm dugout somewheres, where there's a stove, a bunk to set on, and a few magazines to read as mother nature does her best to make the outside miserable.

The last of the beef herd had been turned over to another "wagon" of the Rocking R and shipped, and

Jeff's main herd was from then on made up of cows with big weaner calves, and all stock that'd need feeding thru the winter.

"A couple of weeks more now and we'll be seeing the gates of the home ranch," says Jeff one day, but it was a long three weeks before the stock was tended to and when camp was made for the last time. The wet snow had got flaky and dry by then and six inches of it was covering the ground.

"Now hold on a minute, Smoky, and give a feller a chance, won't you?"

It was Clint a talking, and trying to hold Smoky down till he got his foot in the stirrup. The cowboy being all bundled up couldn't handle himself as he'd like to, the little horse was cold, crusted snow had to be rubbed off his back before the saddle could be put on and he was aching to put his head down and go to bucking so he could warm up.

Clint was only half ways in the saddle when that pony lit into it, but the cowboy didn't mind that, his blood was also a long ways from the boiling point and any excuse to get circulating good was welcome.

Around and around him and Smoky went and all in one spot, all the fancy twists of a bucking pony was gone over and the rider met him all the way, and as Clint rode and fanned and laughed, he'd get fast glimpses of other riders and other horses a tearing up the white landscape and getting down to the earth underneath.

It was the last day of the round up, all the work was done, the cook climbed on his seat, grabbed the lines

the boys handed him, and letting out a war whoop
scared his already spooky team into a long lope towards
the home ranch.

The sight of the big gates was a mighty fine one to
all as the outfit clattered in, specially with the sky a
threatening the way it was, the old cow horses had
their ears pointed towards the big pole corrals. They
knowed what the sight of them meant at that time of
the year and none tried to break away as the wrangler
run 'em in. They was turned out in a big pasture that
night, and the next day a couple of riders came,
bunched 'em up, and took 'em thru another gate leading out of the ranch.

Clint had took it onto hisself to be one of them
riders,—he wanted to get another look at Smoky before letting him go to the winter range and find out
for sure just what condition that range would be in.
The outskirts of it was reached that noon and as
Clint rode along back of the remuda he was more
than satisfied to notice the tall feed that the six inches
of snow couldn't hide, he noticed the breaks and the
shelter they would give, then the thick growth of willows along the creek bottom and which meant more
shelter.

Clint stopped his horse and the two hundred ponies
was left to scatter. His eyes run over the well known
backs for a last time, he wouldn't be seeing them again
till spring round up started and he watched 'em slowly
graze away. Many was in that bunch that he'd broke
and named, and starting from the meanest fighting

bronc of the rough string, and taking all the ponies on up to the best cowhorse of the foreman's string there wasn't one that Clint didn't know and know mighty well as to tricks and good or bad points.

A big old sorrel with a kinked neck and by the name of Boar Hound caught his eye, and Clint remembered how that pony tried to commit suicide rather than be rode and how he'd now changed to wanting to commit murder instead and kill a few cowboys. Then a smile spread over his face as he spotted a tall roman nosed gruller who'd never made a jump till a rope got under his tail. He'd took a sudden liking to bucking from then on and made hisself a reputation at that which scattered over four counties.

Every horse Clint looked at brought to memory some kind of a story, and there was a variety of expressions which changed with every horse that came under his eye. A big shaggy black looked his way and snorted and with the sight of him Clint remembered how that horse had reached ahead one time and kicked to pieces a cowboy that'd been unsaddling him.

His expression was mighty solemn at the thought of that, but it didn't last long. Like a ray of sunshine, something shot out and scattered that dark cloud of memories four ways,—Smoky had showed himself from behind other horses and not over fifty feet from where Clint was setting on his horse.

The cowboy's face lit up with a smile at the sight of the pony, and getting down off his saddle he made tracks his way, but he didn't have to go all the way, for soon as Smoky spotted him he left Pecos, his running pardner behind, and nickering came to meet Clint.

"A feller would think to see you act that you're a sure enough sugar eater," Clint remarked as the little horse came up to him and stopped. He rubbed a hand on the pony's head and went on.

"Well, anyway, Smoky, I'm glad to see that you've got a mighty fine winter range to run on; with all the feed I see here and the shelter that's with it you hadn't ought to lose an ounce of fat," Clint felt for the pony's ribs and grinning resumed, "and if you ever get any fatter than you are now you'll be plum worthless."

Smoky followed Clint as he turned and went to where he'd left his horse, "I wonder," says that cowboy, "if you've got the hunch that you won't be seeing me no more till next spring?—that's a long time ain't it? but never mind old horse, I'm the first cowboy you're going to see when spring does break up.

Clint was about to get on his horse and ride away, but he stopped, and felt of Smoky's hide once more.

"Well, so long, Smoky, take care of yourself and don't let anything drag you down."

Smoky watched him ride away and nickered once as the cowboy went over the point of a ridge and disappeared, he watched a long time even after that and till he was sure Clint was gone, and finally turning went to grazing back till he was by the side of Pecos again.

The winter came and hit the range with the average amount of snow, freeze ups, and cold winds. The cayotes howled the hunger they felt, for there was no weak stock to speak of for them to feed off of, and outside of small varmints they could get once in a while, pickings was mighty poor. Horses and cattle was and

Clint was about to get on his horse and ride away, but he stopped, and felt of Smoky's hide once more.

stayed in fine shape and the stockman could hit his bed after the long day's ride knowing that he could go to sleep right off and not lay awake a wondering what he could do to pull his stock thru.

Smoky met all what the weather had to hand him, with a good layer of fat, a thick skin, and a long coat of hair. He lost a few ounces but he could of spared many pounds and felt as good, feed was aplenty and the little pawing that had to be done to reach it was

like so much exercise and only kept his blood in good
circulating order.

The winter months wore on, the ponies drifted from
ridge to ridge, from shelter to shelter and nothing

Feed was aplenty and the little pawing that had to be done to reach it was like so
much exercise and only kept his blood in good circulating order.

much came to disturb the quiet of the land, nothing
much excepting when a big shaggy black tried to throw
in with Pecos, the same black that'd kicked the cowboy over the Great Divide. But his interfering and
butting in was welcome tho in a way, Smoky and
Pecos had so much good energy going to waste that
they'd been just aching for some excuse to use some
of it for some good.

It came about that the big black had took a liking to Pecos, and at the same time a dislike for Smoky. Pecos was neutral for a while and wondered what the black was up to when he tried to chase Smoky away from him. Smoky wouldn't chase worth a nickel but he was getting skinned up considerable a trying to hold his ground. Things went on that way for a day or so and every once in a while the black made a dive for Smoky like he was going to tear him to pieces,—his intentions was good, but Smoky sure was no invalid. When the snow settled again where he'd held his ground the little horse hadn't give away one inch.

But the black was twice as old as Smoky, more up to the game of fighting, and heavier by a hundred pounds. All that begin to tell on the mouse colored hide, and there might of come a time when Smoky would of had to hightail it, only, as the scraps was repeated off and on, Pecos begin to notice and realize that that black was taking too much territory, and he didn't like him nohow.

So, that's how come, that when the black put down his ears and made another grand tearing rush for Smoky that something struck him from the off side and upset him and his plans of attack all to pieces,—he found hisself jerked off his feet and rolled plum over the top of Smoky and he lit head first on the other side. When he picked himself up out of the snow his spirits was dampened some in wonder, and more so when he shook his head and was able to see and noticed that there was *two* mighty vicious looking ponies a waiting for him to come again. He shook his head once more at that, and as Smoky and Pecos bowed their necks and came his way the black turned tail and started a looking for other company and which would appreciate him more.

But whether it was orneriness or just plain thick headedness the black tried to butt in again the next day, maybe he just wasn't convinced, anyway, Pecos noticed him first and before the black could even get to Smoky. War was started right there, but Pecos was no match for the black and even tho he wasn't for quitting, the worst of the battle was on his side. It was about when the crusted snow was flying the thickest that Smoky, who'd been off a ways, noticed the commotion. He seen his pardner down on his knees and the black a chewing away on him, and right about then the standing Smoky was transformed into a eleven hundred pound bombshell. The explosion came as he connected with the black and then black fur begin to fly and soar up above.—Somehow or other the black managed to gather enough of his scattered senses to know what had happened; them senses told him to act, and act quick, and he did. He tore himself away from the pressing, tearing mixture of flying hoofs and sharp teeth and split the breeze making far apart tracks to where horseflesh wasn't so thick.

The next day he was seen with Boar Hound, the kink-necked sorrel, the roman-nosed gruller, and a few more ornery ponies of the "rough string." A company bunch more fitting to his kind.

The days was getting longer and warmer, the snow

begin packing and melting some, and pretty soon bare patches of ground showed in plain sight. Smoky and

The black was jerked off his feet, rolled plum over, and he lit head first on the other side.

Pecos' hides begin a itching and the two was often busy a scratching one another and starting from the neck went to the withers along the backbone to the

rump and back again. Big bunches of long winter hair
begin a slipping and falling to the ground as they
scratched, and came a time when as they rolled, more

Smoky and Pecos' hides begin a itching and the two was often busy scratching one
another.

of that hair was left till finally patches of short slick
satin like hair begin to show.

Then green and tender grass begin to loom up and
plentiful, and that finished the work of ridding the
ponies hides of all the long hair that was left. Creeks
was swelling from the waters of the fast melting snows,
spring had come and the sunshine and warm winds
that came with it was doing its work.

The round up cook was once again scrubbing on the

chuck box that was on the end of the long wagon, and the cowboys, one by one begin a drifting in from parts near and far anxious to be starting on the spring works again. Some came from the different cow camps of the Rocking R range, a few of the riders that'd been let go when work was done the fall before never showed up, but others rode in and after a few words with Jeff took the places of them that was missing.

Clint had wintered at one of the outfit's camps and drawed his wages regular, and when the range land begin to get bare of snow and the watching out for weak stock was no more necessary he put his bed on one horse, his saddle on another and headed for the home ranch. He was one of the first riders to reach that place, and when the horse round up started he was one of the first to have his horse saddled, topped off, and lined out to sashay in all of the ponies that could be found on the horse range.

Smoky had been feeding on the sunny side of a butte, and for no reason other than to be looking around he raised his head, only his ears and eyes showed as he looked over the top of that butte; but that was enough for him to see a rider coming his direction, and see him before that rider ever had a hunch any horses was around anywheres near.

Smoky snorted and hightailed it down the side of the butte to where Pecos and a few other ponies had also been feeding, and the way he acted left no doubt in their minds but what they should be on the move. They all was at full speed the minute he landed amongst 'em, and when the rider topped the butte where they'd been a few minutes before, they had the lead on him by near a mile.

But the ponies wasn't wanting to get away near as much as might of been thought. It was only that Smoky had got spooked up at the sudden sight of the rider, and him and all the others feeling good as they did wasn't needing much excuse. The cowboy fogged down on 'em and a little to one side so as to turn 'em, they turned easy enough even tho the rider was a long ways behind, and making a big circle that rider finally had 'em headed towards the big corrals of the home ranch.

A big grin spread over the cowboy's features as the sun shined on the slick back of the mouse colored horse at the lead of the bunch, and even tho there was a half a mile between him and that horse, *that cowboy* knowed daggone well it was *him*, for the sun never reflected on no other horse's hide as well as it did on Smoky's, and besides, there was no mistaking the good feeling action of that pony's.

"Told you I'd be the first to see you when spring broke up," says the cowboy as he held his horse down to a lope.

The twenty-five mile run from the time Smoky had been spotted kinda filled the bill far as running was concerned, and when the long wings of the pole corrals at the home ranch was reached the rider was right on the ponies' tails and on the job to keep 'em going straight ahead into the corral;—then the big gate closed in on 'em.

"Guess you don't know me no more," says Clint to

Smoky as he stood afoot in the corral and watched the pony tear around;—then to hisself:

"Maybe he don't know it's *me* that's watching him."

Clint was right, the long winter months of freedom without seeing one human had kind of let him get back to his natural wild instinct, and the first sight of Clint had been of just a human, and it'd spooked him up till he'd have to calm down some before it'd come to him just *who* that human was.

The cowboy spoke to him as Smoky, wild eyed, snorted and hunted for a hole, but Clint kept a speaking, and as the pony tore around and heard the voice, something gradually came to him that seemed far away and near forgot. He stopped a couple of times to look at the cowboy, and each time his getting away was less rushing, till, as the voice kept a being heard, things got clearer and clearer in that pony's brain.

Smoky had stopped once more, and neck bowed, ears straight ahead, and eyes a sparkling, faced acrost the corral to where the cowboy, still and standing, was talking to him.

"Daggone your little hide," says Clint, "are we going to have to get acquainted all over again?—come on over here and let me run my hand over that knowledge bump of yours, and maybe I can get your think tank to functioning right again."

Smoky didn't come, but he held his ground and listened to the talk. Clint talked on and watched him till the horse lost some of his wild look and then slow and easy started walking his way. Something and away in the past seemed to hold Smoky as the cowboy slowly

came nearer and nearer. His instinct was all for him a
leaving the spot he was holding, but that something
which stuck in his memory was the stronger and sort
of kept him there.

Clint came on a few steps at the time, and then
stopped, and talking the while, took his time till he
was within a few feet of Smoky. A little flaw of any
kind right then in that human's actions could of spoilt
things easy and sent the pony a skeedaddling away
from there in a hurry, but Clint knowed horses and
specially Smoky too well to do anything of the kind. He
knowed just what was going on between that pony's
ears, and how to agree with all that mixed in there.

Finally, Clint got to where by reaching out he could
near of touched Smoky. Slow and easy the cowboy
raised a hand and held it to within a few inches of the
pony's nose, Smoky looked at it and snorted, but
pretty soon he stretched his neck and mighty careful
took a sniff of the human paw. He snorted again and
jerked his head away from it, but it wasn't long when
he took another sniff, then another and another, and
each time the snort growed less to be heard, till at last,
Smoky even allowed that paw to touch his nostrils,
the fingers rubbed there easy for a spell and gradually
went on a rubbing along his nose along on up to between his eyes and pretty soon between his ears to that
knowledge bump. Five minutes afterwards Smoky was
following the grinning cowboy all around the corral.

The round up wagons, all cleaned and loaded, was
ready to pull out, the remuda was all accounted for

Slow and easy Clint raised a hand and held it to within a few inches of his nose. Smoky stretched his neck, sniffed at it, and snorted.

and each string pointed out to each rider, and Jeff giving the whole outfit another look over waved a hand, the pilot reined his horse into a bucking start, all took up his lead and thru the big gates of the home ranch, wagons, riders, remuda, and all lined out. The spring round up had started.

Smoky broke the record for learning that year, and when the fall round up was over and the saddle was pulled off him for the last time before being turned out on the winter range, there was two little white spots of white hair showed on each side of his withers and about the size of a dollar,—saddle marks they was, and like medals for the good work he'd done. There was a knowing spark in his eyes for the critter too, for the little horse had got to savvy the cow near as well as the old cowhorses that'd been in the same remuda that year.

There was only one thing that could of been held against the good record of that pony, and that was his bucking;—he just had to have his little buck out every morning, and sometimes he bucked harder than other times—that all depended on how cold the weather was—but Clint didn't seem to mind that at all. If anything he tried to preserve that bucking streak in the pony, and he was often heard to remark:

"A horse ain't worth much unless that shows up some."

But Clint had other reasons for keeping the "buck" in Smoky's backbone.—Old Tom Jarvis, superintendent and part owner of the Rocking R had joined the wagon for a few days that summer and wanted to

see his cowboys work his cattle for a spell. Him being
an old cowman and from away back before cattle
wore short horns made all the working of a herd all
the more interesting and to be criticized one way or
the other. He was present steady on the cutting
grounds, and so was Smoky one day.

Clint felt that the eyes of Old Tom was on Smoky the
minute he rode him to the edge of the herd, and an
uneasy feeling crawled up his backbone as he noticed
that that Old Grizzly seemed to've lost his eyesight
for anything else but his Smoky horse. Clint knowed
Old Tom's failing for a good horse, and he'd heard of
how many a time that same failing had come near
putting the cowman in jail for appropriating some
horse he couldn't buy;—of course them times was past,
but the failing was still in the old man's chest, and
Smoky belonged to him.

The cowboy had started Smoky to cutting out, a
work where all the good points of a cowhorse have a
chance to show up, and Smoky sure wasn't hiding any.
Old Tom's eyes was near popping out of his head as
he watched the mouse colored gelding work, and finally,
as Clint noticed all the interest, he figgered it a good
idea to get out of the herd and hide Smoky somewheres before the old cowman came to him and suggested swapping horses; the cowboy was afraid he'd
already showed too much of that horse, and as he come
out of the herd he made a circle and took his stand
away on the opposite side from where Old Tom was
holding.

But Old Tom was controlling owner of that outfit

and he could be any place he wanted to on that range any time. A steer broke out, Old Tom took after him, circled him around the herd, and when he put him back in and brought his horse to a standstill, there was only a short distance between him and the horse he'd had his eye on.

Clint was scared and he cussed a little. He tried to keep Smoky down whenever a critter broke out that needed turning, and even tried to let a couple of 'em get away, but he couldn't do it without making it too plain to see, and besides, Smoky had ideas of his own about handling them critters.

The cowboy was worried all the rest of the day and lost some sleep that night a wondering how he was going to dodge Old Tom. He knowed the old cowman would be around with some proposition to swap him out of Smoky, and that was one of the last things the cowboy would do. There wasn't a horse in the outfit or anywheres else he'd trade Smoky for.

It's took for granted on any real cow outfit that whenever a horse is swapped or borrowed out of a cowboy's string and handed to somebody else, that that cowboy is requested to quit or be fired, in other words it's an insult that makes any real cowboy want to scrap and then ask for his wages.

Clint was a valuable man to the outfit, but with Old Tom one cowboy more or less didn't matter, that is if that cowboy stood between him and a horse he wanted. He walked up to Clint the next day and not hesitating any he says:

"I'm going to try that mouse colored horse you was

riding yesterday"; and thinking it'd please Clint to hear, he went on, "and if I like him I'll trade you my brown horse Chico for him; he's the best horse I got at the home ranch."

But all that only made Clint get red in the face, and fire showed in his eyes as he spoke.

"Huh! you can't ride Smoky."

"Why in samhill can't I?" asks Old Tom, also getting red in the face.

"Cause you can't," answers Clint, "why you couldn't even put a saddle on him."

Clint was for quitting the outfit right there and hit for some other country, but the thought of leaving Smoky behind kinda put him to figgering another way out;—if he could get Old Tom sort of peeved and let him handle Smoky while he was feeling that way, most likely that pony would do the rest.

"I'll show you whether I can saddle that horse or not," says Old Tom, frothing at the mouth; "why I've handled and rode broncs that you couldn't get in the same corral with, and before you even was born."

"Yep," says Clint, grinning sarcastic, "that was too long ago, and you're too daggoned old now for that kind of a horse."

Old Tom glared at Clint for a second, and not finding no ready come back done the next best thing and got busy. He went to his saddle, jerked his rope off it, and spitting fire, shook out a loop that could be heard a whistling plum to the other side of the corral.

Smoky was surprised into a dozen catfits as that

same wicked loop settled over his head and drawed
tight and sudden around his neck. He bellered and
bucked thru the remuda a dragging Old Tom with
him. The old cowman made a motion and two grinning cowboys went and helped him.

Clint stood on the outside and watched the performance, he rolled cigarette after cigarette and tore
'em up fast as they was made, not a one was lit. He
seen Smoky brought to a choking standstill and that
cowboy felt like committing murder as he noticed the
fear in that pony's eyes as he faced the strangers;
but there Clint noticed something else and which he
gradually recognized as *fight*,—there was more fight
than fear, and at the sight of that the cowboy took
hope.

"Since when does a cowboy get help to rope and
saddle his horse," he hollered as Old Tom was sizing
up Smoky. "Pretty soon you'll be wanting one of us
to top him off for you."

It worked just right, and Old Tom's answer was
only a jerk on the rope that held Smoky. The old cowman knowed better than to handle a horse that way
and as a rule was always easy with 'em, but he was
mad, mad clear thru, and rather than shoot a cowboy
he was taking it out on the horse.

And Smoky by that time was fast catching up with
the spirit of all that went on. He was like a raw bronc
that'd never seen a human or a saddle, and when he
was finally brought up alongside the saddle, there was
all about him to show he wasn't safe for anybody coming near. But Old Tom, even tho it was a long time

Old Tom didn't even get well set that time, Smoky bowed his head and went out from under him leaving him come down on the other side.

ago, had handled many mean horses;—he knowed he was past handling 'em any more, but this time was different and he'd do his best to carry it thru.

The two riders that'd been helping him was waved away; he'd show Clint and the rest of the young fellers that he could still do it. He then spread a loop and caught both of Smoky's threatening front feet; Smoky knowed better than to fight a rope and he stood still knowing he'd soon have another chance. Rawhide hobbles was fastened on his front legs, a bridle put on his head, and then the saddle was reached for and put on his back and cinched to stay.

"Better say your prayers before you climb up," says Clint, still prodding Old Tom, at the same time hoping that he would stop before he went too far. But there was no stopping him, he pulled up his chap' belt, set his hat down tight, and still mad enough to bite a nail in two, loosened the hobbles, grabbed a short holt on the reins and climbed on.

Smoky looked back at the stranger that was a setting on him, and soon as a touch of the rein on his neck told him that all was set, things started a happening from there. He bowed his head, made two jumps, and was just getting started good when he felt the saddle was empty;—he made a few more jumps just for good measure, and then stopped.

Clint was grinning from ear to ear as he walked up to Smoky and put his hand on his neck.

"Good work, old boy," he says,—and then turning to Old Tom, who was picking himself up: "Want to try him again?"

"You bet your doggone life I do," says that old cowboy.

"All right," answers Clint, getting peeved some more. "Go ahead and break your fool neck, there's plenty of buffalo wallows around here we can bury you in."

Old Tom walked over and jerked the reins out of Clint's hands and started to get in the saddle again, but he didn't even get well in it that time,—Smoky bowed his head and went out from under him leaving Old Tom come down on the other side.

It was as the old man was about to try Smoky once more when Jeff Nicks interfered, and told his boss how he'd rather not have him try that horse any more.

"That horse bucks every time he's rode," says Jeff.

Old Tom knowed he'd come to the end of his string but that didn't ease his feelings any, and he was looking for some way of letting some of them feelings out before they choked him. When he spots Clint a standing to one side and by Smoky.

"You're fired," he hollered, pointing a finger at him, "I'll get somebody to take the buck out of that horse, and the sooner you're off this range the better I'll like it."

Clint just grinned at Old Tom, which made him all the madder, and about then Jeff spoke:

"I'm doing the hiring and firing on this outfit, Tom, and as long as I'm working for you I'll keep on a doing it."

Old Tom turned on him like a wild cat. "Fine!" he hollered, "you can go too."

The old cowman had went as far as he could, and as he walked away to catch himself another saddle horse, he had a hunch that he'd also went further than he should; that hunch got stronger as he went on saddling, and as he gave the latigo a last yank, it all developed into plain common sense that he'd sure enough went too far.

But Old Tom wasn't for giving in, not right then anyway. He got on his horse and riding close enough so Jeff could hear, says:

"You and Clint can come to the ranch and I'll have your time ready for you," and then to another rider,— "you handle the outfit till I send out another foreman."

A lot of orneriness was scattered to the winds as Old Tom covered the long fifty miles back to the ranch, and as he opened the big gate leading in, a brand new feeling had come over him,—he was for catching a fresh horse the next morning early and hightail it back to the wagon to sort of smooth things over best as he could.

He unsaddled and turned his horse loose, and was mighty surprised as he came up to the big ranch house to find both Jeff and Clint already there and waiting for him. Not a hint of the good resolutions he'd made showed as he walked up to 'em, and after some kind of a "howdy," Old Tom heard Jeff say:

"All the boys sent word in by me, that as long as you're making out my check you'd just as well make theirs out too. I'm sorry for that," went on Jeff, "and I tried to talk 'em out of it, but it's no use, they're all for quitting if I go."

The old cowman never said a word as he led Jeff and Clint in the big house. He walked to a big table in the center of the living room and there he turned on his two riders. A smile was on his face and he says:

"Daggone it, Jeff, I'm glad to hear that." Then Old Tom, still pleasant, but serious, went on, "for no man does his best work unless he's doing it with somebody he likes and has confidence in. Yes," he repeated, "I'm glad to hear that, but the question is now, you're fired and free to go, ain't you? " he asks.

"Yes," says Jeff, "soon as I get paid off."

"Well, how's chances of hiring you over again? I can't afford to let a foreman like you go, Jeff."

Jeff seemed to figger a while and then looked at Clint, and Old Tom guessing what was on his foreman's mind, went on "and of course, being that I have no say in the hiring and firing of your riders, Clint wasn't fired at all, and he can keep on riding for you."

Finally hands was shook all around, and as Jeff and Clint started back for the wagon the next morning Old Tom was on hand to see 'em go.

"And don't worry about that daggone mouse colored horse of yours, Clint," he says as him and Jeff rode away, "I'll never want him."

The riders reached the big gate leading out of the ranch, and there Jeff remarked as he got off his horse to open it:

"I guess Old Tom didn't have to say that he was sorry."

And Clint more than agreed.

CHAPTER X

"AMONGST THE MISSING"

THE remuda was in the big corrals of the home ranch once more, and after a few "winter" horses was cut out, the rest was hazed towards the winter range, and let go.—Four long winter months went by.—Then one day the round up cook begin to get busy cleaning the chuck box, meadow larks was a tuning up on the high corral posts, and along with the bare patches of ground that could be seen, no better signs was needed that spring had come.

Clint was again the first to spot Smoky that spring and notice the amount of tallow that pony was packing, he was in fine shape for whatever work that'd be his to do that summer, and soon as him and the cowboy got thru with their first "howdys" they both went to work like they never had before.

Smoky took up to where he'd left off the fall before and kept on accumulating science in ways of handling the critter till that critter would just roll up an eye at the sight of the mouse colored pony and never argue as to where he wanted to put 'er;—she'd just go there.

Spring work went on, middle summer came, and sometime after, the fall round up was in full swing again. Thousands of cattle was handled, cut out, and culled. Big herds of fat steers was trailed in to the shipping point and loaded in the cars, and when the

weaning was done and the old stock was all brought in
close to the cow camps, Jeff headed his wagon towards
the home ranch once more. The work was over, the
remuda was turned out and the riders that was kept
on the pay-roll saddled their winter horses and scattered out for the outfit's different camps.

Winter came on and set in, then spring bloomed out
green once again, and with it the cowboys spread out
on the range once more. Season after season followed
one another without a ruffle that way, the same territory was covered at the same time of the year, the
wagon rolled in at the same grounds, and the rope
corral stretched at the same spot, old riders disappeared and new ones took their place, like with the
ponies; the old cowhorses was pensioned, replaced by
younger ones and the work went on, season after
season; year after year, the same outfit rambled out
of the home ranch and combed the range like as if no
changes was taking place.

Jeff, the cow boss, the round up cook, Clint, and a
couple more riders was all that was left of the old
hands as the wagon pulled out one spring;—the others
'd had cravings for new countries and went and throwed
their soogans on some other outfit's wagons.

Five years had went by since that day when Clint,
riding Smoky, had joined the wagon, five summers was
put in when every time Smoky was saddled and rode
Clint was the cowboy that done it, not another hand
had touched Smoky's hide in that time, excepting
when Old Tom had *tried* to appropriate the horse for
his own string, and since that day there hadn't been

any excuse for Clint to worry about anybody taking
Smoky away from him. There wasn't a cowboy in the
outfit who didn't more than want the horse, and if
Clint ever failed to show up when the spring works
started there'd most likely been some argument as to
who should get him; but he'd always been the first to
ride in at the home ranch at them times and none had
the chance to lay claim on the horse.

In them long summers, and as Smoky was rode off
and on, the little horse had got to know Clint as well
as that cowboy knowed hisself; he knowed just when
Clint was a little under the weather and not feeling
good,—at them times he'd go kinda easy with his bucking as the cowboy topped him off. The feel of Clint's
hand was plain reading to him, and he could tell by
a light touch of it whether it meant "go get 'er," "easy
now," "good work," and so on. The tone of his voice
was also mighty easy to understand. He could tell a
lot of things by it, specially when he was being got
after for doing something he shouldn't of done. His
eyes was wide open at them times, his neck bowed,
and he'd snort sorta low, but when Clint would tell
him what a fine horse he was, Smoky was some different,—he'd just take it all in the same as he would warm
sunshine in a cold fall day, and near close his eyes for
the peace he was feeling at the sound of the cowboy's
voice.

The way Smoky could understand the man who rode
him thru and around the big herds had a lot to do in
making him the cowhorse he'd turned out to be, his
strong liking for the rider had made him take interest

and for learning all about whatever he was rode out
to do. There'd come a time when Smoky knowed the
second Clint had a critter spotted to be cut out, and
the pony's instinct near told him which one it was,
till nary a feel of the rein was needed and the dodging
critter was stepped on and headed for the "cut."

The same with roping and where Smoky could do
near everything but throw the rope that caught the
critter. There he shined as he did anywhere else under
the saddle, he'd keep one ear back, watch out and follow the loop leave Clint's hand and sail out to settle
around a steer's horns, and the slack was no more
than pulled when that pony would turn and go the
other way,—he knowed how to "lay" the critter, and
none of the big ones ever got up, not while Smoky was
at one end of the rope.

Of the many happenings that all went to show of
Smoky's knowing how in handling the critter there's
one Clint and the boys liked to tell of. It was only an
average of the others that happened, but there was
something about that one which made the telling easier
as to the wonders of that horse. It was the detail that
counted there.

There was a big steer in the herd with a crooked horn
which had curved and threatened to grow some more
and right thru his eye. Clint and Jeff spotted the steer
at the same time, and while one of the boys went to
the wagon to get a saw to cut the horn off with, both
Clint and Jeff took their ropes down and proceeded
to catch the critter.

The steer was wild, big and husky, and wise, and

soon as he seen the two riders coming thru the herd headed his way, he broke out of it and tail up in the air begin to leave the flat. About then is when Smoky appeared on the scene.

That little horse et up the distance between him and that steer in no time and soon carried Clint to within reach. On account of the crooked horn Clint had to rope the steer around the neck, and that he did neat and quick. Everything went on as it should,—Smoky run on past the steer and Clint throwed the slack of his rope over that same steer's rump and in another second that critter would of been laying with toes up to the sky and ready to tie.

The unexpected happened about that time, and when the rope tightened the steer didn't lay at all. Instead there was a sound of something ripping. Clint went up in the air about three feet, turned a somerset and hit the ground, the saddle stood up on end on Smoky's back and only the flank cinch was holding it there. The stub latigo of the front cinch had been ripped right thru by the tongue of the cinch buckle like it'd been paper.

Every rider around the herd seen the thing happen, and had already figgered how it wouldn't take long for Smoky to get himself out from under the remains of that saddle. For near every horse would go to bucking and raising the dust when being pinched around the flanks that way, and Smoky had seemed so inclined to want to buck that it was thought he'd never overlook that chance.

The boys was already grinning at such a good promise

of seeing a little excitement, but the grins soon faded to looks of wonder, for Smoky, instead of trying to get shed of the saddle, showed he was using his brain to the best way of *keeping it there*. He was a cow-horse and working, and it was no time for foolishness, so, when the rigging reared up on his hind quarters that way he reared up with it, and turned while in the air. When his front feet touched the ground again the saddle was where it belonged and he was facing the steer.

When that story was told to the country around there was many hard-to-be-convinced riders, who laughed and shook their heads and remarked how it was pure luck that the pony acted that way, but if they'd knowed Smoky, if they'd seen how he juggled that saddle and worked to keep his holt on the steer there'd been a different tune.

The steer had stayed up and with his ten hundred pounds of wild weight had fought at the rope and hit the end mighty hard. Then Smoky done another thing which kept the boys a staring and doing nothing— the steer was making another wild dash for open country, and Smoky, instead of holding his ground and waiting for the steer to hit the end of the rope broke out in a sudden run and right after the critter. When the speed of both of 'em was up good and high Smoky of a sudden planted himself till his hocks touched the ground, and when Mr. Steer hit the end of the rope that time it was just as tho that rope had been fastened to a four foot stump. His head was jerked under him, he turned in the air, and when he came down *he layed*.

"There was only one thing that horse didn't do,"
Jeff had remarked afterwards,—"he didn't give the
rope a flip before he set down on it."

Smoky had kept the rope tight and Clint tied the
steer down to stay till the crooked horn was sawed
off. When that was done Clint put up a hand and
spoke, and Smoky gave slack so the rope could be
pulled off the steer's head.

Big herds of Mexico long-horned steers had been
bought by the Rocking R and shipped up into that
northern country, they got fat on that range and
wilder than ever, and there's where Smoky showed he
had something else besides the knowing how. Them
longhorned critters are too fast for the average cowhorse to catch up with in a short distance, but not with
Smoky;—he had the speed to go with what he knowed,
and Clint would have time to whirl his rope only a
few times when the little horse would climb up on the
long legged steer and pack the cowboy to within roping distance.

Many a cowboy had remarked that it was worth the
price of a good show to watch Smoky work, whether it
was around, in or out of a herd, and many a rider had
let a cow sneak past him just so he could see how neat
that pony could outdodge a critter, and when after
the last meal of the day and the cowboys stretched out
to rest some, talk, or sing, none ever had any argument
to put up and no betting was ever done against whatever Clint said Smoky could do or had done. They all
knowed and admired the horse, and came a time as
these cowboys came and went that Smoky begin to

Many a cowboy had remarked it was worth the price of a good show to watch Smoky outdodge the critter.

be talked about in the cow camps of other cow outfits.
One whole northern State got to hear of him, and one
cowboy wasn't at all surprised when hitting South one
fall and close to the Mexican border to hear another
cowboy talk of "Smoky of the Rocking R."

The owner of a neighbor outfit sent word by one of
his "reps"* one day that he'd give a hundred dollars
for that horse; Smoky had been broke only two years
then. Old Tom laughed at the offer, and Clint got
peeved. The next year that offer was raised by the
same party to two hundred, and Old Tom laughed
again, but Clint didn't know whether to get mad or
scared this time. Anyway, things went on as usual for
a couple of years more, and then a big outfit from
acrost the state line sent in an offer of a cool four hundred dollars for the mouse colored cowhorse.

Good saddle horses could be bought by the carload
for fifty dollars a head about that time, but there never
was no set price on a good cowhorse, and as a rule that
kind can't be bought unless an outfit is selling out. The
biggest price that was ever heard offered in that country for any cowhorse had never went over two hundred, and when rumors spread around that four hundred had been offered for Smoky many figgered that
whoever offered it had a lot of money to spend;—but
them who figgered that way had never seen Smoky
work.

Ole Tom came up to Clint that fall after the wagon
had pulled in and showed him the letter offering the
four hundred. Clint had heard about the offer and he

* Riders representing other outfits.

just stargazed at the letter, not reading;—instead he was doing some tall wondering at what Old Tom was going to do about it. He was still stargazing and sort of waiting for the blow to fall, when he felt the old cowman's hand on his shoulder, and then heard him say:

"Well, Clint, I'll tell you"—then Old Tom waited a while, maybe just to sort of aggravate the cowboy, but finally he went on,—"if my cattle was starving, and I needed the money to buy feed to pull 'em thru with, I might *sacrifice* Smoky for four hundred, but as things are now there's no money can buy that horse."

The cowboy smiled, took a long breath, and grabbed the paw the old man was holding for him to shake.

"But I'm hoping," resumed Old Tom, "that some day soon you'll get to hankering to drift to some other country and quit this outfit, so I can get Smoky for myself; I'd fired you long ago, only I'd have to fire Jeff too, and somehow I'd rather get along without the horse till one of you highbinders quit."

Clint had kept a smiling all the while the old man was speaking, then he gave his hand another shake and walked away. He knowed Old Tom had said that last just to hear how his voice sounded.

As usual, Smoky was turned out on the range along with the remuda for that winter. Clint had helped haze 'em to the breaks as he'd always done, and noticed as he stopped and let the ponies graze and scatter that the feed was mighty short and scarcer than he'd ever seen it. The whole summer had been mighty dry and the range short on grass, but this little scope of country that was the saddle horse range had always been good, and the ponies had always wintered there better than if they'd been in a warm stable and fed grain.

Clint thought some of taking Smoky back with him and keeping him up for a winter horse, but then he'd have to turn him out when spring works came on, and the cowboy didn't want to think of going out on spring round up without his "top horse."

"No," he decided, "I'm going to let you run out this winter, but I'll be out to see how you're making it and don't loose too much tallow. You're getting to be too valuable a horse to take any chances of losing," he says to him as he scratched him back of the ear—"but," he went on, "you're not half as valuable to the outfit as you are to me, old pony, even tho Old Tom won't consider no price on you."

Clint was on his way back and had no more than got sight of the buildings of the ranch when Old White Winter hit him from behind and made him clap his gloved hands over his ears.

"Holy smoke," he whistled thru his chattering teeth, "she's sure starting ferocious."

And she had,—the first initiating blizzard of the season was more than just a snowstorm with a wind, it was a full grown blizzard drifting over the country, covering up the feed with packed snow, and freezing things up. It kept up for two days and nights, and as it cleared up, the thermometer went down. The next day Clint was busy bringing in old stock closer to the ranch and where they could be watched, and as another blizzard hit the country again a few days later that cowboy was *kept* on the jump bringing under the sheds and next to the haystacks all the stock he'd hunted up.

Clint was in the saddle all day every day, and some-

The next day Clint was busy bringing the weak stock closer to the ranch.

times away into the night. A month went by and in that time two feet of snow had accumulated on the range;—more was threatening to come, and all the cowboys that was kept on the Rocking R payroll more than had their hands full. The ranch hands would roll up their eyes at every bunch of stock the riders brought in to be fed, for as they figgered they already had all they could handle, and if this kept up, Old Tom would have to hire more hay shovelers and buy more hay.

Clint had worried some about Smoky and figgered to hunt him up sometime, but as on account of the deep snow he couldn't get his horse out of a walk he never could make it. Besides there was always a bunch of cattle somewheres on the way, and amongst 'em there'd be a few that needed bringing in.

But with all them drawbacks, Clint finally reached Smoky's range late one day. The gray sky was getting darker, and night was coming on as the cowboy topped a ridge and spotted a bunch of ponies, amongst the bunch was a long-haired, shaggy-looking, and lean mouse-colored horse, and Clint could hardly believe his eyes or keep from choking as he rode closer and recognized his Smoky horse.

The cowboy was for catching the horse right there and bring him in to the ranch. He wondered if Smoky could travel that far, but as the horse raised his head out of the hole in the snow where he'd been pawing for feed, and spotted the rider coming towards him, Clint was surprised to see so much strength and action. Smoky hadn't recognized the cowboy, and before he'd took a second look, he'd hightailed it from there in a hurry.

Clint watched him and smiled as he seen that the horse wasn't in near as bad a shape as he'd first thought.

"But I'm going to take you in just the same, you little son of a gun, for God knows what you'll be like in a few weeks from now if this weather keeps up."

He started on the trail Smoky and the other ponies had left, it was good and dark by then, but the trail in the deep snow was easy enough to follow. He wondered as he rode if he could get Smoky to stand long enough so as the horse would recognize him under all the disguise of his winter clothes, for at night specially he looked more like a bear than anything; then again, horses are spookier and harder to get near at that time, Clint had his doubts if he could catch him, and he figgered he'd most likely have to take the whole bunch along in order to get him to the ranch.

He was riding along on the trail and trying to get sight of the ponies, when to his left just a little ways, and out of the snow came a faint beller; it sounded like a critter in trouble, and Clint stopped his horse, the beller came again, and he rode towards the sound. —All curled up, shivering, and near covered with snow, a little bitty calf was found,—couldn't been over two days old, figgered the cowboy, and he wondered how the poor little cuss could still be alive.

"Where's your mammy, Johnny?" says Clint as he got off his horse and came near the calf.

But the words was no more out of his mouth when a dark shadow appeared, and bellering, tried to get to the cowboy with her horns before he could get on his horse. In making his getaway, Clint noticed tracks of more cattle, and following 'em a ways, come acrost another cow and with another calf, only this second calf was older and more able to navigate.

"These two wall-eyed heifers must of been missed during last fall's round up," Clint figgered, "and just as luck would have it they both have winter calves. Well, Smoky," he says as he looked the direction the ponies had went, "I guess that leaves you out, *this time*."

It was near noon the next day when Clint showed up at the ranch packing a little calf on the front of his saddle. He found Jeff by the big sheds where the cattle was sheltered and fed, and told him:

"I had to leave this little feller's mammy out about ten miles. There's another cow and young calf with 'er, and maybe you better send a man out after 'em before this storm that's coming catches up with 'em. Me, I'm going to eat the whole hind leg off a beef and roll in between my soogans."

The storm Clint had spoke of came sure enough, and seemed like to want to clean the earth of all that drawed a breath, the snow piled up and up till, as the cowboy remarked, "the fence posts around the ranch are only sticking up about an inch, and soon won't be visible no more."

That storm would of meant the death of all the cattle that was on the range, and most of the horses too, but as the tail of it came, a high wind sprung up, the snow drifted and piled high in the coulees, and at the same time took the depth of it down considerable wherever that wind hit. When it all finally quit raging, there was many patches where the grass was buried only by a few inches, and them patches the wind had cleared was what saved the lives of the range stock that winter.

Clint had worried about Smoky as the stormy weather

came on; he'd tried time and time again to get to him, but always some helpless critter made him branch off and finally turn back. "Tomorrow," Clint kept a saying, but the "Tomorrows" came and went and the cowboy always a fretting hadn't got near Smoky's range.

The great liking Clint had for the mouse colored horse made him fret and worry more than was necessary. That liking made him imagine a lot that was nowheres near true, and many a time that cowboy rolled in his bunk, tired, and wore out, and dreamed of seeing Smoky caught in a snow bank, weak, starving, and wolves drawing near.

Smoky had sure enough lost considerable fat, and his strength was reduced some too, but he was nowheres weak;—that is, not so weak that he couldn't get up easy once he layed down, or be able to travel and rustle for his feed. The last big storm had took him down some more, but he was still able to plow thru the snow banks that'd gathered on the sides of the ridges and get on the other side where the feed was easier reached.

If it didn't snow too much more there was no danger for Smoky and the bunch he was with. Him and Pecos had got to know that range so well, they knowed where the best of shelter could be found when the winds was cold or the blizzard howled, and then again, they knowed of many ridges and where the snow was always the thinnest. They had a spot to fit in with or against whatever the weather had to hand out, and whether the next on the program was to be sunshine or more snow they was still well able to enjoy or compete with either.

Weeks had passed since Smoky had raised his head out of the hollow in the snow and spotted the rider,

Heavy drifts was lunged into and hit on a high run as they tried to leave the rider behind.

who'd been Clint coming onto him, and then one day, here comes another rider. Smoky had been the first to spot that other rider, and as was natural, him and the rest of the bunch made tracks away from there till the rider couldn't be seen no more.

A mile or so on the bunch went to pawing snow and grazing again, night was coming on, a wind was raising,

and pretty soon light flakes of snow begin to
Then, when night was well on, and as the wi
stronger and the snow heavier, the rider showed up
again, right in the middle of the bunch this time and
before Smoky or any of the others could see him.—
The ponies scattered like a bunch of quail at the sight
of him and so close, but they soon got together again,
and on a high lope went along with the storm.

The rider followed on after 'em, and as mile after
mile of snow covered country was left behind the
ponies realized there was no dodging *him*. Heavy drifts
was lunged into and hit on a high run as they tried
to leave him behind, and then as they'd cross creek
bottoms a mile or so wide, and where the snow was
from two to three feet deep, the run begin to tell on
'em. They finally slowed down to a trot, and as the
rider wasn't pressing 'em any, there came a time when
going at a walk seemed plenty fast. They was getting
tired.

The night wore on with 'em a traveling that way, the
heavy wind pushed 'em on and their long hair was
matted with snow, but tired, and hard as the deep
snow was to buck thru, it all seemed better to drift on
that way than stand still in such as the storm had
turned out to be. They drifted on, not minding the
rider much no more.—Then after a while it begin to
get light, slow and gradual, the new day come, and
the rider, finding a thick patch of willows let the ponies
drift in the shelter. He tried to look on the back trail
as he let 'em drift, and he grinned as the thick stinging snow blurred his view.

"That old blizzard will sure do the work of covering up my trail," he remarked as he looked for a sheltered spot amongst the willows.

He soon found the sheltered spot and where the wind was more heard than felt, and getting off his tired horse begin tamping himself a place where he could move around a little and not have the snow up to his waist. He tied his horse up where he'd be within easy reach, and soon had a fire started out of dead willow twigs. Rice and "jerky" was cooked in a small lard bucket, and et out of the same. When that was gone, a few handfuls of snow was melted in the same bucket and coffee was made. Then a cigarette was rolled, a few puffs drawed out of it, and the man, curled up by the fire, was soon asleep.

All of him, from the toe of his gunny sack covered boots to the dark face which showed under the wore out black hat, pointed out as the man being a half-breed of Mexican and other blood that's darker, and noticing the cheap, wore out saddle, the ragged saddle-blanket on a horse that should of had some chance to feed instead of being tied up, showed that he was a halfbreed from the *bad* side, not caring, and with no pride.

He slept, feeling sure that no rider would be on his trail in this kind of weather, for the trail he'd made was wiped out and covered over near as soon as he made it, and as for the horses he'd stole, he knowed they wouldn't be facing this storm and trying to go back; they'd be more for staying in shelter instead and try to find something to eat.

Seventeen head of Rocking R saddle stock, counting Smoky, was half a mile or so further down the creek bottom from where the halfbreed was sleeping. They hugged the thick willows for the shelter they'd give, and feed off the small green branches the rye grass, and everything they could reach which they could chew on. Smoky and Pecos, side by side, rustled on thru the deep snow, sometimes ahead and sometimes behind the other horses, all a nosing around or pawing for whatever little feed could be found, but many cattle had been there ahead of 'em, and when darkness came on they showed near as drawed as they'd been that morning.

The snowing had let up some during the day, but as night drawed near the wind got stronger, the snow was drifting, and there'd be another night of travel when no trail would be left to show.

The breed woke up, looked around and grinned, then got up and shook himself. The fire was started again, another bait was cooked and consumed, and after all was gathered, he mounted his horse and went to looking for the ponies he'd left to graze down the creek bottom. He run onto 'em a couple of miles further and where he'd figgered they'd be, and as dark settled over the snow covered range, he fell in behind 'em and started 'em on the way.

An hour or so of traveling, and then Smoky, who was in the lead, found himself between the wings of a corral, a corral that was made of willows and well hid. The breed had built it for *his purpose*, and signs showed that it'd been used many a time before. Long willow poles made the gate, and after he run the ponies in, and put up the poles, he went after his rope on his saddle.

Many a brand had been changed in that corral, and on both horse and cow, other times he'd used it just to change horses, and that's what he wanted just now, a fresh horse. He wasn't changing for the sake of the tired horse he'd been riding, it was just that he didn't want to take chances of having a tired horse under him in case somebody jumped him.

His loop was made, and thru the dark he was trying to see just what horse to put his rope on, the white background helped him considerable in making out the shapes of the ponies, and there was one shape he was looking out for before he let his loop sail, the shape of a mouse colored blazed faced horse which he'd noticed and watched all along. Pretty soon, and furthest away from him, he got a glimpse of Smoky's head,—he recognized the white streak on his forehead, and his rope sailed.

Smoky snorted and ducked, the rope just grazed his ears and went on to settle over another horse's head. In the dark, the breed couldn't follow his rope, and he didn't know but what he'd caught Smoky till he pulled on the rope and brought the horse to him. He cussed considerable as he seen he'd caught another horse than the one he wanted, but as he noticed that this horse was good size and strong looking, he let it go at that, and didn't take time to make another try for Smoky.

"I'll get you next time, you——" he says as he looked Smoky's way and saddled the horse he'd caught.

Letting the poles down the breed mounted the fresh horse, let the ponies out, and turned 'em out of the creek bottom onto a long bench. The strong winds had blowed most all the snow off there, and excepting for a few low places where it had piled deep, traveling was made easy. He kept the ponies on a trot most of the night, and sometimes where the snow wasn't too deep he'd crowd 'em into a lope.

Steady, the gait was kept up, and finally, after the breed seen that the ponies was too tired and weak to travel much more, he begin to look for a place where he could hide 'em and where they could rustle feed during the day that was soon to come. On the other end of the ridge he was following, he knowed of a place, and taking down his rope, he snapped it at the tired ponies and kept 'em on the move till that place was reached. There, another stop was made.

The storm had dwindled down and wore out till nothing was left but the high wind, it kept the snow drifting, which would keep on covering tracks and make traveling easier. But the breed didn't need the storm to help him no more, for, as he figgered, the country ahead and where he was headed was all open, he expected no riders would be found on the way at that time of the year, and as he'd been on that route many a time before with stolen stock, he knowed just how far it was between each good hiding and stopping place, both for himself and stock.

There was corrals on the way, some built by him, and others built by more of his kind. Sometimes he

would change the iron on the ponies he'd just stole, but
as the hair was too long for anybody to be able to read
the brand that was on 'em, that could wait a while
till he got further away and he could travel in daytime
more.

He was pleased with everything in general as he
left the ponies and started hunting a shelter for himself, he grinned, satisfied, as he melted snow for his
coffee and figgered on the price the ponies would bring.
He knowed good horses, and even tho they was in
poor shape now he knowed what they'd turn out to be
after a month's time on green grass.

And then there was "Smoky," that mouse colored
horse;—he'd heard how four hundred dollars had been
offered for that pony, and allowed that some other
cowman to the south would be glad to give at least
half that price for him, once it was showed what a
cowhorse he really was.

A few hundred miles to the south was the breed's
hangout, a place in a low country and where the snow
hardly stayed. Once there he could take it easy, let
the ponies fatten up, and after the brand was well
"blotched" so nobody would recognize the original,
he'd sell 'em one at a time for a good price or ship 'em
out to some horse dealer. In the meantime he had
nothing to worry about, the storm had took his trail
off the face of the earth, there was a good seventy miles
between him and where he'd started with the horses,
and near a hundred miles to the Rocking R home ranch.

CHAPTER XI

"THE FEEL OF A STRANGE HAND"

A LONG month had passed since Clint had rode
out to get Smoky and came back with a calf instead. Every day since, that cowboy had been for
going after Smoky again, but the deep snow and storms
had more than kept him breaking trails for snowbound
cattle that was weak and needed bringing in, he could-
n't find no time and hadn't been able to frame no excuse so as he could hit out for Smoky's range. Then
one morning he got up with a hunch. He tried to keep
it down, but every morning it got stronger till finally
Clint just had to saddle up the best horse he had and
hit out for where Smoky had been wintering.

The last big storm had let up a few days before, and
many fresh tracks covered the horse range, Clint trailed
and trailed, he found and went thru many bunches of
ponies, but no Smoky. Even the bunch that pony was
running with when last seen had seemed to evaporate
into thin air, and there Clint wondered. He wondered
if somebody'd stole him and the bunch, but he put
that off, figgering that no horse thief would steal horses
packing as well known a brand as the Rocking R, unless he was a daggone fool, or a daggone good one.
Anyway, as worried as Clint was, he felt some relieved
in not finding the bunch Smoky had been with, for if
he'd found them and no Smoky that'd been proof

enough that the pony had went and died somewheres. The other ponies he'd seen that day still looked good and strong, and that was proof enough that Smoky must be the same.

"Most likely him and his bunch just drifted with that last storm and went back to their home range," Clint thought, as he headed his horse back for the ranch, but the hunch that was still with him didn't seem to agree with that thought none at all.

Two weeks later found the cowboy on the horse range once more, and making a bigger circle, but Smoky and his bunch still kept being amongst the missing. He told Old Tom about it as he got back to the ranch that night, but the old man didn't seem worried; he waved a hand as Clint said how he'd finally got to believe that the whole bunch had been stole.

"Don't worry," he says, "we'll find him and all the rest during horse round up."

Finally, spring broke up, the deep drifts started to melting and the creeks begin to raise, then after a while, and when the "hospital stuff"* had been turned out on the range a couple of weeks, riders begin stringing out towards the horse range and gathering the remuda. Clint lined out by himself and hit for the country where Smoky had been raised. He reached the camp where he'd started breaking him, and from there he rode, every morning with a fresh horse and running down every bunch of stock horses a hoping to get sight of the mouse colored gelding.

He rode for a week and seen every horse that was

---

* The old cattle which 'd been kept and fed under the sheds thru the winter.

on that range, strays and all, and finally after he'd combed the whole country where Smoky had run as a colt, he rode back to the ranch, feeling disappointed but a hoping that the other riders had found him.

The remuda was in the big corrals, when he got there, all of it, excepting for the seventeen head which couldn't be found nowheres. Smoky was one of the seventeen.

There was a few more days riding, and then of a sudden Old Tom decided Clint had been right, the horses was sure enough stolen—. His big car hit only the high spots as the old man headed for town,—jack rabbits was passed by and left behind the same as if they'd been tied, and when he hit the main street he was doing seventy. He put on his brakes and passed the sheriff's office by half a block, but he left his car there, and hoofed on a high run all the way back.

That official was notified of the theft, and notified to notify other officials of the State and other States around, and Old Tom stuck close to see that that was done and mighty quick. A thousand dollars reward was offered for the thief, and the same reward for the return of the horses, naming one mouse colored saddle horse as special.

The spring round up went by, summer, and then the fall round up and the close of the season's work. Nothing of Smoky, nor any of the ponies he'd run with or the horse thief was heard of; it seemed like one and all had left the earth for good, and if what all Old Tom often wished on the thief could of come thru, that hombre would of sure found himself in a mighty hot place.

Clint rode on for the Rocking R thru that summer and fall, and always as he rode, he kept an eye on the country around and hoping that sometimes he'd run acrost his *one* horse, Smoky. He didn't want to think that the horse had been stolen, and he kept a saying to himself as he rode: "he's just strayed away somewheres."—There wasn't a draw, coulee, or creek bottom passed by without the whole of it was looked into, and never before was the Rocking R country looked into so well. Every rider, on down to the wrangler, kept his eyes peeled for the mouse colored horse, and even tho *cattle* is what the wagons was out for, there was more eyes out for Smoky, and cattle was only brought in as second best.

It wasn't till fall round up was near over that Clint begin losing all hope of ever seeing Smoky again in *that* country, and as them hopes left him, there came a hankering for him to move. Maybe it was just to be moving and riding on some other range for a change, but back of it all, and if Clint had stopped to figger some, he'd found that his hankering to move wasn't only for seeing new territory,—there was a faint hope away deep, that some day, somewheres, he'd find Smoky.

For that pony had got tangled up in the cowboy's heartstrings a heap more than that cowboy wanted to let on, even to himself. He couldn't get away from *how* he missed him. He'd thought of him when on day herd and how the horse had seemed to understand every word he'd said. On the cutting grounds, he'd kept a comparing whatever horse he'd be riding with

And even tho cattle is what the round up wagons was out for, there was more eyes out for Smoky, and cattle was only brought in as second best.

Smoky, and find that pony (no matter how good he was) a mighty poor excuse of a cowhorse alongside of the mouse colored pony that was missing.

Clint'd keep on comparing whatever horse he'd be riding with Smoky, and find that pony (no matter how good he was) a mighty poor excuse as compared with the mouse colored horse that was missing.

But all them good points of Smoky's was nothing as compared to the rest of what that horse really had been *as a horse*, and there's where Smoky had got under Clint's hide, as a horse, one in a thousand.

The last of the wagons had trailed into the home ranch, and the next day, the remuda was hazed out to the winter range.—Clint wasn't along that fall to see the ponies turned loose. Instead he was in the big bunk house at the home ranch, and busy stuffing his saddle into a gunny sack. A railroad map was spread on the floor and which the cowboy had been studying.

Jeff opened the door of the bunk house and took in at a glance what all Clint was up to;—he noticed the railroad map laying by his foot and smiled.

"I figgered you would," he says, "now that Smoky is not with the outfit no more."

The first of winter had come and hit the high mountains of the southern country. Big, dark clouds had drifted in, drenched the ranges down to bedrock with a cold rain, and hung on for days. Then the rain had gradually turned to a wet snow, kept a falling steady, and without a break, till it seemed like the country itself was shivering under the spell.

Finally, and after many long days, the dark clouds begin to get lighter and lighter and started lifting and drifting on—then one evening, the sun got a chance to peek thru and smile at the country again. It went down a smiling that way and after it disappeared over the blue ridge a new moon took its place for a spell, and like as to promise that the sun would smile again the next day.

And it did, it came up bright and real fitting to that Arizona country. The air was clear as spring water in a granite pool, and as still. The whole world seemed dozing and just contended to take on all the warmth and life the sun was giving. A mountain lion was stretched out on a boulder, warm and comfortable, where the day before he'd been in his den all curled up and shivering, then a few deer come out of their shelter, hair on end and still wet thru, but as they reached the sunny side of the mountain it wasn't long when it dried again, and layed smooth.

Further down the mountain and more on the foothills, a little chipmunk stuck his head out of his winter quarters and blinked at the sun. He blinked at it for quite a spell like not believing, and pretty soon came out to make sure. He stood up, rolled in the warm dirt, and in more ways than one made up for the long days he'd holed away. Other chipmunks came out, and then he went visiting, more seeds was gathered as he went from bush to bush and even tho he already had a mighty big supply already stored away, he worked on as tho he was afraid of running short long before spring come.

He was at his busiest, and tearing a pine cone apart for the nuts he'd find inside, when he hears something a tearing thru the brush and coming his way. Away he went and hightailed it towards his hole, and he'd no more than got there when he gets a glimpse of what looked like a mountain of a horse and running for all he was worth.—A long rope was dragging from his neck.

The chipmunk went down as far in his hole as he could, stood still and listened a minute, and then storing away the nuts he'd gathered, stuck his head out once more. He chirped considerable as he looked around to see if any more out of the ordinary or dangerous looking was in sight, and he'd just had time to blink at the scenery a couple of times, when he gets a glimpse of another horse,—this one was packing a man, and at the same speed went right on the trail the other had left.

The chipmunk never wondered what this running was all about, he just chirped and ducked out of sight, but it wasn't long when he stuck his head out again and gradually showed all of himself. He stood up on a rock close to his hole, and looking around from there, he could see two objects out towards the flat, moving fast, and seeming like one trying to catch up with the other. He watched 'em, till a raise finally took 'em out of sight, then he watched some more and in other directions and seeing nothing that'd need watching, he went to visiting again and to gathering more nuts.

Out on the flat, and on the other side of the raise the two objects went on. How glad that one object in the lead would of been to've changed places with the chipmunk and like him been able to crawl down a hole and hide for a spell. For hours and hours thru the night he'd been trailed, his hoofs had sunk deep into the mud every step he'd took, but acrost foothills and adobe flats he'd went on, always the human close behind.

Twice that human'd disappeared and he'd took hope, but soon he'd show up again, and mounted on a fresh horse would chase him some more. A rope had settled around his neck once,—he'd fought till it broke, and run on a dragging it.

He was getting tired, mighty tired, and beginning to

feel with each step he took that the country was in cahoots with the man and trying to hold him back. His feet went ankle deep in the soft, rain-soaked ground, and pulling out and placing 'em ahead steady, on and on, was getting to be more and more of an effort.

Once again the man disappeared, only to show up mounted on another fresh horse, the man's relay string had been well placed and as the horse he'd been chasing was getting tired and easier right along to turn the way he wanted him, he could near see how the end of the chase was going to be.

The sun was getting well up in the sky when skirting along the foothills and going thru a thick bunch of cedars, the tired horse noticed dead cedars piled up in a way that made a fence. Any other time he'd whirled at the sight and went some other way, but his vision wasn't very clear no more, nor was his brain working very good. He'd went on his nerves and kept on long after his muscles had hollered "quit," and he'd got to the point where he was running because something away back in his mind kept a telling him that he should, really not knowing why. He was past caring where he went, and even if the rider behind had stopped and quit, he'd kept on running just the same and till he'd dropped.

He followed the cedar fence hardly realizing it was there. Then from the other side of him appeared another fence, it gradually pinched in on him as he went, till finally both fences led up to a gate and into a corral hid in the thick trees. There he stopped, realizing somehow that he couldn't go no further, and legs wide

A rope had settled around his neck once, he'd fought till it broke,—and run on a dragging it.

apart, breathing hard, sweat a dripping from every part of him, he stood still.

The halfbreed closed the pole gate, and turned looking at the horse.

"Now, you ornery mouse colored hunk of meaness, I guess I got you."

But Smoky, eyes half closed and not seeing, head near touching the ground, and the rest of him trying hard to stay up, never seemed to hear.

Many months had passed and many things happened since Smoky had been hazed away from his home range on the Rocking R. There'd been long nights of traveling when many miles was covered and very little feed was got on the way. Then long, weary miles of travel had accumulated till near a thousand of 'em separated him from the country where he'd been born and raised.

Many strange looking hills and flats he'd crossed as he was kept on the go with Pecos and the rest of the bunch, and when he'd come to the desert it'd been a great relief,—the deep snow had gradually been left behind by then and the bare sagebrush flats had took the place of the snow covered prairie. Many bunches of wild ponies had been seen on the way and once in a while a little bunch of cattle was passed by. The country had kept a changing, from rolling prairie it went to low hills, low hills to mountains, and on the other side more low hills and then sagebrush, the sagebrush had stayed in the landscape from then on and only added some yuccas as the southern country was reached, then spanish dagger, barrel cactus, and cat-claw.

Finally a wide river in a deep canyon of many colors had been reached and swimmed acrost. A few days more travel, and then it seemed like Smoky and the bunch had got *there*,—anyway there'd been no more traveling. The next day, the half breed had corralled all the ponies, and with a running iron, blotched the Rocking R brand over with what looked like a wagon wheel. The original brand was disfigured complete, and then the horses was shoved up on a high knoll while the new brand healed. The knoll was a high flat mesa, with rimrocks all around and where it could be got up on only in one place, that place had then been closed with a rope and a blanket stretched over it. There was good feed up there, and enough snow and rain water in a natural reservoir to last many days.

All would of been well for Smoky, and the long trip with the bucking of snow, hard traveling, and all with the changes of the country would of been took in as it come, but along with that trip, there'd growed some-thing between that pony's ears which had got to chafe. It was a hate, a hate with poison and all for the breed that'd kept him and the others on the move.

Smoky was born with a natural fear and hate of the human, he'd carried it always, excepting when Clint, *that one man*, was around, but hating humans had never bothered him, not till the dark face of the breed h showed itself over the skyline.

With him in sight, that hate had got to grow til

murder showed in his eye, and the little fear that was still with him, was all that'd kept him from doing damage to the dark complected human that'd trailed along behind all the way. He'd boiled over to himself, stayed in the lead, and far away from the breed as he could.

The breed had throwed a rope at him one day, and missed. Smoky had never been missed that way before, and from that once he'd learned that by ducking at the right time there was such a thing as dodging a rope. The next day the breed had throwed his rope at him again, and Smoky watching, had ducked at the right time and once more the loop had missed. The breed begin cussing as he spread another loop and tried to place it around Smoky's neck, but his cussing didn't do him any good, and the loop had fell short a foot from the dodging pony's head.

Smoky would of enjoyed all that, if he hadn't meant it so much, and what's more the breed had got ferocious, which all made things more serious for the horse. He'd hated the sound of that breed's voice as that hombre, fighting his head, and cussing for all he was worth, had coiled up his rope once more and made ready for another try.

And in that third throw the breed had fooled Smoky. He'd swung his rope like as to throw it, but the loop had never left his hands. Smoky had dodged and dodged thinking sure that the rope had come, but it never had, and finally when he'd quit dodging, it did come, and with the speed of a "blue racer" had circled around his neck.

Smoky had fought like a trapped grizzly as the rope had drawed up, and the breed had to take a few turns around a corral post to hold him.

"I'll fix you now, you——"

Cussing a blue streak, the breed had broke a limb off the willows that hung over the corral, and coming towards Smoky had been for showing that horse who was boss. He'd went to work, and tried to break the limb over the fighting pony's head. Orneriness had stuck up in the breed's gizzard, and anything would be done, even killing the horse right there would of been hunkydory so long as he could ease his feelings some.

He'd pounded and pounded till the limb begin to break, and as he'd noticed it give that way he was going to keep on till it did break, but there again, luck had been against him. The rope that'd held Smoky went and separated at the honda and set the horse free.

The breed had raved on some more at seeing his victim getting away, and throwed the club after him as the pony staggered back amongst the other ponies, and then somehow realizing that then was no time to fool with ornery horses, the breed had caught another horse.

"I'll tend to you some more," he hollered at Smoky, and getting on the other horse he'd let the bunch out and started 'em on the trail.

Two hundred miles of that trail was covered, and in the time it took to cover that distance, Smoky had fed on hate for the breed till that hate growed to a disease. Killing the breed would be all that could cure it. Every blow that human had pounded on his head that day, a couple of weeks past, had left a scar, a scar that healed on the surface, but which went to his heart instead, spread there, and stayed raw.

Then one day, on the edge of a big desert flat and amongst the junipers the breed spotted a high, strong, corral. A log cabin with smoke coming out of the chimney was off to one side a ways, and standing in the door was a man, the first man the breed had seen since starting out with the stolen horses. But he felt safe, five hundred miles had been covered, the brands on the horses had all been "picked"* and besides, as he figgered, it'd be a good place to stop a while and re-cuperate; and as he seen the place was a cow camp, he thought maybe he could get the cowboy to help him some with that mouse colored horse he was still want-ing to "tend" to and packing a grudge against.

The cowboy wasn't much for the breed the minute that hombre rode up, but as company was scarce, he kinda stood him, and even agreed to help him with the horse.

Smoky watched the two walk in the corral the next day, and knowed something was up. His ears layed back at the sight of the breed and hate showed from every part of him;—he was ready to fight, and if any-thing he was glad of the chance.

But Smoky had no chance, too many ropes settled on him at once, and the first thing he knowed, he was flat on his side and tied down before he could use either hoof or teeth.

The horse was no more than down and helpless,

* Changed for a time by just cutting the hair.

when the breed, seeing his victim within reach and where he couldn't get away, begin to get rid of what'd been on his chest for so long, and when Smoky even tho tied down, reached over and near pulled the shirt off of him with his teeth, was when the breed figgered he had an excuse to beat that horse to a pulp even tho the horse had no chance.

The cowboy, not understanding the breed's tactics for a spell, stood off a ways, and watched. There was all about the horse to show that he'd been right in his first dislike for the dark faced hombre. At first he was for interfering and shove the club the breed was using right down his throat. Then as he noticed how the pony would like to do the damaging instead, he thought of a better way and walked up.

"Listen, feller," he says to the breed, "what's the use of beating a horse up that way. Why don't you give him a chance and try to do it *while you're setting on him?*"

"Maybe you think I can't do it," says that hombre, bleary-eyed and mad clear thru.

The scheme had worked fine—the cowboy grinned to himself as he helped the breed put the saddle on Smoky. Once he'd got a little too close to that pony's head while helping that way, and that horse come within an inch of getting his arm, the cowboy overlooked it, and to himself remarked: "the poor devil had sure got a reason to be mean, and I guess he's at the point where he figgers no human is his friend any more."

The cowboy was right, anything on two legs, whether

it was the breed or any other human, had sure enough got to be Smoky's enemy,—a crethure to scatter into

And while the breed was getting as much of the saddle under him as he could, the cowboy took off the foot ropes.

dust and put out of the way whenever a chance showed up.

The saddle was cinched on, and while the breed was getting as much of the seat under him as he could, the cowboy took off the foot ropes, and soon as the last coil was pulled away, he made long steps for the highest part of the corral and where he could watch everything to *his heart's content*.

The cowboy had no more than reached the top pole of the corral when a sudden commotion, which sounded like a landslide, made him turn. Smoky had come up, and at last given a chance had more than started to make use of it. It was his turn to do some pounding, and he done it with the saddle that was on his back and which went with every crooked and hard hitting jump he made.

The breed had rode many hard horses and he was a good rider, but he soon found that Smoky was a harder horse to set than any he'd ever rode before, and as good a rider as he was there was many a twist brought in that he couldn't keep track of,—they kept a coming too fast, and it wasn't long when he begin to feel that setting in that saddle on such a horse was no place for him. The saddle horn and cantle was taking turns and hitting him from all sides, till he didn't know which way he was setting. Pretty soon he lost both stirrups, and once as he was a hanging over to one side, one of them stirrups came up and hit him between the eyes. That finished him—, he hit the ground like a ton of lead.

The cowboy up on top of the corral had laughed and enjoyed the performance all the way thru, and when the breed dug his nose in the dust of the corral he laughed all the more, he'd never been more agreeable to seeing a man get "busted" in his life.

The breed layed in a heap, never moving, and then the cowboy, finally getting serious, was for getting him out of there before the horse spotted him, and reduced him into thin air. Somehow, he wasn't caring to see a human get tore apart and right before his eyes that way even if that human did deserve killing, but Smoky's interest was all for shedding the saddle right then and all that carried the breed's smell; finally *it* begin to slip;—higher and higher on his withers it went till the high point was reached, and then it started going down. When it reached the ground the hackamore had come off with it, and before Smoky, slick and clean, straightened up again, the breed had picked himself up, and without the help of the cowboy, sneaked out of the corral.

The next few minutes was used by that cowboy in telling the breed to get another horse saddled and hit the trail while the hitting was good, and helping him getting his horses together, boosted him out of camp. —But the breed wasn't thru with Smoky, he was going to "tend to him" again, some other time.

Months had went by before that other time come, and it'd been away late in the next fall before that hombre ever put his hands on Smoky again. In that time, the other ponies, which all had seemed inclined to behave, had been sold. Smoky had been kept in the corral, treated with a club regular, and fed "post hay," till, as the breed figgered, he'd break that pony's spirit, or break his neck, but he was going to *make* him behave some way, so as he'd get the price he'd be asking for him.

Then one night a high March wind had sprung up,

rattled the corral gate, and finally worked it open. Smoky hadn't been long in seeing the opening, and when a few days later the breed, hunting for the horse, spotted him, the mouse colored gelding had took up with

Smoky's interest was all for shedding the saddle right then and all that carried the breed's smell.

the wild bunch, and only a glimpse of him did he get.

Every once in a while that whole summer the breed had tried cutting Smoky out of the wild bunch and run him in, but that pony had been harder to get near than any of the wild ones he was with. He knowed what was on the program for him if that breed ever caught him again,—the steady beatings he'd got from him had made his hate grow for the human till a striking rattlesnake looked like a friend in comparing.

But the breed hadn't been for quitting,—he couldn't stand to have anything get the best of him, not even an ornery pony, and as Smoky enjoyed his wild freedom them summer months, the breed had kept a studying which circle Smoky and the wild ones would take whenever they was being chased, and getting a good lay of the land he finally figgered a plan.

And, that's how come, when he started out after Smoky again in the fall he knowed just where to place a relay string of ponies. At the other end was a trap corral and well hid— Then the breed spotted the horse late one afternoon, and fell in behind him and the other wild ones he was with. It had been a long chase, the wild ones had dropped out of the run one by one and branched to one side, but Smoky and the rest of the strongest had kept on right along on the trail where the breed had stationed his fresh relay horses. Finally, and as the breed kept a coming in on 'em with fresh horses, the strongest of the mustangs kept a branching out, but Smoky had kept on straight ahead, till, leg weary and staggering, he'd found himself in the wings of the trap corral, and then inside, past being able to see the grinning halfbreed who'd closed the gate on him.

A few days went by when Smoky seemed in a trance. He remembered some of being led and jerked all the way back to the breed's hangout, of being saddled the next day and jerked around some more, and then rode out and with spur and quirt, made to trot around. He didn't realize the breed had set on him or he didn't

That pony had been harder to get near than any of the wild ones he was with.

seem to care. The little hay that was throwed out to him wasn't noticed, and hardly did he drink,—only if by chance he happened to mope around the corral and find himself standing in the stream that was running in one side of it.

There was everything about the horse to indicate that in a few more days he'd be laying down, never to

get up no more; his trail seemed fast coming to an
end, and the heart that was left in him had shrunk till
nary a beat of it could be felt. The breed kept a riding
him out, thinking he at last and for sure had the horse
right where he wanted him.

"I'll make a good horse out of you, you scrub," he'd
say as he'd beat him over the head with his quirt and
at the same time cut him with the spur. Smoky had
seemed to feel neither the quirt nor the spur. He didn't
flinch nor even bat an eye as both would come down on
him and leave the marks. There seemed to be no sign
of hopes or life left in the horse, and the abuse went
on till, finally, and one day the breed happened to
cut the horse a little deeper and in a more sensitive
place.

That cut had stirred the pony's shrunk up heart,
and a faint spark had showed in his eyes for a second.
The next day Smoky even snorted a little as the breed
walked into the corral, and he tried to buck some as
he climbed into the saddle. The breed was surprised
at the new show of spirit, and remarked as he took
down his quirt:

"I'll take *that* out of you."

From that day on Smoky's heart begin to expand
towards natural size once more— But it wasn't the
same kind of heart that had once been his,—that first
one had died, and this one had took root from abuse,
growed from rough treatment to full size, and with
hankerings in it only for finding and destroying all that
wasn't to his liking. And there was nothing to his
liking no more.

The breed he hated more than anything in the world, but Smoky, with that new heart of his, wasn't for showing them feelings much. He'd got wise in ways of how and when to do his fighting, and where it'd do

The breed would often watch him thru the corral poles and wonder, he'd sometimes wonder if it wouldn't be best to just place a forty-five slug between that pony's ears instead of fooling with him.

most good;—he'd wait for a chance. In the meantime he'd got to eating every stem of what little hay the breed would hand him; he'd have to live to carry out them new ambitions of his.

But somehow, a hint of Smoky's new ambitions must of leaked out; anyway the breed had a hunch that it wouldn't be well for him to come too close to that pony's teeth and hoofs. He'd often watch him thru

the corral poles and wonder, he'd sometimes wonder
if it wouldn't be best to just place a forty-five slug between that pony's ears instead of fooling with him,
but the hopes of still being able to sell the horse for a
good price would always keep him from drawing his
gun.

"A good long ride'll fix you," says the breed one
morning as he drug his saddle near the corral chute.
"And I've got a hell of a long one ahead for you to-day."

Smoky was prodded into the chute with a long pole,
and saddled where he couldn't move. Then the breed
climbed in the saddle, opened the chute gate and
started the horse out on a long run.

Ten miles of country was covered which Smoky
didn't see; his instinct made him dodge badger holes
and jump washouts, and his eyes and ears was steady
back and on the human he was packing, if he could
only reach with his teeth and get him down.

The breed's spurs kept a gouging him, and along
with the quirt a pounding, Smoky was kept into a
high lope. With that kind of tattoo being played on
him the pony gradually begin to warm up and getting
peeved, it wouldn't be long, if that gait was kept up,
when he'd be reaching the boiling point, and then get
desperate.

A steep bank was reached by the edge of a creek,
and there Smoky sorta hesitated a second. His ears
and eyes was pointed ahead for that second and looking for a place where the going down wouldn't be so
sudden, when the breed, always looking for some
reason to deal the horse misery, put the steel and

layed the quirt to him at once. That took Smoky by surprise, and the flame that'd been smoldering in his heart loomed up into a active volcano all at once.

Down over the bank he went, and when he landed he had his head between his front legs and went to bucking from there. By some miracle the breed stuck him for half a dozen jumps, then he made a circle in the air and landed on all fours at the foot of the bank.

A shadow on the ground and right by him made the breed reach for his gun near as quick as he landed; it was the shadow of the horse and *too close;* his gun was out of the holster and he turned to use it; but he was just the splinter of a second too late, and the six-shooter was buried in the ground as Smoky, like a big cougar, pounced on him.

CHAPTER XII

"WHEN THE GOOD LEAVES"

BIG posters was tacked on the telegraph poles all around the little town of Gramah. Them posters could be seen in many windows of the town's stores, and advertised the coming rodeo and cowboys' reunion. Amongst the prizes that was wrote down on the poster was prints from photographs of bucking horses and steers, and taking most of the room in the center of it was the picture of a bucking horse which outdone all the others. It showed that horse throwing his rider in a way few riders ever get throwed. Then in big letters underneath was the words: THE COUGAR CHALLENGES THE WORLD'S BEST.

The Cougar was the name of a bucking horse, the main attraction, and challenger to all the good riders of the country. No line was drawed as to where them riders came from or how far, and the purse that was offered for the one who could ride that horse and scratch him was enough to make any good rider want to come a long ways and try.

Many had come and tried him at other rodeos and where The Cougar had performed, and found that that pony was no ordinary bucking horse, and as all that tried him could tell, afterwards, there was more than his bucking to contend with; he was mean, there was murder in his eye, and if it wasn't for the "pick-up"

The horse had been found out on the desert, amongst a bunch of wild horses and packing an empty saddle.

men who hazed him, many a cowboy would of been pawed to pieces even before he could of hit the ground.

That pony seemed to have a grudge against humans in general; his ambition was for exterminating 'em all off the face of the earth. But there was one thing which the riders noticed in him as most queer, and that was in the way he seemed to hate some humans worse than others,—his hate was plainest for the face that showed dark.

A story followed the horse, and which kept a being repeated as rider met rider at different rodeos and frontier day celebrations. It was that the horse had been found on the desert, amongst a bunch of wild horses and packing an empty saddle. There'd been dried blood sticking to the hair along his jaw, and some more on his knees; the horse had been roped and tied down and the riders had looked for signs of wounds or cuts on his hide but nary a scratch had been found.

The horse was then advertised in the county and State papers and described as "A mouse colored, blaze faced, stocking legged gelding, and packing a brand that looked like a blotched wagon wheel." The advertisement was kept running for two weeks and nobody showed to claim the horse. He was kept in the pasture for a few days more, and then one day one of the riders run him in the corral.

The cowboy had liked the looks of the pony from the day he'd set eyes on him; he'd figgered him as an ordinary horse that'd been spoiled a little, and shaking out a loop, there'd been no doubt in his mind but what that could be took out of him easy enough. But

he hadn't got very far when he found that the pony
would have to be throwed before a saddle could ever
be put on his back. There was a look in the horse's
eye which he didn't like, and that cowboy having
handled all kind of horses knowed mighty well what
that look meant.

He kept his distance, and from there worked his
ropes till the horse went down to his knees and then
flat to the ground. The saddle was cinched on tight,
and seeing that the hackamore was on the pony's head
to stay, the cowboy took his seat while the horse was
down, and reaching over took the foot ropes off.

What went on in the next few minutes was past ever
being described with talk, and as that cowboy felt,
telling about it would be a disgrace as compared with
what really happened—something like trying to paint
the Grand Canyon of Arizona on black canvas with
black paint.

Anyway, that cowboy had reached for the top pole
of the corral and got on the other side of it before the
pony had really got started to whatever he was up
to, and there on the safe side he done a mental round
up, and it all came to him. He remembered the empty
saddle that was on the pony's back when found that
day two weeks past—then the dried blood that'd been
on his jaw and more of it on his knees—.

The cowboy had remarked as thru the corral poles
he'd watched the man killer:

"A twelve hundred pound mountain lion is what
that horse is."

That's where his name Cougar had come in, and no

horse never lived up to a name like the mouse colored
gelding did to his.

Then had come rumors of a Fourth of July celebration which was going to be pulled off in some big town
to the south; there was to be bronc riding and everything that went with it. A prize of a hundred dollars
had been offered for the best bucking horse, and that's
how come one day that The Cougar made his first
appearance before a grandstand. A warning was given
to the "pick-up" man and "hazers" to be on hand
and watch out nobody got hurt, and them few words
of warning that way had proved to sound mighty right
before that day was over.

The Cougar had been *tried* out, and then a hundred
dollars was handed to the rider who'd brought him
in. He'd won the prize. There was no doubt in anybody's mind but what that pony was by a long ways
the meanest and hardest horse to ride there, and not
only there, but anywhere else and wherever hard bucking horses was rode. Fifty dollars additional was offered for the right to keep the horse for rodeo purposes.
That was refused, and when the last day of the doings
come, and the riders came up for the "finals" another
fifty was added to the first offer, and accepted. A bill of
sale was made out, and The Cougar from that day on
was drove from stockyard to stock car and from arena
to arena.

In front of the crowded grandstand is where his
fame as a fighting, man hating, bucking outlaw begin
to spread, and from State to State, town and range
folks alike was on hand and whenever he was to be

rode and handled; for watching that horse perform was alone worth more than the price that was asked for the ticket at the gate of the rodeo grounds.

It wasn't long when the folks thru whole of the southwestern states begin to talk of The Cougar as

In front of the crowded grandstand is where his fame as a man-hating, bucking outlaw begin to spread.

they did of their favorite movie actor, actress, or the Prince of Wales. Tourists from Europe and from all parts of the U. S. came and went, and carried stories with 'em about the wonders of the wickedness of that horse. Then rodeo committees begin to perk up their ears, and at the same time started bidding for him. The Cougar's presence got to be valuable, and came a time when five hundred dollars was offered by a rival who also made a business of furnishing rodeos with strings of bucking stock. The offer wasn't considered, none at all, and the riders around had their doubts if even a thousand would change the ownership of that horse.

Every summer thru, the mouse colored outlaw was skipped along with the others more or less of his kind and unloaded at some different rodeo grounds; every few weeks and for three or four days he was *rode at*. Twice or three times a day during the doings, some strange rider would climb him, the chute gate would fly open, and out would come a tearing, bellering hunk of steel coils to land out a ways, and like a ton of lava from up above, jar the earth even up to the grandstand.

The judges, pick-up men, and others around would find themselves short about ten pairs of eyes as all tried to catch every crooked move that pony put into his work. All breaths seemed to be held up during that time, but never no time was them breaths held up for very long, cause, very soon, there'd be a scattering of a tall cowboy, who, from the chute had started on top, took a lot of wicked jars while setting there, and so high, and good rider as he'd have to be, soon come to conclude that it sure was no disgrace to be separated from his saddle and flung out a ways — not on that horse.

Very seldom would the rider have to walk back very far, and sometimes only a few feet was between the rider who was picking himself up and the chute where he'd rode out from so fast and furious.

As an all around outlaw and bucking horse The

Cougar had no rival; there wasn't a horse in the state or any state neighboring that could compete with him

The chute gate would fly open, and out would come a tearing, bellering hunk of steel coils to land out a ways, and like a ton of lava from above, jar the earth even up to the grandstand.

in either fighting or bucking, and folks seeing or studying the horse often wondered; for anybody who knowed horses could see that that horse hadn't been born a

natural outlaw like most of the rodeo's bucking horses
generally are; that pony had brains, a big supply of
'em and which showed in the way he'd go about throwing his man. He wasn't like the average bucking horse,
who'd often buck back under the man that was already loosened, and instead, when The Cougar felt a
man lose an inch, that inch was never got back. The
saddle kept a getting away from him from then on.

But there was more and which was all proof as to
the amount of brains that pony carried, there was his
hate for the man, and which showed the same as the
hate one human would have for another, only it was
more dangerous. And then again, and as the cowboy
who took care of him often remarked:—

"The way that horse packs a grudge, somebody sure
must of dealt him a dirty deal some time or other. I
know there's sure something on his mind besides that
too, and like he's pining for something that's gone and
hopeless; at them times he acts like he wants my company the same as tho he was craving for somebody,
but them spells don't last long, and soon he seems to
come back to earth and realizing things. Then's when
I'm not within reaching distance no more—but by
golly, I sure wish sometimes that horse would like me
as well as he hates."

The first two years he put in as The Cougar and bad
horse was the most ferocious two years any horse went
thru. It was wicked times, not only for the horse, but
for all who handled and tried to ride him. There was
so much poison in that pony's heart that the only way
he could live was by hating and being hated; he fed

on it, and the bars or poles that was between him and whoever he wanted to get at in his fits of wickedness showed signs a plenty of his hankering to murder,—the destroying ability of that pony's teeth and hoofs sure was visible, and convincing.

He wasn't at all the same horse that'd faced a cowboy some eight years or so past. He hadn't wanted to fight then, he'd just wanted to get away and be left alone and he'd only fought the rope that held him, and even tho his suspicions and hate of the human had been natural he hadn't seen anything about that cowboy he wanted to disfigure.

He'd done a mighty neat job of bucking in the Rocking R corrals and made Clint pay attention to his riding pretty well; but his bucking then, even tho it was hard, didn't compare much with the bucking of The Cougar. He'd just been bucking thru instinct, it was the natural thing for a brainy range horse to do, and when he bucked it wasn't for meaness but just to see if he couldn't get out from under that rig and man. He'd felt like it didn't belong up there in the middle of him, and he'd only wanted to make sure that it all could stick.

He'd given it all a mighty good test of course, but as compared with the way Smoky had acted with how he was now acting as The Cougar, it would match well with a man playing a peaceful game of solitary and a gambler dealing for his life with some hated enemy.

The Cougar would of killed himself to get his man, he was past caring for his own hide and only lived to hate, but even as strong as that hate was, it was queer to see that he wasn't interested to do damage only to the men that handled or tried to ride him. Maybe that was because there was always so many around,—the grandstands was full of people and it was the same around the chutes and corrals of the rodeo grounds. Them crowds might of confused him to a standstill and sort of made him keep neutral till only one or two come near.

Another thing that might of fooled a few was the way The Cougar carried his ears. Most every town person has noticed how some horses in the city's streets have some kind of leather muzzles to keep 'em from biting passing folks. Them horses have their ears back most of the time and whenever somebody comes near, they have a mighty cranky look too, but as a rule they're not as wicked as they look,—it's just that they're tired of having everybody that goes by stop and try to feed 'em peanuts or apples and such, or being petted and sometimes rubbed the wrong way. Some horses' disposition can't stand it, and them few seem to get so that they can't keep their ears forward and look pleasant any time;—they're always laying 'em back and looking like they would do some damage, but the most they would do if they had no muzzle would be to maybe just nip a little hunk of hard-twist serge or a little silk off different folks' arms.

Like a feller says to me one time, "it's just that they're bored."

The horse out on the range, no matter how mean he might be, hardly ever puts his ears back at a human; when he does, it's only once in a coon's age and only for the split of a second,—in the next split of that second *something has happened*.

The Cougar, being a sure enough range horse and with real mustang* blood to boot carried his ears in the ways of that kind. He'd look at a man thru the chute timbers and with his ears *straight ahead*, but in them eyes under the shadow of them ears was a fair picture of what would happen if that man ever stepped in that chute with him. It didn't need no imagination to see it either.

Never did The Cougar lay his ears back unless he was sure of his victim. When he did there'd be an ambulance wagon racing thru the arena and remarks in queer low tones passed by white faced folks up in the grandstand, which all kept accumulating and piled up in The Cougar's reputation as a bad horse.

A little bit of a freckle faced hombre who'd made the "grand finals" was along the chute one day and "up" to ride The Cougar. He'd come from acrost the border, and thru the first three days of the rodeo had proved himself to be a "ranahan"† in bronc riding as well as in steer roping.

"By golly," he was heard to say as The Cougar was hazed into the saddling chute, "I've come a long ways to get a setting at that pony." He felt of his taped spurs to make sure they was there to stay, "and if you watch close," he went on, grinning, "I'll give you all a few lessons on how to play a tune with a spur rowel at the tip of a pony's ears."

* Of the early Spanish.   † Top hand.

The little "vaquero"* was feeling good, he hadn't been to town for a year or more, and a chance to ride a mean horse where there was folks around was a big change to him; barrel cactus and Spanish dagger had been the only witnesses to his riding ability, and riding a side-winding pony on dobie flats or high mesas wasn't so apt to bring out the best in a rider as when in a nice arena where there's a band playing and folks a cheering.

"There's a horse to my liking," he says as he took a look at The Cougar. The way that pony was acting while being saddled didn't faze the rider none at all, the grin on his face kept a spreading all the wider as he made ready to climb the chute; he'd handled many a fighting horse, and to him they all could do only one thing, and that was their worst.

As a true rider of the range he welcomed anything that'd test his skill and ability, and if The Cougar had come straight up from hell, wore horns, a forked tail, and cloven hoof, he'd of grinned all the more and bet his year's earnings that he could send him back to where he came with his tail between his legs and hollering "enough."

"Rider up," hollered the hazer, but the judges was already watching, for it was The Cougar "coming out."

The cowboy let out a war whoop and grinned as the chute gate flew open and The Cougar came "uncorked," he packed that grin past the judges and at the same time "reefed" (spurred) the earth jarring

* Cowboy.

The Cougar reared up while the rider was still in the air, then turned, and with his ears back, teeth a flashing, hoofs a striking with lightning speed, went to carry out his heart's craving.

outlaw with *taped* rowels from back of the ear to the back of the saddle skirts.

"Yee-e-e-ep!" he howled, as the bellering Cougar left the earth once more. A cloud of dust went up which kept the judges from seeing what went on, but even if there'd been no dust they couldn't of followed what all had happened, it had happened too fast. In the next particle of time a twisting hunk of mouse colored horse flesh was tearing up the arena towards the chutes and the fence along it. The cowboy was still war whooping and fanning but he was to one side and being snapped around like a whip lash. The Cougar had found his stride and, as usual, was getting his man.

The "pick up men" rode up to grab holt of the horse's head and before the man was throwed, but they was just too late and in another second something happened that made everybody in the grandstand turn pale and hang on to each other, for the cowboy, still a fanning, was, by a wicked jolt, loosened from his saddle and headed for the ground, The Cougar reared up while the rider was still in the air, then turned, and with ears back, teeth a flashing, hoofs a striking with lightning speed, went to carry out his heart's cravings.

The man was juggled up there for a second and then came down, the horse, like the cougar he was, right after him and to finish what he'd started.

It was then that Providence or something seemed to interfere, for as the rider came down and reached the earth he was on the other side of the fence, which kept him from being totally reduced to dust. But even with the fence separating, The Cougar wasn't thru. There was a noise of splintering timbers as he tried to reach the cowboy, and it wasn't till two ropes settled around his neck and pulled him away that it was what you'd call ended.

A few riders rushed up to find the cowboy setting up and shaking his head like a trying to get back amongst the living. Pretty soon he looked up at the men around him and a sort of vacant grin spread over his features; then he looked at his clothes, noticed his shirt was most tore off of him. He wrinkled his face as he moved his body and felt kinks along his ribs and back, and looked at his hand-made rawhide chaps which showed marks where hard hoofs had connected. The sight of them made him grin again, and after a while he says:

"Daggone good thing I had these chaps on or I'd be setting here and going Adam one better."

From that day on the freckle faced cowboy was, or tried to be, at every rodeo and near whatever chute The Cougar honored by his presence. He'd run up against a horse he couldn't ride; it was hard to take and he couldn't get it into his head how it was done. He'd never seen a horse he couldn't ride before, but there was more and which all kept the cowboy to following the outlaw, the unnatural meanness of that pony had him guessing, and he sort of wanted to figger it out while a setting on top— *There* was a horse that not only called for skill and nerve, but the thinking ability of the pony was sure worth a trying to match.

Winters and springs and falls found him on the range and doing his work there, he was getting all kinds of good practice with his every day work, and when summers come he was always on the trail of The Cougar and with new hopes that he could go back to the range and tell his "majordomo" that he "rode him, slick and clean and to a standstill."

For two summers he followed him, in that time, competing with other good riders, he'd had three chances at him and each time them chances wound up with him hitting the ground, and running as he hit.

"That horse sure means what he does," he was heard to say to one of the riders one time, "and by golly that's just what makes me keep after him."

Three more long summers of rodeo work went by, and The Cougar kept on a challenging the world's best riders. Another spring came, more rodeos was followed and where it was advertised that "The Cougar Will Be Present." The posters went on a telling how in five years time no rider had been able to set the horse till the gun was fired, and as the cowboys remarked, "That was one truthful statement."

Smoky kept on a throwing men right and left that spring and on thru the summer. He kept his record and back clean that way till away along towards the fall, and then one day at the start of another rodeo, a cowboy from the Wyoming country, and who'd come south for the winter, happened to hear of the doings. A couple of days later that bronc fighter showed himself at the rodeo headquarters, and remarking how he'd heard of The Cougar, signed his name and entered on bronc riding.

He qualified and went thru the "tryouts" and "semi-finals" like it all was so much play. The Cougar was a horse kept for the finals only, and that's the pony the cowboy had been trying to reach, the others he'd had to ride had only been a means for him to get to The Cougar.

He'd easy won the right to ride that horse, and also the chance to win the thousand dollars that was up for any rider that could. He hung around the chute and mighty close the next afternoon. Soon the time would come for him to really try his ability, and while waiting he was using that time to seeing that the latigos and cinch had no weak spots, and would be able to stand the strain of staying around the middle of that Cougar horse.

Then the judges hollered out his name as the next rider out, and about that time the mouse colored out-law peeked thru the bars of the chute at him and snorted, the rider whistled at the sight of the mean looking head, and, grinning a little, remarked:

"I got a hunch that this pony is going to be totally different than any horse I ever rode, but here goes, and I got to wish myself luck."

"You'll need lots of that," says one of the cow-boys.

The saddle was on, the cinch reached for and drawed up to stay, and then the rider climbed over the poles of the chute and took his seat on a back that'd throwed the country's best riders. He pulled the rope rein up just tight enough, worked his feet ahead a little, and setting back some to sort of meet the first jolt. He took off his hat, layed all the balance he could in it, and then hollered:

About that time the mouse colored outlaw peeked thru the bars of the chute at him and snorted.

"We're coming out."

"Coming out" was right, but "shot out" would of been more fitting in that case; anyway, the judges hardly seen either the horse or the man till both was *out there*, and both a fighting to win.—There was a mighty big surprise showing on all the faces around when as the first big cloud of dust cleared, it was noticed the rider was still *up there*, and what's more, all indicated that he was going to stay there.

The judges was a setting on their horses, and pop-eyed with the miracle of the performance looked on petrified. Such a rider on such a horse was seldom seen, and they was so all took up with the goings on, they didn't notice that the rider had rode past the limit, and forgot to fire the gun marking the end of the ride, then somebody hollered and jarred 'em out of the trance they was in.

The shot was fired, and the report had no more than died down when the rider seemed to quit from there and fell off the horse,—the punishment he'd took in that ride had been enough to do him for many a day to come. He'd felt like his backbone was going to be pushed thru his throat from the first jump, and that feeling had kept a repeating right along with each fast coming jolt till he was near unconscious. Being the rider he was, he stuck there and tried to fight away the dizzy feeling and keep track of the horse at the same time; then after what seemed an hour, he heard a faint echo of the shot, and realized in a way that he'd qualified for first money. *He'd been the first man to ride that horse past the judges*, and that was enough,— he wasn't caring right then if it would be said that he didn't ride the horse to the finish.

One of the riders who knowed The Cougar *mighty*

well had watched the horse "come out" with the same
thrill that'd always been his at that time. He'd seen
the pony come out many a time before, and as that
last performance came to an end, he leaned over to
one of the boys near him, and says:

"Do you know, it strikes me like The Cougar is beginning to fade out as a bucking horse. I don't think
that pony's been keeping up his standard the last few
times he's been rode, and specially this last time.—If
that cowboy who's just left him had straddled him last
summer, I'm sure and certain that he wouldn't of
stuck as long as he did."

"Well, I've been sort of noticing that too, and figgered the horse had slowed down some," agrees the
other rider, "but that's got to be expected, consider-
ing that The Cougar's been in the arenas for going on
six years now—I don't see, myself, how them legs of
his has been able to stand the strain *that* long."

Them remarks was true,—nothing was meant against
the cowboy who'd been the first to stick him past the
judges; and as them words was said they meant just
that, with no hint that *they* could of done the same,
and what's more, other cowboys had noticed the same
what these two had spoke of. The Cougar was beginning to slow down,—but that last would maybe give
some idea of what a bucking horse The Cougar really
was, *or had been.*

That pony slowing down that way begin to be noticed more and more every time he was rode. The little
vaquero from acrost the border went back satisfied
that fall: he'd been the second man to *ride* The Cougar,

and when the last rodeo of the year had been pulled off The Cougar had been rode twice more, *and to a finish.* The folks in the grandstands was surprised,

He wasn't caring right then if it was said that he didn't ride the horse to the finish.

and come to the conclusion that he wasn't so much of a bucking horse after all, but they didn't realize.— Anyway, the thousand dollar purse that'd been offered for anyone who could ride him had dwindled down to

five hundred, and The Cougar was fast losing the reputation he'd made as a man-hating bucking horse.

Even his hate for the human had seemed to die
down. He'd throwed a rider one day who'd landed
right in front of him; the crowd had held their breath,
expecting to see that cowboy mangled to pieces right
before their eyes. All that would of happened, and
mighty quick a year or so before, but this time the
outlaw didn't seem to notice the man. He'd bucked
on right over him and seeming like careful how he
placed his hoofs as he'd went so as to miss him.—
There was murmurs in the grandstand afterwards that
The Cougar was no outlaw at all, maybe just a pet
and trained to buck, and like his man killing reputation, which was most likely only a sort of a draw
card and advertising for the rodeo.

But whatever the folks in the grandstand thought,
Smoky had reasons of his own for gradually getting
away from being The Cougar. It wasn't that his legs
was getting stove up or giving away on him so much
as the way things had come to him as year after year
he met up with the strange riders that'd come to try
him, and even tho none of 'em seemed to want a *close
acquaintance* with him, there was nothing about them
boys for the hate he was packing to feed on.

Not once, since that day he'd bogged his head in
front of the first grandstand, had a club, nor even a
twig, ever been layed on him. For the first couple of
years, Smoky had let the heart the halfbreed had
transplanted in him, control his actions. The poison
of hate in that heart had kept him from noticing or go

according to the good treatment he'd been getting, and it was close on to the fifth year before his ears begin to perk up to the show of admiration and respect that was handed him from all around.

The name of The Cougar lived on for a spell, but the horse that had been packing that name was fast getting away from having the right to such.—Then the next spring came and with it rodeos begin to be pulled off here and there, good riders begin following The Cougar again as before, and with the hopes that some day, sometime or other, they'd be able to pull their riggin's off that pony's back and be able to say:

"I rode him."

But long before middle summer come, them hopes had died down in many of the boys, for The Cougar wasn't The Cougar no more. Them fast, crooked, and hard hitting jumps of his, and which had jarred the thoughts and balance out of so many a good rider, had died down, and put the horse as an average with the other bucking horses. Rider after rider forked him, and sorta disappointed, had rode and fanned him easy enough, where a year or so before no fanning had been required to qualify.

The Cougar kept a bucking on and on every time he was saddled, and he was rode thru to the finish oftener and oftener till finally, no rider was ever throwed no more, not from that pony's back.

The heart of The Cougar was shriveling up and leaving space for the heart that was Smoky's, and that heart, even tho older and weaker was making a mighty strong stand, and steady coming back.

Soon, there came a time when the mouse colored outlaw didn't have to be handled from a distance no more;
no high corral was needed for protection against his
teeth and hoofs, and like most of the other buckers he
could be led from the stock car to the rodeo grounds
without any other ropes holding him back, and away
from the man that was leading him.

Then one day, a rider brought in a big raw-boned
grey, remarking that "*here* was an outlaw," and an
outlaw he was, sure enough. From his Roman nose
on up to his sunk, dead looking eyes, and taking in his
lantern jaws on to his thick neck and along with the
rest of him, all indicated the *natural* outlaw, but what
made him as a most valuable horse for the rodeos, was
in the how he could buck; that's all he knowed, and
like all natural outlaws that way, that's all he wanted
to know.

Right away, he was called "The Grey Cougar," the
same as to try and bring back the real Cougar. But
there was no comparing the grey outlaw with The
Cougar, not when that last one had meant business.
To begin with, the grey horse was mean only because
it was his natural instinct to be that way, he didn't
have the special ambition nor the brains that The
Cougar had. With the grey it was just jug headed
orneriness, and in no way could he compete with the
mouse colored man killer, but he made a fine outlaw
just the same, a second best that'd do.

He managed to buck a few men off from the start,
and right then is when the Old Cougar begin sliding
into the background, for it'd been quite a spell since

that pony had made a man ride for his money.—The appearance of the grey outlaw had kinda marked the downhill start for Smoky's career as a bucking horse, and then one day the end came sure enough, and in a few minutes.

As usual, The Cougar was announced to the crowd, and them in the grandstand who'd often heard but never seen that wicked pony in action was naturally mighty interested as that notorious horse made his appearance in the saddling chute. Many in the crowd had seen him buck before, and some of them stopped breathing for a spell and while the gate was opened, most anything was expected, from that horse, and all of them that looked on felt sure of seeing something that'd come up to their expectations, and then some.

The gate was opened, and out came a streak of a mouse colored horse with a cowboy on top, and The Cougar, that famous outlaw, lined out acrost the ground *on a long lope*.

Anywheres, and in any line, very little respect is ever showed for a "has been." If The Cougar had fought and tore things up as he'd once had, all would of been hunkydory, and the crowd would all been satisfied, but the horse had come to the end of his fighting streak. Not a jump was left in him, for the Smoky heart had growed over and smothered the heart that'd been The Cougar's. He was a "has been" and only willing to be the plain behaving Smoky again.

The crowd was disappointed, they felt they wasn't getting their money's worth, and there was hollers of "take him away and hook him up on a milk wagon," or "sell him for a lady's saddle horse," and so on.— It was queer, but only natural, to notice that them loud mouth remarks was passed only by the most useless, and of the kind that's plum helpless whenever away from their home grounds. Others hollered more to kind of show off, but the looks they'd get from the sensible folks around only went to prove that the show off was of just plain *ignorance*.

The cowboy rode The Cougar till the other side of the grounds was reached. There he stopped him and climbed off, and hearing the hurrahs from the grandstand, he touched the horse on the neck and says:

"Never mind, old horse, you've done yours—and I'd liked mighty well if I could of turned you loose amongst that bunch that's making all that noise up there, and watch 'em scatter,—but you're not fighting any more."

The rodeo was on its last day, the prizes was handed out that night, and the next morning the bucking horses was loaded in the stock cars on the way for some other town where another rodeo was going to be pulled off. In them box cars there was one place where The Cougar had stood while on the road, but this time, and in that same place was a grey horse who snorted as the train begin to move— The Cougar had been left behind, and from the inside of the stock yards watched the train pull out of sight.

CHAPTER XIII

"A MANY–MEN HORSE"

THE Cougar being he was useless for rodeo purposes, had been sold to the livery stable man for
twenty-five dollars.

It was figgered that at least twenty-five dollars worth
of use would be got out of him there,—the horse was
fat and strong looking, could be broke to harness, and
made to do his share with any of the six and eight
horse teams which was kept on the road acrost the
deserts as freight teams.

But one day, and before the harness ever disgraced
The Cougar's hide, a bunch of tourists had flocked
into town to stay for a spell, and one of the crowd
suggested a little horseback riding. The livery stable
man was at once swamped with orders for saddle
horses, and before he got thru tallying up how many
he could furnish, he found he was short of about
three. By scouting around, he dug up two more, but
he was still short one, and then his eye fell on the
mouse colored horse.

At first, he was for overlooking that horse entirely,
but as he needed one more to finish up the party, he
couldn't very well afford to overlook any horse that
might do. He caught the horse and saddled him, and
scared but game, he got in the saddle. If that pony
still had one jump left in him, it was up to that old

boy to find out, and one jump from *that horse* would be that much too many. He'd never do for no tourist then.

But The Cougar never even humped up as he was rode around the stable corrals. The man's legs begin to quit shaking, and as he sat there, his face gradually turned from blank white to natural color again, and then he begin to grin and show pleasant surprise as he noticed how well the horse reined whichever way was wanted.

"By japers," he remarked to the stable door, "this feller is a real saddle horse."

So, when the tourists, all togged up in their shiny riding habits, appeared some time later, the stable man was all ready and waiting for 'em. He sized 'em all up as to which would get along with each horse best, and being he was still dubious as to what The Cougar might do, he looked 'em all over careful once more till the strongest and most able looking young man in the bunch was spotted.

The Cougar's reins was handed to him, and sort of cautious, he asked:

"I suppose you know how to ride well?"

That young man turned on him, surprised at such a question, and answered sarcastic:

"Why certainly."

The stable man grinned as he watched him and all ride up the street; "Why certainly," he says to himself, and grinned some more. "I hope he's just as *certain* on his riding when he gets back."

It was evening before the party, slouching all over

their horses, returned to the stable. The stable man smiled, satisfied, as he noticed that the young feller, not at all mussed up, was still riding The Cougar. He'd been worried about letting that young feller have the horse, but everything was O.K. now and the folks seemed to've all enjoyed their ride considerable, and so well that they wanted the horses again for the next day.

"This is a very fine horse," says the young feller as he got off The Cougar. There was all about him that as much as went on to say, "Why certainly I can ride."

The stable man had seen many like him, and knowed exactly *how well* he could ride, but he was relieved in learning that The Cougar had behaved so well.

"And what's this horse's name?" asks the young feller.

For a minute the stable man done some tall thinking; if the horse's real name was given out, the young feller would sure swell up and bust in learning that he'd rode the famous outlaw nobody else had been able to ride for so long, and even tho the horse hadn't made a single jump with him, his *"certainly"* would get more conceited than ever. And then again, he maybe wouldn't want the horse any more. So after hesitating a while he finally came onto a new name for the horse.

"Cloudy, is that horse's name," he says.

That name sounded sort of pleasing all around, and it fitted the color of the pony mighty well, but then the good points for it would never loom up like the name of Smoky had in the cow country to the north,

nor would it ever be mentioned about from state to
state and give thrills just at the sound like the name
of The Cougar had often done; but then again that
horse wasn't the same no more,—he'd went from top
cowhorse, to champion bucking horse and all around
outlaw, only to fade away in a livery stable, and there
for every Tom, Dick, and Harry to ride as they
pleased. Cloudy, was just a livery plug.

As a raw bronc and then cowhorse, Smoky had been
for learning all that could be learned. As The Cougar
and outlaw, he'd been for killing and disfiguring every
man that gave him the chance. There'd been something that called on him to do his best while on the
Rocking R range, and there he went to the top as a
cowhorse. Something else, and very different, had
stirred his interest while in the arena of the rodeo
grounds; he'd shined there as a fighting outlaw, and
in a way that'd made all the others seem to be out of
sight.

He'd had something big to work for, both on the
range and in the arena, but now it seemed like as the
big livery stable doors closed on him after his first
day of use there, that the end of his string had come,
he'd sort of felt it in a way, soon as the last car of the
bucking horses he'd been with went and disappeared
over the skyline. He hadn't tried to get away, or even
snorted when the stable man came in the corral where
he'd been left, and led him out.

He'd followed the man to the big stable, and as he
was kept there, he found nothing about the place nor

the folks around that suggested anything worth while working for. He was just a horse *there*, a plug that could be rented by the hour or day, and even tho all seemed strange and new compared to what he'd been used to, there was nothing in the goings on which could put a spark in his eye.

Maybe it was that his heart was growing old, but anyway, and after getting acquainted some with the place, the pony sort of took things as they come without snorting out his opinions. He was fast getting past caring,—his main interest in life soon begin to be only for the manger of hay and the little grain that was fed him when the day's work was done. One day the stable man came and curried him, that was a new experience for the horse; never had a curry comb ever touched his hide before. Somehow he didn't mind it, and then come a time when the feel of that performance was looked forward to, it felt near as good as a good roll in the dirt. The currying, his feed of grain, a rest, and to be left alone, had got to be the remains of the mouse colored pony's ambitions.

But he had to work, and earn what hay and care was handed him, he didn't mind working, but all this aimless chasing around he was took out to do most every day wasn't at all to that pony's liking. He'd been broke to doing something useful, and which *had* to be done. Afterwards, and with his bucking, there was a reason, but with these *equestrians*, as they was called, they didn't seem to know themselves what they wanted to do, or where they wanted to go. They'd just wander around and handle him with a rein in each hand like he was a plow horse. They'd run him up and down streets where the ground was hard on his feet, and let him walk where the going was soft and level. It was no wonder that the end of the day, and the stall at the stable was looked forward to so much.

Never before had that horse appreciated his night's rests as he was now doing. He'd near close his eyes for the peace he'd feel then, and eat his hay and grain slow, the same as tho he was fearing that as soon as it was gone, he'd have to be out again, and going. There'd be a short spell thru the night when he'd close his eyes all the way, and his tired mind, like his tired body, would be at rest, and then after a while, when his eyes would open again, he'd clean up what little hay he'd left the night before, and that way, gather all the strength he could for the day's work that was soon to begin.

Near every morning, early, a grey haired man, and sort of stout around the middle, would come. A little "pancake" saddle with flapping iron stirrups, would be put on the pony's back, and after a lot of hard work and puffing, the equestrian would finally get up and on the horse, and the early morning ride would begin.

The man was heavy, and set his saddle mighty awkward, but with all his weight and awkwardness, and as Cloudy got acquainted some with the man, he finally sort of took a liking for him. That one seemed to know where he wanted to go, and when he got there, even tho it was no place in perticular, the old feller would always get down off of him, sometimes he'd talk to him, and Cloudy would listen,—it didn't matter if he couldn't make heads or tails of what the talk was about, he just liked the sound of his voice.

Them morning rides was always on the outside of town, up some canyon or lane, and Cloudy felt better at them places, besides, he never was rushed, and if he was put into a trot or a lope, it was done proper and in a way both man and horse enjoyed. Seldom would any sweat ever show after the ride was over and the stable was reached again.

But the day's work would be just beginning for Cloudy, and the stable was no more than got into sight, when saddles would be changed and another person, fresh, and aching for a *jaunt*, would get on him and start out on another ride. When he'd be brought back at noon, he'd just have time to eat his grain, when another equestrian would darken the stable door, and ask for Cloudy.

"I enjoy riding that horse so, don't you know."

Everybody preferred Cloudy to any horse the stable man had, and being that feller wasn't running that business for his health, he rented him out every chance he got, and fed him an extra feed of grain so the horse could stand up under the work. Sometimes that horse would be rode till away into the night, then brought in dripping with sweat and often staggering. But the next day his work went on just the same.

Folks of all ages, sizes, built, and packing from none to a big amount of brains, came and rode Cloudy. Once in a while he'd be handled right and like it was known that a horse has feelings, and brains, but most of the time, his feelings wasn't at all considered, no thought would be given that the horse might of already

went a long ways, or that he might be tired. But
amongst all that rode him, the boys was the worst,
and fast running the old pony downhill and towards
the end.

The most of 'em would start the horse on a high
lope, and from the time they got on him till he was
brought back, that high lope, instead of being let up
on, would most always wind up into a high run. Up
and down the side streets they'd race him, loan him
to other boys to race him some more, and each would
do their best to show off on how fast they could make
the tired horse go.

There was times as the spur, a quirt was layed on
the old horse, to make him go faster; when The Cougar
heart which had died in him near showed signs of
coming back to life again, but the pony's spirit had
dwindled down as the years accumulated, and he
couldn't back the way he felt. He was weary both in
mind and body, and no chance was ever given him so
as to let either rest, and if once in a while the heart of
The Cougar did make a try at coming back it wasn't
for long, the flame would only sputter and go out, and
another wrap with the quirt would only make him try
to do his best once again, as just plain Cloudy, the
livery stable plug.

The boys, girls, and grown ups kept a setting on
the old horse, and not knowing, but sure and steady
was riding and dragging him down to a death that'd
be away ahead of the time when it should come—
They'd compared well with a pack of wolves, for like
that kind, none of 'em would ever wanted to come
within a hundred yards of the horse when he was up

and a fighting. None of 'em would ever dreamed of wanting to set on his back when he was The Cougar and hankering to fight and kill, but now, and at last he was down, there was no fight in him no more, and like the pack of wolves they compared so well with, they all closed in on him.

The only difference was, the wolf pack killed their victim quick, they don't leave the life drag on for days, weeks and months, nor let the victim suffer to finally die slow and by degrees— Then again, the wolf killed to eat and live.

But there was no blame ever attached to these human wolves who was killing the horse only for the pleasure they'd get in riding him, and the fine exercise that went with it, most of 'em meant well— Only they didn't know. Cloudy, always true in whatever he done, was so willing, no jab of the spur was needed to make him go, and his willingness to do his best that way, was often if not always mistaken, and took for granted that he was feeling good and rearing to go.

They didn't know the difference between a tired, wore out horse and one that's fresh and fit to be rode— Then again, there was many who never stopped to realize, to them, a horse was just a horse, and they didn't know nothing about horses— That kind figgered a horse to be like an automobile, always able to go and as fast as was wanted, and instead of stepping on the gas like is done with a car, just give the horse the whip, and that way keep him right on a going.

A winter came and scattered the bright fall days

four ways. The coming of the long, cold winter, along
with the raw winds that swept down from the divide,
brought to the folks around a dread of the dreary
months that was to follow; them folks wasn't for enjoying being out much any more, and instead found
a lot of comfort in being where there was a roof
over their heads, and a fire roaring between the four
walls.

The tourists had all left, and scattered back to where
they came. "The town was dead," and many heads
was got together a trying to figger ways to break the
monotony that'd took hold of the community. For
two weeks a cold wind had blowed down off the mountain and once in a while would bring along light flakes
of snow that kept a skipping and never seemed to
light.—The weather was cussed at by some, while
others kept busy bringing in wood and coal, and not
any had a good word put in for Old Man Winter, not
any excepting one, and that one was only an old livery
stable plug.

That old plug couldn't of said anything anyway,
but he done better, he *felt* what he couldn't say. He
felt that the coming of winter that way and the evaporating of the tourists and the others, as it came, was
all that saved what little life he had left. There was
saddle sores on his back, and he'd got to where there
was nothing to him but a rack of bones on which a
hide hung,—that hide was faded from many a sweating,
and in spots the hair had wore off and left it bare. His
weary legs near buckled under him, and was hardly
able to pack the weight he'd reduced to, and another

couple of weeks more the old pony would of been done for—he'd long ago been going on his nerve, and that had been fast wearing out on him.

But now, it looked like Old Man Winter had come just in time and saved him from the bone pile. There'd been two weeks when the cold winds howled, whistled thru the cracks of the stable and shook it, and in them two weeks, the old horse had recuperated some till he was able to listen to the howling wind and feel the while that no equestrian would be showing up to interrupt the rest he was needing so bad.

Every person around wondered when that awful wind was going to stop, but with Cloudy, and if he could of, he'd wished that wind would last forever. It'd got to be sweet music to his ears, and he dozed to his heart's content only to be woke up out of his dream to stare at a fresh forkful of hay once in a while. Then he'd eat a spell, listen to the wind some more, and on the sound of it, go to dozing again. Maybe dreaming of a winter range, somewheres, and far away. Pecos is by him maybe, while he dreams, then other ponies of the Rocking R, and on a ridge watching him is Clint—the only real friend he'd ever knowed.

The winter months wore on and Cloudy begin to look like a horse again; then spring come, and the air that came with it got the folks to wanting to be out. One day the gray haired gent who'd rode Cloudy in mornings of the summer before showed up again and was picked on as one steady customer for the pony; then a few days later a young lady came to the stable who "just loved horses," and asked if she could get

Cloudy every afternoon and whenever the weather was fit to ride in.

The stable man let her have the horse once and noticing what good care she'd took of him, figgered her as another steady customer for the old horse. With her and the grey haired man showing up every day he allowed how that would be enough work for him, and none of the other equestrians ever got a chance to set on that horse from then on.

A few years before, and if Cloudy had been the kind of a horse folks would want to ride, that pony would of been able to take on a couple more equestrians and stand up under the work easy enough, but now, he was getting too old for much more riding, and the stable man realizing that, was trying to make him last as long as he could. But Cloudy was getting stiff mighty fast along the shoulders and front legs, he couldn't reach out no more in the same stride that'd been his, and instead, whenever a front foot touched the ground for another step, it was like he was placing it on needles, and careful so as not to jar his shoulders and the rest of his body any more than he could help.

There was times when he felt like he wanted to split the breeze the same as he used to, but that feeling was mostly in his heart, and his old legs couldn't follow up. Them old legs had hit the ground too hard, too many times and jarred too many riders out of the saddle at the rodeos where he'd performed as a bucking horse. Then the first year of livery stable work where he was jammed around on the town's hard and rocky streets put the kibosh on him for fair. The old tendons had been called on to do too much.

But neither the old gent nor the young lady that was riding him every day noticed the stiffness crawling up on the old horse. He still went, and he still seemed willing to go some more, and far as they could tell he was as good as any four year old. Both took care of him so well that no hint ever came to either of 'em that they was riding an old horse what had along ago earned freedom and a rest for what few years was still his to live.

Every afternoon the girl came, her pockets loaded down with lumps of sugar, and refusing help, saddled Cloudy and headed him for a trail from where the scenery around could be seen and well. She'd pet him on the neck and run her fingers thru his mane, and talk while the pony, given plenty of time, would pick his way thru the rocks and brush. She'd let him rest often while in the steepest climbs, and sometimes would get out of the saddle so as to give him a better chance. At them times, she'd reach in the pocket of her white riding habit and get a few lumps of the sugar she'd brought for him.

Cloudy hadn't been much for sugar when it was first introduced to him. He'd sniffed and snorted at the white lump, but the young lady had kept it under his nose till he finally nibbled at it. It didn't taste so bad, and he'd nibbled at it again, and some more, till came a time as the girl kept a feeding it to him right along he'd got to looking for it. He'd even stop sometimes, look back at her while she was on him, and make it mighty plain that he wanted another one of them white lumps, and when she was by him on the ground he kept a trying to stick his nose in her pockets and reaching for 'em. He knowed where she carried it.

What a surprise it would of been for the cowboys who knowed Cloudy when he was The Cougar, the man killer, to've seen him in the act of bumming a young lady for sugar that way, and what a surprise it would of been for that same young lady to've learned that not so very long ago that horse would of took her hand and snapped it off at the wrist if that hand had ever come to within reaching distance.

It would of been a surprise sure enough, and afterwards, she'd figgered the horse being mean that way would of been on account of rough treatment by some one,—she'd been right, even if that some one was only a scrub of a degenerate halfbreed and not fit to be classed amongst humans. Without him coming into the life of that pony there wouldn't of been no such a horse as The Cougar, and he'd still be known around to the northern country as Smoky, the best cowhorse that ever busted a critter.

But anyway, and whatever had been in the past of the horse that was now better known as Cloudy, didn't worry the young lady any. To her he was "the sweetest horse" she'd ever seen, and she kept a supplying him with sugar. If she knowed that lumps of sugar wasn't the best thing there is to feed to a horse, she'd filled her pockets with a handful or so of grain instead, or something that's more fitting to a horse's stomach that way, but she didn't know, and she sure meant well.

Fine warm spring days came, the kind of days when folks and animals alike hunt for a place where the sun shines the best. The last storm of the season had left, and as it went the last of Cloudy's rest had come to an end. That pony was rearing to go (as best as he could) when the young lady came and saddled him one bright afternoon, and as she'd been cooped up considerable herself, her spirits more than agreed with that of the horse.

Out of the stable old Cloudy went, his legs hardly feeling the stiffness that was in 'em, and seeming like his hoofs was more for flying and not at all for touching the ground. The old pony acted like he wanted to go so bad that the girl didn't have the heart to hold him back, besides the stable man had told her one time that it wouldn't hurt to let him run once in a while, if for a short ways, so, leaning ahead on her saddle, she let the horse go.

Cloudy et up the distance and brought up sudden changes of scenery as mile after mile was covered and left behind. With the warming up of the run, the stiffness went out of his legs, he felt near young again, and was taking the steep hills more like a four year old than the old stove up horse he was. Sweat begin a dripping from him, and as the gait was kept up, that sweat turned to a white lather.

His whole hide was soaked and steaming from the heat of his body, but he kept right on a wanting to go, and like the girl, the excitement of the run had got a holt of him till neither realized they was carrying a good thing too far. The girl's hair was flying in the

breeze that was stirred, she'd lost her hat, but she
wasn't caring. To be going and splitting up some more
of that breeze had got to the girl's head, and cheeks
flushed and a smiling she was sure getting a heap of
joy out of just being alive and a going.

The trail followed along a stream and up a canyon;
it kept a getting steeper and steeper, and the old horse
begin to breathe harder and harder, till finally, his
wide open nostrils couldn't take on enough air to do
him no more. He had to slow down or else drop in
his tracks, but Cloudy didn't slow down, and not a
sign showed on him that he was wanting to. He was
the kind of a horse that never quit and would keep
right on a going till his heart stopped.

The girl, not at all realizing, kept a riding and enjoying the fast pace for all she was worth. She might
of rode the old pony to his death that afternoon, only,
the trail stopped and she couldn't follow it no further.
It had washed out during the spring thaw, and a
place ten feet wide and as deep had cut the trail in
two.

She stopped there, and coming out of the trance the
fast ride had put her in, she started looking for a place
to cross, but there wasn't any, and the only way left
was to go back on the trail she'd come.

She put her hand on Cloudy's neck like to tell him
how it was "too bad the trail stopped short that way"
but she never got to say the words— The feel of the
sweat and lather that covered the horse left her dumb,
and then she noticed how hard he was breathing.

The thrill of the run had turned to sudden worry

and fear for what she might of done, and another sort of excitement took a holt of her as she realized and then wondered what to do. She stepped away from the horse and wide eyed looked at him, she'd never seen a horse shake and quiver all over like that one was doing, he seemed like hardly able to stand up, rocked back and forth like he was going to keel over any minute. Cloudy was "jiggered"* and his staggering scared her all the more. She must do something, and quick.

The first thing that came to her was to try and cool him off before, as she figgered, he fainted from being overheated. She tore at the saddle and worked at the latigos till it was loosened, then she pulled it off and with the blanket throwed it to the ground. Steam raised off the pony's back, and at the sight of that the girl got excited all the more. Then she spotted the mountain stream below and just a little ways.

She led the horse careful and over to it, and then, thinking steady of quick ways to cool the horse off, she figgered it a good idea to lead him in the water and where it was the deepest. She skipped from boulder to boulder till finally a place was found where the water came up above the pony's knees, and there she let him stand, while with her cupped hands she splashed the cold snow water on his chest, shoulders, and back.

A half an hour or so of that, and the horse at last quit quivering, showed signs that he was cooled off and got his breath all O. K. again. After a while he drank, and then drank some more, and the girl watching him felt sure that the worst was over and that the

* Overrun.

horse was saved. She smiled, petted him on the neck, and felt relieved at the natural way he'd got to acting again.

The sun was hitting for the tall peaks to the west when the girl finally decided Cloudy was all right again and fit to start back. He was good and dry by then and felt cool; she'd kept him in the shade all the while, and being that mountain shade is not at all warm at that time of the year, the old pony was near shivering from the cold by the time the girl led him back to the saddle and put it on him again.

The ride back to the stable was like a funeral march as compared with the one starting out, the horse was kept on a slow walk all the way, and every care was taken by the girl so that only the easiest trail was followed; she worried as she rode along and noticed that the horse didn't seem to be the same as before, his step wasn't so sure and he'd stumble when there was nothing on the ground for him to stumble on, and then he'd sway like he was weak.

It was away after dark when finally the stable was reached, the stable man was there and waiting, and greeting the young lady with a smile he asked:

"Did you water Cloudy before you left?"

"No," says the girl, "but I watered him on the mountain where I turned to come back."

"The reason I asked, is because the new stable boy I hired forgot to water him this morning, or he thought *I* did."

The grey haired man didn't get to ride Cloudy the

next day, nor did anybody else, for that horse was hardly able to even get out of the stall; his legs was like so many sticks of wood and with no more bend in 'em than them same sticks have. His head hung near to the ground, and not a spear of the hay that'd been put in the manger had been touched.

The girl came to the stable that noon, and would of cried at the sight of him, only the stable man came up, and she held the tears back best as she could.

"Looks like he's done for," says that feller as he came up. He didn't ask the girl what she'd done, cause a look at the horse told him the whole story better than the girl could of, and as he figgered, a man has to take them chances when he's renting horses out that way, besides, the girl looked so downhearted about it that he didn't have the heart to do any more but try to cheer her up.

"I'll doctor him up the best I can, and maybe get him to come out of it a little."

The girl took hopes at them words, and her eyes a shining, asked:

"And can I come and help you?"

Every day from then on the time the girl had used a riding Cloudy was spent in the stable and by that horse. Liniments and medicines of all kinds was dug up and bought and used, and as the stable man watched her trying to do her best, he'd only shake his head. He knowed it was no use, and if the horse did come out of it, he'd never come out of it enough to ever be of any use as a saddle horse again.

The horse had been foundered.—The twenty-four

hours without water, the hard run and sweating up, and then cooled off sudden in ice cold water, and drinking his fill of that same water, and all at once, had crippled him and stoved him up in a way where he'd be plum useless only maybe for slow work and hooked to a wagon.

A month went by, and the doctoring went on, the girl always a hoping, and then one day she came to the stable to find the horse gone. She hunted up the stable man and finally, after a lot of running around, found him up in the hay loft.

"I figgered," says that feller on finding himself cornered, "that it'd be best to turn him loose. There's good range up north a ways and thinking it'd do him more good to be loose that way on good feed, I just took him up there."

But there was no good range in that country, not for many miles. The stable man had lied to save the girl's feelings,—and instead, realizing that he couldn't turn the horse loose only maybe to let him starve, and being he couldn't afford to keep and feed a useless horse, there'd been only one way out. He'd sold him to a man who bought old horses and killed 'em for chicken feed.

CHAPTER XIV

"DARK CLOUDS, THEN TALL GRASS"

THE man collecting old wore out and crippled horses
had come along and led him away. He had a little salt-grass pasture a short distance out of town, and
there's where he took the old horse. He turned him
loose amongst a few more old horses, and would keep
him there till the time come when some "chicken man"
around town would need the carcass of one of the
horses to feed to his chickens; then the horse what
looked like it had the shortest to live would be killed
and hauled away.

It didn't look like the end was very far for the mouse
colored horse. All the work he'd done and the interest
he'd had while under the names of Smoky and The
Cougar, had stopped being accounted for and sort of
pinched out under the name of Cloudy, and now he
had no name. He was just "chicken feed," and soon,
if he stayed in that pasture, all what he'd been and
done would be blotted out with the crack of a rifle
shot.

But the old pony had no hint of that, and as it was
he wasn't for quitting as yet. His old stiff legs was still
able to carry him around some, the doctoring he'd got
at the stable had helped him more than what had been
hoped, and then getting out in a pasture where he
could keep moving around as he wanted to was help-

ing him some more. Besides, his old heart was still
strong, quite a bit solid meat was covering his ribs,
and with the salt and wire grass to graze on he could
still make out and mighty well.

A few weeks went by when once in a while and every
few days, one of the old horses he was pasturing with,
was caught, led out, a rifle shot was heard, and he'd
never be seen no more. Other old horses was brought
in and they'd pasture on with him till one by one they'd
also disappear only to be replaced by more of 'em.

The old mouse colored horse must of looked like he
was good to live for a long time yet; anyway, the
"chicken horse" man had kept him, maybe for emer-
gency, and so he wouldn't be out of horses if an order
for one, and that kind was hard to get.

Then one day, a man came, looked all the old horses
over. And finally, like he'd decided, pointed a finger
towards the horse that'd last been known as Cloudy.
That pony was caught and led out the same way other
horses had disappeared, but no rifle shot was heard.
Instead, a lot of parleying went on.

Cloudy was led alongside of an old bony something
that'd once been a horse, the old rack of bones was
hooked onto a light wagon and seeming like hardly
able to stand as the eyes of the two men went from
him to Cloudy, to sort of figger out which of the two
was worth the most, and *how much* the most.

Finally the dickering came to an end and seemed
like agreeable to both parties. Three dollars to boot
was handed, and the trade was made. The rack of
bones was unhooked, the harness pulled off of him,

and turned loose in the chicken horse pasture. Then Cloudy's old heart missed a few beats as that same harness was picked up again and throwed over his own back.

As true a saddle horse, and once hard to set on, as the mouse colored horse had been, the feel of that harness on his back was as much the same as if a shovel or a hayfork had been handed to a cowpuncher with the idea of his using 'em. The old horse felt it a plain disgrace and snorted as it was buckled around him to stay, but the black whiskered hombre that buckled it on never seemed to notice or care that the horse had no liking for the collar and all the straps.

He kept on a fastening the harness, and when that was done, he jerked the old pony around and backed him into the shafts of the same old wagon that the rack of bones had been unhooked out of. Cloudy kept on a snorting and looked on one side and then the other as the shafts of the wagon was raised. If only he could act the way his heart wanted him to, but he didn't have the strength, the action to put in it, nor the energy no more. The most he could do was to snort, quiver, and shake his head.

But, as he was all hooked up and the man jumping in the wagon grabbed his whip, Old Cloudy done his best to try and get back to some of the life and tearing ability that'd once been his. He kicked a couple of times at the rattling thing on wheels and which he was fastened to, then he tried to buck some and finally wound up by wanting to run away, but the harness held and the rattling thing behind came right along wherever he went, and worse yet, he felt the stinging lash of the man's whip as he fought on and tried to clear himself. Then the jerking of the bit thru his mouth, and with all that to show how useless his fighting and wanting to get away really was, the old pony soon lost heart. He finally settled down to a choppy lope, then a trot that was just as choppy, and at last to a walk.

Another sting of the whip was felt on his flank, and at the same time, the line was jerked at the bit, and Cloudy, still pulling the wagon, was made to turn up a lane. At the end of the lane was a shack made of old pieces of boards and covered over with the tin of old oil-cans. To the right of that and a little ways further was another shack that looked like a mate to the first, only worse, and that one was going to be Cloudy's place of rest and shelter whenever work was over.

There he was pulled to a stop, unhooked, led to the manger, and tied. The stable door was closed with a bang, and after a while the old horse, still wanting to cling to life regardless of what came, stuck his nose in the manger to nibble on some of what was in it. He reached for a mouthful of what he'd naturally took for hay, and chewed for a spell, but he didn't chew on it long. There was a musty taste about the long dirty brown stems that didn't at all fit in with any hay he'd ever et. The kind that'd been put in the manger for him to eat was the same that the livery stableman had used to put in the stalls and bed the horses down with. It was straw, only this was musty straw and wouldn't even make good bedding for horses.

Cloudy felt hungry long before the next morning came, and often thru the night he'd nosed into the musty straw with the hopes of finding a few stems that'd do to fill an empty space, but there wasn't any to be found. The old rack of bones that'd been there before him had looked for some too, and with no better luck.—Cloudy's new owner figgered it cheaper to swap horses with the "chicken man" and give him a few dollars to boot whenever any horse of his give out; he wasn't going to buy no high-priced hay for no horse. The straw was given to him for the getting and would keep any horse alive and working for at least six months, and then, or whenever the horse would be too weak to go any more, he'd trade him for another. Any kind of a horse, fat or thin, could always be used by the chicken man, and in trade, he'd always take one of the fattest to take the place of the one he'd just starved near to death,—that way, year in year out, he'd keep a draining the last of the life of every horse he'd get his claws onto.

His property, and where he starved the horses into making a living for him, took in a couple of acres. Half of that land was rocks, mostly, and where he kept a few chickens, he bought, or stole a little grain for *them*, but they well repaid him, every time he went to town there was a basket of eggs in his wagon and which he sold well. The other half of his land was cultivated, and where vegetables of all kinds had been made to grow. There's where the help of a horse was needed, to pull the cultivator or the plow, then the hauling of the vegetables to town, and once there, any odd job that could be got and which would bring a few dollars for the use of the horse and wagon.

It was bright and early the next morning when the work begin for Cloudy. The man showed his teeth in a grin as he looked in the manger while putting the harness on the horse, and noticing the straw in there hadn't hardly been touched, remarked:

"You'll be eating some of that before you get thru."

Cloudy was made acquainted with many different kinds of implements and work that day. All was mighty strange and plum against the ways of working which he'd been broke to do. It was pull, and pull, one contraption and then another, back and forth thru furrows, turn at the end and then back again. If he slowed down, or hesitated, wondering what to do, there was the whip always on hand to make him decide and mighty quick.

His muscles, having developed under the saddle, used to pack weight, and set that way, wasn't for getting next to the change very easy. Looking thru a collar and pulling steady was so different to heading off and turning a wild-eyed critter. It wasn't at all like coming out of the chute in front of a grandstand and seeing how many jumps could be put into one, nor didn't compare even with packing equestrians around. He'd felt some free under the saddle, and even tho all of it had been real work, there'd always been something that fitted in and which made him feel natural.

But now, with all these straps a hanging onto him, there was a feeling that he was tied down,—them straps even seemed to wrap around his heart at times and keep it from beating. And taking all, the strange hard work, the sting of the whip-lash on his ribs, nothing fit to eat after he was tired out and the day was over, it was no wonder that the old pony's heart begin to shrivel up on him.

As the long days run into weeks and the work in the field and in the town got to bearing down on him, the old pony even got so he couldn't hate no more; abuse or kindness had both got to be the same, and one brought out no more result or show of interest than the other. He went to the jerk of the lines like without realizing, and when he was finally led into the stable when night come the feeling was the same. There he et the musty straw because it was under his nose, he didn't mind the taste of it, he didn't mind anything, any more.

Of the odd jobs that Cloudy's owner would get to do around town and whenever he could get away from his truck and chicken farm, there was one which he looked forward to the most, and which the thought of made him rub his hands together with pleasure. It was that of scattering the posters advertising The Annual Rodeo, and Celebration, that was pulled off in town and every early fall. But that wasn't all, there was many other things for him to do at that time for which he could charge without anybody ever finding out whether all he'd been paid to do really had been done.

That year as usual, he was ready, and right on the dot to take on some more of that kind of work. He'd hooked up the old mouse colored horse and taking a load of vegetables on the way in, stuck around town doing the different kinds of work the rodeo association had furnished him with. He'd be on the go all day and prodding the old horse into a trot, sometimes even if the wagon was loaded.

It'd be away into the night before he'd turn the tired horse towards home. Every day was a great day, *for the man*, there was so many people around to make the town lively, and being most of 'em was strangers, he could get to within talking distance of 'em easy enough, and a few would even stand to have him around for a few minutes at the time.

Them strangers had come to see the rodeo, most of 'em was from other towns around, and mixed in the crowd once in a while could be seen the high-crowned hat of a cowboy who'd come to ride, rope, and bull-dog. Then at the Casa Grande Hotel, and registered there, was many cattle buyers from the northern States.

They'd come to bid on the big herds of cattle that was being crowded acrost the border from Mexico, for Pancho Villa and the Yaquis was making it hard for the cattleman of that country. Villa took the cattle to feed his army, while the Yaquis run off whatever Villa overlooked, and the cowman that could, and had any stock left, soon seen where if he wanted to save anything of what he'd worked to accumulate, he'd have to rush whatever that was to the border and get it on American soil mighty quick.

That's how come that the stockyards of the border towns was filled with cattle and that the hotels along

The long horned "Sonora reds" begin to spread all over the range countries of the U. S. plum up to the Canadian line.

them same towns was filled with cattle buyers. The
Casa Grande Hotel was the most filled on account that
along with the business of buying cattle, a little pleasure
could be got there afterwards. A rodeo was in that
town, and night celebrations, and being that them
cattle buyers was still as much cowboys as ever, a good
bucking contest and the fun afterwards couldn't be
overlooked, not if it could be helped. "Yep, the town
was sure lively."

Two of the buyers was setting in the lobby of the
hotel one morning and a talking on the first day's
event of the rodeo. A telegraph pole which stuck up
right before their vision and on the edge of the side-
walk, and nailed to that pole was a poster advertising
the rodeo, and with a photograph of a bucking horse
in action on it, told all about "the great bucking horse
and outlaw The Grey Cougar, the only one that could
compare, in wickedness and bucking ability, to The
Cougar, that once famous man killing horse."

The two went on to talking about the rodeo, and
naturally the talk drifted on about The Grey Cougar,
and "*how* he could buck."

"The boys tell me," says one of the men, "that this
Grey Cougar horse couldn't hold a candle to the real
Cougar when it come to bucking and fighting. Accord-
ing to that, the other horse must of been *some* wicked."

The man was still talking on the subject, when an
old mouse colored horse, pulling an old wagon loaded
down with vegetables, came to a stiff legged stop, and
right by the telegraph pole on which the poster telling
all about The Grey Cougar was nailed. The man in

the lobby grinned a little at the sight of the old horse
a standing there like in comparison with the famous
grey outlaw, and pointing a finger in his direction, he
remarked:

"There must be the Old Cougar right there, Clint.
Anyway he's got the same color."

The man called Clint grinned some at the joke, but
the grin soon faded away as he kept a looking at the
old horse, and noticed the condition he was in,—then
he seen the saddle-marks that was all over the pony's
back, and he says:

"You can never tell, that old pony might of been
mighty hard to set at one time too—but the way he
looks like now, them times are sure done past and
gone."

"Yep," agreed the other man, "it's a miracle that
pony can navigate at all—I wonder how it is that this
Humane Society hombre that's sticking around the
rodeo grounds don't happen to notice such as this.
I'd like to help hang a feller for driving a horse like
that around."

The conversation was held up for a spell as the two
men watched the bewhiskered man come out of the
hotel with an empty basket and climbed the wagon
on which the old mouse colored horse was hooked. He
grabbed the lines and the whip both at the same time
and went to work a putting the horse into a trot.

Clint was for getting up as he seen the whip land on
the old pony's hide, but the other man grabbed a
hold of his arm and says:

"Never mind, old boy, most likely that Humane

Society outfit'll fall on that bolshevik's neck before he gets very far."

The man called Clint set down again, but he was boiling up inside, and he didn't at all look pleasant as the conversation was resumed and noticed how his friend turned it to other things and away from the subject of old horses and such. He wasn't for answering very quick when that same friend went on to talking about that country to the north;—how he'd heard rumors that the Rocking R might be selling out in another year or so. "I wonder why?" he asks.

Clint, turned to his friend and grinning at his idea of changing the subject that way, finally answered: "I guess it's because Old Tom feels the end a coming, besides he's getting crowded all around by small outfits, and his range ain't holding up like it used to."

"But what are you going to do when the Rocking R sells out?—you left that country quite a few times the last few years, and I notice you always go back like there was no other that suited you."

"I've got that fixed," says Clint gradually taking more heart in the new subject, and there he tried to describe some;—"you know abouts where that camp is where I used to break horses when I first started working for the Rocking R? it's where the outfit used to run their stock horses. Well, I bought that camp from Old Tom Jarvis,—that is, I talked him into selling it to me, and four thousand acres of the fine range around to go with it.

"I'm thinking that this shipment I'm getting together now will be the last Old Tom'll ever buy, and

No remuda got by that Clint didn't ride thru.

by the time I get this train-load of Sonora Reds north
and delivered to him, I'll have enough money to make
the final payment on my place and still have enough
left to buy a few head of cattle and start stocking
it."

Clint often thought of his little place up in the heart
of the cow country to the north. He could picture his
own cattle ranging there and packing a brand of his
on their slick hides,—he'd a long time hoped for the
likes, and at last he was getting it. A couple more days
now, and he'd be heading north again, and there to
stay, this time.

The last day of the rodeo had come, and Clint was
to start with his train load of stock that night. Him
and his friend was setting in the lobby of the hotel
that evening a talking and wondering when they'd be
seeing one another again, when outside and by the
telegraph pole, came the same old mouse colored horse
and stopped not an inch from where the two men had
seen him a couple of days before.

Both was quick to spot him again this time, and
right then, for some reason or other the conversation
died down. The first sight of that old pony hadn't
been forgot, and when he showed up this second time,
right before their eyes, he was like reminding 'em, and
natural like, set the two men to thinking. That old
shadow of a horse told some of the hard knocks of life,
of things that was past and gone and which could of
been bettered while the bettering could be done.

It was while the thinking was going on that way,

that Clint sort of felt a faint, far away something a knocking and from down the bottom of his think tank. That something was trying hard to come back to life as that man's eyes kept a going over the pony's blazed face and bony frame, but it was buried so far underneath so many things that'd been stacked there. that the knocking was pretty well muffled up. It'd have to be helped by some sort of a sudden jolt before it could come out on top.

The jolt came as the vegetable man got his seat on the wagon and as usual reached for the whip. Clint's friend a trying to keep him from running out and starting a rompus had tried to draw his interest by asking:

"What's become of that cowhorse *Smoky*, that used to—— ?"

But the question was left for *him* to wonder about, for Clint wasn't there to answer, instead the hotel door slammed and only a glimpse of that same cowboy could be seen as he passed by the lobby window. In less than it takes to tell it, he was up on the wagon, took a bulldogging holt of the surprised vegetable man, and by his whiskers, drug him off his seat and down to earth.

The telephone on the desk of the sheriff's office rang till it near danced a jig, and when that feller lifted the receiver, a female voice was heard to holler: "somebody is killing somebody else with a whip, by the Casa Granda Hotel. *Hurry! Quick!*"

The sheriff appeared on the scene and took in the goings on at a glance. Like a man who knowed his business, his eyes went to looking for what might of caused the argument as he came. He looked at the old horse whose frame showed thru the hide, then the whip marks on that hide. He knowed horses as well as he did men, and when he noticed more marks of the same whip on the bewhiskered man's face, he stood his ground, watched, and then grinned.

"Say, cowboy," he finally says, "don't scatter that hombre's remains too much, you know we got to keep record of that kind the same as if it was a white man, and I don't want to be looking all over the streets to find out who he *was*."

Clint turned at the sound of the voice, and sizing up the grinning sheriff, went back to his victim and broke the butt end of the whip over his head, after which he wiped his hands, and proceeded to unhook the old horse off the wagon.

That evening was spent in "investigating." Clint and the sheriff went to the chicken-horse man and found out enough from him about the vegetable man and his way of treating horses to put that hombre in a cool place and keep him there for a spell.

"I'm glad to've caught on to that feller's doings," remarks the sheriff as him and Clint went to the livery stable, their next place of investigation.

There Clint listened mighty close as he learned a heap about the mouse colored horse when he was known as Cloudy. The stable man went on to tell as far as he knowed about the horse and the whole history of him, and when that pony was known thru the Southwest and many other places, as *The Cougar*, the wickedest bucking horse and fighting outlaw the country had every layed eyes on.

Clint was kinda proud in hearing that. He'd heard of The Cougar and that pony's bucking ability even up to the Canadian line and acrost it, and to himself he says: "That Smoky horse never did do things half-ways." But he got to wondering, and then asked how come the pony had turned out to be the kind of a horse, that, the stable man didn't know. It was news to him that the horse had ever been anything else, and as he says:

"The first that was seen of that horse is when some cowboys found him on the desert, amongst a bunch of wild horses, and packing a saddle. Nobody had ever showed up to claim him, and as that pony had been more than inclined to buck and fight is how come he was sold as a bucking horse—and believe me, old timer," went on the stable man, a shaking his head, "he was *some* bucking horse."

"Well," says the sheriff, "that's another clue run to the ground with nothing left of, but the remains."

That night, the big engine was hooked on to the trainload of cattle as to per schedule and started puffing its way on to the north. In the last car, the one next to the caboose, and the least crowded, a space had been partitioned off. In that space was a bale of good hay, a barrel of water, and an old mouse colored horse.

The winter that came was very different to any the old mouse colored horse had ever put in. The first part of it went by with him like in a trance, not realizing and hardly seeing. His old heart had dwindled down till only a sputtering flame was left, and that threatened to go out with the first hint of any kind of breeze.

Clint had got the old horse in a warm box stall, filled the manger full of the best blue joint hay there was, and even bedded him down with more of the same; water was in that same stall and where it could be easy reached, and then that cowboy had bought many a dollar's worth of condition powders, and other preparations which would near coax life back even in a dead body.

Two months went by when all seemed kinda hopeless, but Clint worked on and kept a hoping. He'd brought the old horse in the house, and made him a bed by the stove if that would of helped, and far as that goes, he'd of done anything else, just so a spark of life showed in the old pony's eyes; but he'd done all he could do, and as he'd lay a hand on the old skinny neck and felt of the old hide, he'd cuss and wish for the chance of twisting out of shape who all had been responsible. Then his expression would change, and he'd near bust out crying as he'd think back and compare the old wreck with what that horse had been.

As much as Clint had liked Smoky, the old wreck of a shadow of that horse wasn't wanting for any of the same liking. It was still in the cowboy's heart a plenty, and if anything, more so on account that the old pony was now needing help, and a friend like he'd never needed before, and Clint was more on hand with the horse, now that he was worthless, than he'd been when

Smoky was the four hundred dollar cowhorse and worth more.

Finally, and after many a day of care and worrying, Clint begin to notice with a glad smile, that the pony's hide was loosening up; then after a week or so more of shoving hay and grain, condition powders, and other things down the old pony's throat, a layer of meat begin to spread over them bones and under that hide. Then one day a spark showed in the pony's eye, soon after that he started taking interest in the things around.

As layer after layer of meat and then tallow accumulated and rounded the sharp corners of Smoky's frame, that pony was for noticing more and more till after a while his interest spread enough, and with a clearer vision, went as far as to take in the man, who kept a going and coming, once in a while touched him, and then talked.

Clint liked to had a fit one day, when talking to the horse and happening to say *Smoky*, he noticed that pony cock an ear.

The recuperating of the horse went pretty fast from then on, and as the winter days howled past and early spring drawed near, there was no more fear of Smoky's last stand being anywheres near. As the days growed longer and the sun got warmer, there was times when Clint would lead the horse out and turn him loose to walk around in the sunshine, and that way get the blood to circulating. Smoky would sometimes mosey along for hours around the place and then start out on some trail, but always when the sun went down, he

was by the stable door again and then Clint would let
him in.

Clint would watch him by the hour whenever the
horse was out that way, and he'd wonder, as he kept
his eye on him, if that pony remembered, if the knocks
he'd got from different people in different countries,
didn't forever make him forget his home range and all
that went with it. Not many miles away was where
he was born; the big mountains now covered with
snow was the same he was raised on, and which he
tore up with his hoofs as he played while a little colt,
and by his mammy. The corrals by the stable and
sheds was the ones he was first run into when branded,
and in them, a few years later, broke to saddle; but
what Clint would wonder the most, as he watched, is
whether Smoky remembered *him*.

The cowboy had kept a hoping that sometime he'd
be greeted with a nicker as he'd open the stable door
in the morning. Clint felt if the horse remembered, he
would nicker that way at the sight of him and like he
used to, but morning after morning went by, and even
tho Smoky seemed full of life and rounded out to near
natural again, no nicker was ever heard.

"Somebody must of stretched that pony's heartstrings to the breaking point," he remarked one day,
as he'd stopped, wondering as usual, and looked at
the horse.

Finally spring came sure enough, and broke up the
winter. Green grass covered ridges took the place of
snow banks, and the cottonwoods along the creeks
was beginning to bud. It was during one of them fine

As he stepped out to get a bucket of water the morning sun throwed a
shadow on the door.

spring days, when riding along and looking the country over, Clint run acrost a bunch of horses. In the bunch was a couple of colts just a few days old, and knowing that old ponies have such a strong interest and liking for the little fellers, the cowboy figgered the sight of 'em would help considerable in bringing Smoky's heart up a few notches, and maybe to remembering. He fell in behind the bunch and hazed 'em all towards the corrals, and as Smoky, turned loose that day, spotted the bunch, his head went up. Then he noticed the little fellers, and that old pony, gathering all the speed there was in him, headed straight for the bunch and amongst 'em.

Clint corralled him and all the rest together and setting on his horse at the gate, watched Smoky while that horse was having the time of his life getting acquainted. The pony dodged kicks and bites and went back and forth thru the bunch, and a spark showed in his eye which hadn't been there for many a day.

The cowboy could near see the horse smile at the little colts, and he was surprised at the show of action and interest the old pony had reserved, or gained. He was acting near like a two-year-old, and Clint grinned as he watched.

"Daggone his old hide," says the cowboy, "it looks to me like he's good to live and enjoy life for many summers yet"; then thinking strong, he went on, "and maybe in that time he might get to remembering me again—I wonder."

He watched Smoky a while longer and till he got acquainted some, and at last deciding it'd be for the best to let him go, he reined his horse out of the gate and let the bunch run by. The old pony seemed to hesitate some as the bunch filed out, he liked their company mighty well but something held him back; then a horse nickered, and even tho that nicker might not of been meant for him, it was enough to make him decide. He struck out on a high lope and towards the bunch;—one of the little colts and full of play waited for him, and nipping the old horse in the flanks run by his side till the bunch was caught up with—Smoky was *living* again.

Clint sat on his horse and watched the bunch lope out over a ridge and out of sight, and with a last glimpse at the mouse colored rump he grinned a little, but it was a sorry grin, and as he kept a looking the way Smoky had gone, he says:

"I wonder if he ever will."

With the green grass growing near an inch a day, Clint wasn't worried much on how old Smoky was making it. He figgered a horse couldn't die if he wanted to, not on that range at that time of the year, but some day soon he was going to try and locate the old horse and find out for sure how he really was. Then a lot of work came on which kept the cowboy from going out soon as he wanted to, and then one morning, bright and early, as he stepped out to get a bucket of water, the morning sun throwed a shadow on the door, and as he stuck his head out a nicker was heard.

Clint dropped his bucket in surprise at what he heard and then seen. For, standing out a ways, slick, and shiny, was the old mouse colored horse. The good care the cowboy had handed him, and afterwards, the ramblings over the old home range, had done its work. The heart of Smoky had come to life again, and full size.